FINAL
JUSTICE

OTHER BOOKS BY AL LACY

Angel of Mercy series:
A Promise for Breanna (Book One)
Faithful Heart (Book Two)
Captive Set Free (Book Three)
A Dream Fulfilled (Book Four)
Suffer the Little Children (Book Five)
Whither Thou Goest (Book Six)

Journeys of the Stranger series:
Legacy (Book One)
Silent Abduction (Book Two)
Blizzard (Book Three)
Tears of the Sun (Book Four)
Circle of Fire (Book Five)
Quiet Thunder (Book Six)
Snow Ghost (Book Seven)

Battles of Destiny (Civil War series):
Beloved Enemy (Battle of First Bull Run)
A Heart Divided (Battle of Mobile Bay)
A Promise Unbroken (Battle of Rich Mountain)
Shadowed Memories (Battle of Shiloh)
Joy From Ashes (Battle of Fredericksburg)
Season of Valor (Battle of Gettysburg)
Wings of the Wind (Battle of Antietam)

Hannah of Fort Bridger series (coauthored with JoAnna Lacy):
Under the Distant Sky (Book One)
Consider the Lilies (Book Two)
No Place for Fear (Book Three)

FINAL JUSTICE

BOOK SEVEN

AL LACY

Multnomah Publishers *Sisters, Oregon*

This book is a work of fiction. With the exception of recognized historical figures, the characters in this novel are fictional. Any resemblance to actual persons, living or dead, is purely coincidental.

FINAL JUSTICE
© 1998 by Lew A. Lacy

published by Multnomah Fiction
a division of Multnomah Publishers, Inc.

Cover design by D^2 DesignWorks
Cover illustration by Vittorio Dangelico

International Standard Book Number: 1-57673-260-6

Printed in the United States of America.

For information:
Multnomah Publishers, Inc.
Post Office Box 1720
Sisters, Oregon 97759

Library of Congress Cataloging–in–Publication Data
Lacy, A156 F5 1998
    Final justice/by Al Lacy.
        p.cm—(Angel of mercy series: bk. 7)
    ISBN 1-57673-260-6 (alk. paper)
        1. Cheyenne Indians—Fiction. I. Title. II. Series: Lacy, Al.
Angel of mercy series: bk. 7
PS3562.A256F5   1998   98-5547
813'.54—dc21   CIP

98 99 00 01 02 03 04 05 06 — 10 9 8 7 6 5 4 3 2 1

For Kevin Marks,
my friend and brother in Christ...
who knows how to sell good novels!

I love you, Kevin—
3 JOHN 2

PROLOGUE

✦

I WANT TO TELL YOU A STORY about a Cheyenne Indian woman named Silver Moon. Like our Angel of Mercy, Breanna Baylor Brockman, Silver Moon is fictional, but representative of bold and brave American Indian women of the late nineteenth century, as Breanna is representative of the bold and brave white women of the same time period.

If the average United States citizen were asked to name a half-dozen of the North American Indian women who left their mark on U.S. history, few would be able to do it. Most would probably say Pocahontas and be stumped for another name. Some no doubt would name Sacajawea. A small number would probably be able to name both of them, but when asked what tribes they were born into, and why their names stand out, very few would know the answer.

Pocahontas, born in 1595, was daughter of Chief Powhatan of the Powhatan tribe (which was so named in his honor) of Virginia. History tells how Chief Powhatan's warriors captured an English soldier, twenty-eight-year-old Captain John Smith, who was leader of the tiny colony at Jamestown.

Around the chief stood a crowd of his people, along with his wife, sons, and daughters. At Powhatan's command, the warriors flung Smith to the ground, placing his head on a stone altar. Two warriors then took heavy clubs in hand. There would be a slight ritualistic pause, then at the chief's signal, Smith's skull would be crushed.

The slight figure of Powhatan's favorite daughter, twelve-year-old Matoaka, affectionately called Pocahontas—or Playful One—was all but lost in the crowd. Before the signal came from her father to bring the clubs down on Smith's head, the girl dashed to the altar and flung herself across the young Englishman's body. She laid her head over Smith's own, sending her long black hair cascading over his face as she begged her father not to kill him.

Because of his love for Pocahontas, Powhatan allowed Smith to live and return to Jamestown unscathed. In a book he published in 1624, titled *Generall Historie of Virginia,* Smith told of his dramatic rescue by the beautiful young girl Pocahontas.

In 1614, Pocahontas became a Christian and married Englishman John Rolfe. Two years later he took her to visit his native Great Britain, where she was received by the royal family as a princess...a result of having saved the life of John Smith. She took sick there and died shortly thereafter at the age of twenty-two.

Pocahontas is buried in Gravesend, England.

Sacajawea, a Shoshone Indian, is known for being the sole woman and guide of the Lewis and Clark Expedition, 1803–1806. When the expedition began, Sacajawea was nineteen. She had been captured by white men and sold to a Mandan Indian, then traded to Toussaint Charbonneau, a Frenchman who traveled with the Lewis and Clark Expedition as an interpreter. Sacajawea also served as an interpreter between whites and Indians on the expedition.

Historians tell us that after the four-year journey with Lewis and Clark, Sacajawea returned to her native people in Wyoming, where she died at the age of twenty-eight. Twice my wife, JoAnna, and I have visited Sacajawea's grave near Lander, Wyoming.

Other North American Indian women who have made their mark on this country's history are Pretty Shield, of the Crow; Tissewoonatis, of the Cheyenne; Brown Weasel Woman, of the Blackfoot; Woman Chief, of the Gros Ventre; Dahteste, of the Apache; White Buffalo Calf Woman, of the Sioux; Our Grandmother, of the Shawnee; Yellow Corn Girl, of the Zuni; Cousaponokeesa, of the Creek; and Tsistunagiska, or Cherokee Rose, of the Cherokee.

My JoAnna is one quarter Cherokee, and quite proud of it. She could tell you much about Wilma Mankiller, a name that is well loved among the Cherokee people.

In 1985, Wilma Mankiller became the first woman chief of the Cherokee tribe, making her home in Stilwell, Oklahoma. Since then she has twice won reelection to her leadership position, under which a resurgent Cherokee nation is living up to the hopes and dreams of generations past.

Some women's liberation movement leaders have stated that the Bible puts women down. This is just not true. God made women special, and has put them on a pedestal. As a Christian man and a Bible believer, I hold the same concept.

Our Creator has laid the responsibility of leadership in human society on men. This is why most of what we read in history is about men. But it has long been my opinion that women haven't been given their fair share of space in the history books, for they most certainly have played a powerful part in shaping this nation of ours.

It certainly is true in the Old West, among both white women and Indian women.

Much of the history about the North American Indians makes it appear that Indian women were downtrodden and browbeaten by Indian men. In some cases, this is true, but not in all.

In the minds of most nineteenth-century North American Indian tribes, the women were known as the sustainers of the people. A great Iroquois sachem once said about their women, in a public gathering, "They are the esteemed mistresses of the soil. Who brings us into life but our mothers? Who cultivates our lands, boils our pots, cooks our food, but the women?"

The Iroquois believed, as did all other North American Indian tribes, that the soil would not bear fruit unless it was cultivated by women. The female power of fertility was deemed necessary in order for crops to grow. It was also believed that women could enrich the soil merely by their presence in the fields, dragging the hems of their garments on the ground.

This is why we see photographs and paintings of nineteenth-century Indian women, not the men, working the fields. It was not a case of making slaves of their wives, mothers, and daughters, but a heartfelt belief that the soil would only produce for them.

In all tribes, women were valued for their labors. They contributed 80 percent of the labor needed to produce the family food supply—not only planting and raising the vegetables, but also butchering and cooking the meat brought in by the men.

They were treasured as well for their roles as midwives and healers. In their pagan religions, many tribes had medicine *women,* as well as medicine men. Women were also prized for their labor in producing the clothing worn by all, and for their skills in crafting material goods. The Navajo hogan, the Apache wickiup, and the tepees of the Great Plains tribes were designed and constructed by women, while the men hunted and carried on the war with the white man.

However, there were many Indian women who took up arms and fought alongside their men, especially when it came to defending their villages. Often women would pursue men who had killed a kinsman or a husband with the intent of exacting justice upon them.

One Sioux woman, Minnie Hollow Wood, won the right to wear a war bonnet for the way she fought against the U.S. cavalry!

For Native American women, the end of their childbearing years marked an important passage into a different realm of respect and influence. In the minds of the people, old age was synonymous with wisdom. Older women frequently assumed new ritual duties, and their views on important tribal issues carried more weight.

Thus we see that North American Indian women were highly regarded by their men for a good many reasons.

Let me take you now to my story, where along with our Angel of Mercy, you will meet the lovely and valorous Silver Moon....

1

As MORNING CAME ACROSS the Colorado plains, the sun painted the horizon a vermilion hue, then lifted its flaming head over the edge of the world to send bright beams of light across the rolling hills around Fort Lyon and the rippling surface of the nearby Arkansas River.

Within the stockade, situated on a two-acre plot of grassy soil, was a scattering of low buildings. The parade ground had deep ruts worn into its hard surface by the iron-shod wheels of the water wagon that made a daily trip to the river and back. Beyond the quadrangle were the stables and corrals. Atop the gate tower, Old Glory waved in the morning breeze.

It was Sunday, September 4, 1864, and already the air had a fall feel to it. The two sentries in the tower scanned the surrounding hills as the rising sun drove away the shadows in the low spots. Suddenly one of them elbowed his comrade. "Look, Tom! Indians!"

Corporal Tom Corbin swung his gaze in the direction where Private Wesley Oldham pointed. "Mm-hmm. Six of 'em under a white flag. Must want a powwow. Who do you suppose it is?"

"Well, since they're comin' from the northeast, I'd say it's probably Black Kettle or Crooked Neck...maybe War Bonnet."

Corbin picked up his binoculars and focused them on the incoming riders. After a few seconds he said, "There's no chief among 'em. Definitely Cheyenne, though."

"Must be carryin' a message."

"Or wantin' somethin'."

Soon the six riders drew rein and thundered their pintos to a halt below the tower.

Corbin noted that the one who rode in the lead had his left eye sewn shut. "It's One Eye, Wes. Black Kettle's toughest warrior." Corbin leaned over the rail and called, "Morning, One Eye. What business brings you here?"

The square-jawed Cheyenne warrior held a folded paper in his hand. "Have letter for Major Wynkoop. From Chief Moketavata."

"Mokie—what?" whispered Oldham.

"Moketavata. That's Black Kettle. His Cheyenne name."

"I'll come down and get it," Corbin called, hurrying down the stairs.

Private Oldham was on his heels, and he held the gate open just wide enough to let Corbin slip through.

As Corporal Corbin approached the mounted Indians, One Eye shook his head. "No. Chief Moketavata say One Eye must deliver it to Major Wynkoop personal."

Corbin hesitated, then said, "All of you come inside. Have your man keep the white flag up high."

One Eye turned around and spoke in Cheyenne to the warrior who held the broken tree limb bearing the white flag. The warrior nodded.

Tom Corbin hurried ahead of the Indians toward the headquarters as Wesley Oldham ushered the six riders through the gate. Men in blue all over the fort looked on, noting the white flag.

Major Edward Wynkoop had just left his small cabin and

was headed for his office in the headquarters building when he saw the Indians.

"Major," Corbin said, dashing up to Wynkoop, "these warriors are from Black Kettle's village. One Eye has a letter for you from Black Kettle and says the chief directed him to give it to you personally."

"All right," Wynkoop said with a nod. He had been the fort's commandant for nearly two years and had met Chief Black Kettle on several occasions. Black Kettle trusted few white men. Wynkoop was one of them.

Private Oldham halted the Indians in front of headquarters. Only One Eye dismounted.

As soldiers gathered from every direction to watch, Captain Charles Axton limped across the parade ground, angling toward Wynkoop. Axton had been wounded in a battle with Kiowas a month before—the same battle in which the fort's only other captain had been killed along with nearly twenty men. A new captain and some thirty troopers were on their way from Fort Larned, Kansas, as replacements.

As Axton approached, One Eye raised his hand in a salute of peace to Wynkoop, and the major did the same.

"Good morning, One Eye," said Wynkoop. "I understand you have a letter for me from my friend Chief Black Kettle."

"Mmm," said One Eye, extending the folded paper. "Chief Moketavata want One Eye wait. You read letter. Give One Eye letter take back to Chief Moketavata."

Captain Axton leaned heavily on his cane as he walked up to his commandant and watched him unfold the paper. "I knew Black Kettle could *speak* English," said Axton, "but I didn't know he could read or write it."

"I'd heard that he could," said Wynkoop. "I don't know how he learned it."

"George Bent," said One Eye.

"Who's George Bent?" asked Axton. "He related to William Bent...the one who runs the trading post down the river a few miles?"

Wynkoop nodded. "George is William's son from his marriage to a Cheyenne woman. She died giving birth to George." Wynkoop looked at One Eye for confirmation as he said, "If I recall correctly, it was George who taught many of the Cheyenne how to read and write English."

"He taught Black Kettle and his squaw," said One Eye. "They teach daughter and son. You right. Many Cheyenne learn read, write English from George Bent. One Eye, too."

Wynkoop nodded, then turned his attention to the letter. It was written in cursive by Black Kettle's own hand.

Cheyenne Village at Smoky Hill River
August 29th/64
Major Wynkoop.

Sir, we received a visit from William Bent wishing us to make peace. We Cheyenne chieves held a counsel in regard to it. All came to the conclusion to make peace with U.S. army providing you make peace with the Kiowas, Comenches, Arapahoes, Apaches, and Siouxs.

We are going to send messengers to the Kiowas and to the other nations about our desire to make peace with you. When we held this counsel there were a few Arapahoes present. We want true news from you in return, that is, a letter.

Black Kettle and Other Chieves.

One Eye kept his gaze on the major's face, trying to read his expression as he scanned the letter.

Axton glanced at One Eye, then said, "What's Black Kettle want, Major?"

"He wants peace, Captain. The same thing I want." Then to One Eye: "I will write a response for you to take back to your chief." As he walked away, he handed the letter to Axton.

Fifteen minutes later, Wynkoop emerged from his office and placed a white envelope in One Eye's hand. "Take this to your chief, One Eye. Tell him he will hear from me or see me soon."

When the gate had closed behind the Indians, Charles Axton turned to his commander and said, "So what did you tell Black Kettle, sir?"

"I told him I would go to Denver and have a talk with Governor John Evans, since Washington has given him authority over the U.S. Army in Colorado Territory. If I can talk the governor into signing a peace treaty with the Indians, we can stop bloodshed between whites and, at least, the local tribes."

"I can see that Black Kettle wants a treaty, sir," said Axton, "and possibly the Arapaho chiefs he mentioned mean business about it, but I don't know about the other tribes."

"I seriously doubt we'll be able to get the others to even consider attending a peace treaty."

"Major!" came the voice of Corporal Corbin from the tower. "Troops from Fort Larned are here!"

While the gate swung open, Captain Axton limped alongside Major Wynkoop to greet the men. Most of the fort's all-male population joined them. Replacements for men killed and wounded in the latest battle with the Kiowas were a welcome sight.

There were smiles on everyone's faces as Major Wynkoop

welcomed the new men. The officer who led them, Captain Nate Wyman, had faithfully served under the commandant at Fort Larned since the fort opened in 1859.

The newcomers were guided to their quarters, and after settling in, Captain Wyman reported to the major's office for an introductory talk. Captain Axton was in the office with Major Wynkoop when Wyman entered.

Wynkoop would be gone from the fort for a few days, he told Wyman, a sturdy and ruggedly handsome man who was all military. Wynkoop then explained the basic workings of the fort and informed the new captain that he would be in charge, with Captain Axton as his advisor. Axton's injury, he explained, prevented him from carrying the load of acting commandant.

"I just received a letter from Black Kettle that says he wants peace with the army. So I'm going to Denver—some 150 miles to the northwest—for a meeting with Governor Evans. If I can get a peace treaty meeting set up, I'll go to Black Kettle's village on the Smoky Hill River and let him know the time and place.

"If I can, I'm going to try to persuade Black Kettle to bring the other chiefs and ride with me from Fort Lyon to whatever spot Governor Evans designates for the meeting. It sure would look good to Evans and whoever else he has with him to see the chiefs riding in with white soldiers."

Upon Major Wynkoop's arrival in Denver, Governor Evans graciously welcomed him into his office, saying he had heard good reports of the major's leadership at Fort Lyon and was glad to finally meet him.

Wynkoop sat in one of the chairs in front of Evans's desk, briefly explained why he had asked to see him, and handed him Black Kettle's letter.

The governor read the letter with little expression on his face, then handed it back to Wynkoop and said, "Do you really think Black Kettle and his pals want peace, Major?"

"I can't speak for the chiefs of the other tribes, sir, but I'm positive Black Kettle is serious about it. I've spent quite a bit of time with him. I have also spent time with War Bonnet, White Antelope, and Crooked Neck. They're definitely of the same mind as Black Kettle."

"The letter speaks of Arapaho that were in the council. Do you have any idea who they might be?"

"Probably Left Hand and Little Raven. I know they're close to Black Kettle."

Evans sighed. "I'm skeptical, Major, but it sure won't hurt to try. Let's set up the meeting—" He reached for a small calendar on the desktop. "Let's set it for…Wednesday, September 28. That'll give Black Kettle time to assemble all of his interested friends, and it'll give Colonel Chivington and me time to work on the wording of the treaty."

"Colonel Chivington, Governor?"

"Yes, that's right, Major. I've found Colonel Chivington quite helpful when it comes to dealing with Indians. You don't object to him being a part of these negotiations, do you?"

"Well, I—"

"Because if you do—" Governor Evans gave Wynkoop a tight smile—"we can put an end to this discussion right now."

Wynkoop sat quietly looking at Evans. Finally he said, "All right, Governor. Wednesday, September 28, it is. Where and what time?"

"Let's make it Camp Weld at two o'clock in the afternoon. That way lunch will be over and we'll have the entire afternoon to talk."

Rising to his feet, Wynkoop said, "All right, sir. I'll meet with Chief Black Kettle and have him and whatever chiefs he can muster at Camp Weld no later than two in the afternoon on September 28."

It was midmorning on Friday, September 16, when Major Edward Wynkoop and the unit of twelve men who'd escorted him arrived back at Fort Lyon. Captains Axton and Wyman were there to meet them, along with most of the men, as they passed through the gate, and they fired questions at the major about the treaty situation. As Wynkoop dismounted and turned his horse over to an adjutant, he said, "I'll address all of you in the morning, men, and fill you in. Right now I'm going to take a bath. Then I'll meet with Captains Axton and Wyman."

An hour later, the two captains entered Wynkoop's office and took seats in front of his desk.

"How's the leg, Captain Axton?" the major asked.

"About the same, sir. I'm not sure I'll ever be able to walk without the cane." He paused, then said, "And I know what that means—I'll have to retire from the army."

"Sure hope it doesn't come to that." Wynkoop eased back in his chair. "Well, gentlemen, it's all set. Governor Evans agreed to September 28 for the peace treaty meeting. It'll be held at Camp Weld."

"Camp Weld," said Wyman. "That's near Denver, isn't it, sir?"

"Yes. East a few miles."

"So who's coming?" asked Axton.

"Black Kettle received word from four Cheyenne who said they'd be there: War Bonnet, White Antelope, Crooked Neck, and High-Backed Wolf. Black Kettle's sure that from the

Arapaho he'll have Left Hand. He couldn't get a rider to Little Raven's village and back in the time we were there, but Black Kettle feels pretty certain Little Raven will join us."

"So other than the governor," said Axton, "who's on the treaty committee?"

Wynkoop wiped a hand over his salt-and-pepper mustache and said, "Chivington."

Axton's eyebrows arched. "That's all? Just Chivington?"

"Yes, other than myself."

"Pardon me, Major," Wyman said. "Is that Chivington as in Colonel John M. Chivington? The hero of Glorieta Pass?"

"Mm-hmm," said Wynkoop with a nod.

"Why is he on the treaty committee, sir?"

"Because he's commander of the First Colorado Cavalry, stationed at Camp Weld, and he's commander of the Military District of Colorado. Not to mention that he and the governor are good friends."

Wyman frowned. "I get the feeling you're not happy about Chivington being a part of this peace meeting."

"You're right, I'm not. Chivington is an Indian hater, and he makes no bones about it. But it seems that because he was the hero at Glorieta Pass, he can get away with anything. He's even been heard to say, 'The only good Indian is a *dead* Indian, and I like to make *good* Indians.'"

Axton shook his head. "And he's on the peace treaty committee? What's the governor thinking of, Major?"

"I don't know. I wanted to say something about it, but... Governor Evans might well have called the whole thing off if I'd voiced any objection."

"You said Chivington can get away with anything, Major, because he's the hero of Glorieta Pass," Wyman said. "What do you mean, *anything?*"

"Well, murder, for one."

"Murder?"

"Yes, but bear with me…this'll take some explaining. Shortly after John Evans was appointed governor of Colorado in May 1862, he informed President Lincoln that, with a few exceptions, the Indians in his territory were peaceful. The chiefs of all the tribes in Colorado were denouncing their young bucks who spoke of war with the whites. A month later, the governor changed his mind.

"A white man who lived among the Arapaho picked up false information about the Sioux having meetings with other tribes to plan attacks on white settlements. The man went to Governor Evans and reported that all the Plains tribes had agreed to make war against white settlements 'as soon as the grass was up in the spring.' The governor was convinced the territory was in grave danger, and he decided the only thing to do was to force the tribes onto reservations. Among those who agreed with him was the hero of Glorieta Pass.

"So Evans and Chivington joined together in a plan to force the Indians onto reservations before summer. By the governor's authority, Chivington led his First Colorado Cavalry Regiment across the plains as soon as the snow started to melt in April. How much the governor knew about Chivington's hatred toward Indians, I don't know, but when Chivington led his men toward the first Cheyenne villages to be forced onto a reservation, he ordered every detachment to 'kill Cheyennes wherever and whenever found.' That way there would be less Indians to herd to the reservation."

Captain Wyman's eyes were riveted on the major. "Are you going to tell me they murdered women and children in those villages?"

Major Wynkoop nodded. "That's it exactly. In a series of

attacks on Cheyenne camps and villages, Chivington and his troops murdered hundreds of peaceful Cheyenne—innocent men, women, and children. They ran off their horses and set fire to their tepees. The public was told these were 'battles' instigated by the Indians."

Wyman slowly shook his head. "And you know this for a fact?"

"Eyewitnesses, Captain. Some of the men who rode with Chivington hated what they were doing, but they were forced to follow his orders or face charges that could stand them before a firing squad."

"Whew! What a spot to be in!"

"One Cheyenne chief named Lean Bear had obtained papers from government officials in Washington that attested to his friendship toward whites. When he saw Chivington and his cavalry unit coming, Lean Bear rode toward them waving the papers and crying out for the soldiers to stop and look at them. But at Chivington's command, the chief was shot off his horse and killed."

"Hasn't somebody gone to the governor and told him the facts?" Wyman said.

"Not that I know of. They're afraid to. Without positive proof, a tattletale would be in serious trouble. You don't mess with Chivington."

As Wyman shook his head in puzzlement, the major said, "Anyway, to the tribes of the Plains Indians, these brutal attacks signified the start of a war. There were many attacks on whites after that, and comparatively few friendly Indians left on the Colorado plains. And that remains so today."

"But in spite of it all," said Axton, "here's Black Kettle, still willing to talk peace."

"He's a good man," said Wynkoop.

Wyman looked apprehensive as he said, "Well, Major, do you trust the governor? I mean, to work out this peace treaty...with Chivington at his side?"

"I have to, Captain. I won't say that I'm not a little on edge, but this is the man I have to go to if there's going to *be* a peace treaty. His authority comes from Washington. He told me he wants to see peace between the Indians and us. So I have to trust his word and hope he'll overshadow Chivington."

Axton let out a sigh and said, "If Chivington does something to throw a kink in this treaty, sir, it could result in all-out war. We might win it in time, but there'll be a lot of white men's blood shed before it's over."

"I know," the major said in a voice barely above a whisper. "I know."

2

THERE WAS A NIP IN THE AIR on September 28 as riders approached Camp Weld, and the wind that came down from the north across the flat, tawny prairie added to its bite. High drifting clouds periodically covered the sun, stealing what little warmth lay on the land.

Camp Weld was a tightly knit complex of squat wooden buildings with flat roofs that surrounded the small parade ground on three sides. There was no stockade fence. The barracks and quartermaster sheds took up one long side of the rectangular-shaped compound, and the officers' quarters took up the short space between the other side, which was made up of stables, corral, infirmary, and mess hall.

In the center of the open place was a flagpole. The red, white, and blue flag atop it snapped in the wind.

At precisely one-thirty, Major Edward Wynkoop and a dozen troopers, accompanied by nine chiefs of the Southern Cheyenne and Southern Arapaho tribes, rode up to the camp's boundary. The soldiers' hats were pulled low and their coat collars turned up. The Indians wore buckskin coats with fur collars. A stiff wind plucked at the Indians' feathers, and the soldiers bent their heads and tugged at their hat brims. The horses snorted and blew, some snuffling up the wind.

In the lead, riding beside Major Wynkoop, was Black Kettle, the man chosen by the other chiefs to be their spokesman.

A lieutenant and four other soldiers who stood by the flagpole stepped out in unison.

Men stood at different spots on the compound, eyeing the Indians warily.

The lieutenant smiled at Fort Lyon's commandant and said, "Welcome back to Camp Weld, Major Wynkoop."

"Thank you, Lieutenant…Adams, isn't it?"

"Yes, sir. Lloyd Adams, sir."

"Colonel Chivington and Governor Evans are expecting us, Lieutenant Adams."

"Yes, sir. Colonel Chivington asked that you meet with him and the governor in his quarters, and we have orders to escort the Indians to the mess hall where the meeting will take place. I'll take you to the colonel's quarters, sir, and Corporal Wilson will take the Indians to the mess hall. Your men are to wait for you in the south end of the barracks, over there, where they will be comfortable and out of the cold." He indicated the two corporals and two privates with him. "These men will take all the horses to the corral."

Wynkoop twisted in the saddle. "You men hear that?"

There was a general nodding of heads and verbal acknowledgment.

The major looked at the venerable Cheyenne leader next to him and said, "Will you make sure all the chiefs understand, Chief Black Kettle?"

Black Kettle turned in his saddle and spoke quickly in Cheyenne, then in Arapaho, telling the chiefs to dismount and follow him. Then he slid from his horse's back and said to Corporal Wilson, "We will follow you."

↑

Lieutenant Adams escorted Major Wynkoop across the parade ground. When they stepped up to the colonel's office door, Adams knocked and called out, "Lieutenant Adams, here, Colonel! I have Major Wynkoop with me!"

Heavy footsteps sounded above the whine of the wind in the eaves, and the door opened. John Chivington filled the door, which was probably six feet high, and had to stoop below the lintel to see. "Thank you, Lieutenant," was all he said. Then his eyes went to Wynkoop's face and he said, "Come in, Major."

Chivington, at forty-three years of age, had a thick head of dark hair lightly speckled with gray, and a full but well-trimmed beard. His eyes were black as midnight, and his face had a stern look.

Governor Evans was standing beside the desk. He smiled in greeting and offered his hand to Wynkoop. "Good to see you, Major."

"Same here, Governor," said Wynkoop, taking his hand in a firm grip.

Both men waited for Chivington to offer his hand, but the colonel, whose voice was deep and gruff, gestured to the chairs sitting before his desk and said, "Be seated, gentlemen. We wanted to have a chat with you before the meeting starts, Major. How many chiefs have come with you?"

"Nine."

Chivington sat down, picked up a stub of a pencil, and pulled a blank sheet of paper from a desk drawer. "I need their names. I assume Black Kettle is one of them?"

"Yes. There are seven Cheyenne and two Arapaho."

"No other tribes represented?" asked Governor Evans.

"No, sir. Black Kettle contacted chiefs from every tribe in the territory, but to no avail. They don't trust the U.S. Army."

Chivington had written Black Kettle's name on the paper. "Give me the names of the other Cheyenne chiefs, Colonel."

Wynkoop spoke slowly so Chivington could keep up. "War Bonnet, White Antelope, Crooked Neck, High-Backed Wolf, Big Mountain, and Gray Fox. The Arapaho are Left Hand and Little Raven."

Chivington picked up a piece of paper from the right side of his desktop and laid it in front of the major. "Here are the terms of the treaty. Go ahead. Read them."

After Wynkoop read the terms, he said, "You may get some resistance about taking all but enough of their weapons to hunt with. And…why do they have to relocate their villages?"

"If they don't have an overabundance of firearms," Evans said, "they'll be less likely to start trouble. And—"

"Looks like the only one who'll have to relocate is Black Kettle," cut in Chivington, "now that I know who the other chiefs are. The rest of them are close enough to forts to be watched, but Black Kettle's village is way out there on the Smoky Hill River, almost to Kansas. Too far from a fort."

"So where do you propose to put him?" asked Wynkoop.

A map of Colorado Territory hung on the wall behind Chivington. He rose from his chair and stabbed a finger at the wall. "We're gonna put him in your neighborhood, Major. Right here at the big bend of Sand Creek." With his finger on the spot, he added, "That'll put him less than thirty miles from Fort Lyon. He'll be your responsibility. Since I'm told you and he are friends, that'll be all right, won't it?"

"It's all right with me, but I don't think Black Kettle's going to take to the idea of being forced to relocate. His village has been on the Smoky Hill for a long time."

Chivington's mouth curved down, and his eyes flashed. "If the guy wants peace with us, he'll do what we say, Wynkoop. The governor and I agreed to this, and that's the way it's gonna be!"

Wynkoop shrugged. "All right. We'll see how he takes it."

"Well, if he doesn't take it good, that's just too bad!"

In the mess hall, Evans, Chivington, and Wynkoop were seated at a long table, facing the chiefs. The Indians regarded Evans and Chivington with wary eyes.

Major Wynkoop shifted uneasily, then said, "My Indian friends, this is Colorado's Governor John Evans, and Colonel John Chivington, commander of the Military District of Colorado. I have given them your names and which tribes you represent. They've drawn up the terms of the peace treaty. I will let one of them read the terms to you. Chief Black Kettle, you are spokesman for these other chiefs. Would you please interpret for those who do not understand English?"

Black Kettle nodded, then interpreted Wynkoop's introductory remarks.

Chivington read the terms of the peace treaty slowly and paused after each line so Black Kettle could interpret it in both Cheyenne and Arapaho. It wasn't long before the Indians began to frown. When Black Kettle translated the words that they would have to give up most of their firearms, he stopped translating and argued against this point, but was told by both Evans and Chivington that if they wanted peace, they must abide by it. The U.S. government would leave them enough weapons to hunt game, but that was all.

Evans was quick to point out that if the villages would not attack whites, would not steal from them or molest them in any way, and if they would obey the rest of the treaty, the U.S. Army would not only be at peace with them but would give them protection. The Indians would not need an abundance of weapons.

When the chiefs heard that the treaty could force any village designated by Evans and Chivington to relocate, they began to murmur. And when Chivington said the only village that would have to relocate now was Black Kettle's, the chief stopped interpreting and objected.

"Black Kettle," said Wynkoop, "you will be closer to Fort Lyon...less than thirty miles from the fort, on the banks of Sand Creek, where the southbound creek makes a big bend and heads east for several hundred yards, then curves south again."

"Yes, Black Kettle," said Evans. "It's for your own protection. You and your people will have the protection of Major Wynkoop and his troops. The villages of War Bonnet, White Antelope, Left Hand, and Little Raven are already under Wynkoop's protection by virtue of their proximity to the fort."

Black Kettle looked at his friend and said, "Major, does this relocation meet with your approval?"

"Yes, Chief. It would make me very happy to have you and your people close to my fort. Now, I believe that you and the other chiefs understand these gentlemen want each village reasonably close to the forts for another reason—for the army's periodic inspection to make sure each village is keeping the treaty."

Black Kettle interpreted, and all the chiefs acknowledged they understood.

Chivington ran his dark gaze over the faces of the chiefs and said, "Are we in agreement then?"

Black Kettle spoke to the chiefs in their own tongue, and all agreed.

"Good," said the governor. "This means that routine inspections will be made by Colonel Chivington's First Colorado Cavalry, as well as the commanders of forts near your villages."

"To prevent any misunderstanding," said Chivington, "we'll provide each of you with a United States flag and a white flag. Every day in your villages, at sunrise, you are to fly the United States flag from a pole. And you will take it down every day at sunset. The white flag must fly beneath the U.S. flag. This will signify that you are at peace with the army and with all white people."

Black Kettle interpreted, and the chiefs said they understood, their dark faces showing they were relieved to finally have a peace treaty with the white man's army.

"Black Kettle," Chivington said, "we will have army units at your villages in the next few days to confiscate most of your firearms."

Before Black Kettle could interpret the words to the other chiefs, Wynkoop said, "You'll not confiscate surplus weapons from Black Kettle and his people until they're moved to Sand Creek, right?"

Chivington stiffened. "And why not?"

"Because they will be in transit for a few days between Smoky Hill River and Sand Creek, with no fort designated to protect them. That's why not." Wynkoop's voice was edged with challenge.

Chivington remained silent for a tense moment, then said, "Well, of course. That goes without saying. We'll be at Sand Creek to confiscate the firearms within a week or so after they get settled."

"Well!" said Evans. "All that's left now is for everyone here to sign the treaty papers."

After all nine chiefs signed the papers, Chivington, Evans, and Wynkoop put their names to the treaty. Even so, Major Wynkoop had an uneasy feeling in his stomach.

Chivington and Evans stood by the flagpole and watched Wynkoop and the chiefs ride away; then they strode toward the colonel's quarters. Once they were inside, Chivington poured generous shots of whiskey for Evans and himself, and they sat down at a small table.

The colonel took a healthy swig of the amber liquid and said, "John, this is gonna work out really good! Bringing those nine villages into subjection is sure gonna be easier when they don't have but a few guns."

"*Much* easier," Evans said, setting his half-empty glass on the table. "Wish it could be that way with all of them."

"Well, every little bit helps." Chivington laughed again. "You know my motto: The only good Indian is a *dead* Indian! What Indians get killed when resisting the move to reservations will only make them *good* Indians!"

Evans chuckled appreciatively. "I wonder what that lame-brained Wynkoop would say if he knew we were planning to move his friend Black Kettle to a reservation in Wyoming?"

Chivington's mouth pulled tight. "Speaking of Wynkoop, John…he's gotta go. He's wary of us. You and I both know what he'll do when he finds out what we're really planning."

"You're right. I'll contact Washington and get him transferred. Probably take a couple weeks or more, but I'll get it done. Do you have somebody in mind to take his place?"

"Sure do. Pal of mine. Major Scott Anthony. Fought beside me at Glorieta Pass. He's at Fort Craig, New Mexico. Been commandant there for about six months and has fought the

Apaches tenaciously. Hates them with a passion. I'm sure he feels the same way about all Indians. Scott would make Fort Lyon a real tool in our hands."

"Then I'll go to work on it as soon as I get back to my office."

Chivington drained his glass. "I can't get over the gullibility of those Indians…and that thickheaded Wynkoop!"

"You'd think Wynkoop could at least figure out that an honest peace agreement with the Indians is out of the question. There's a lot of people who want revenge for what those savages have done to white people in the last few years. They'd sure cause a stink if we actually meant to abide by this treaty!" Governor Evans's expression turned suddenly serious. "I've got to say, though, I'm a bit worried about how you're going to handle Washington when they learn about all those dead Indians."

Chivington snorted. "When the bloodbath starts, I'll merely report to you and to Washington that the dirty savages resisted with guns they'd hidden from us. We had no choice but to defend ourselves."

"Can't happen soon enough for me," said Evans.

"Me, either," said Chivington as he poured himself another glass of whiskey.

Evans gave the colonel a mocking look and said, "What would your Methodist elders say if they knew you were in on this kind of skullduggery, John?"

"The same thing they'd say if they knew I drink whiskey and smoke cigars. But then, what they don't know won't hurt 'em…or me!"

The setting sun painted the buffalo-hide walls of the tepees a golden orange, while smoke lifted from the air vents, carried away by the wind off the Smoky Hill River.

Chief Black Kettle's squaw, Gentle Dove, and fifteen-year-old daughter, Silver Moon, were inside their tepee, cooking the evening meal. Though both had learned to speak, read, and write English, they conversed in their native Cheyenne.

"I wish Father would come home," said Silver Moon as she sliced bread with a sharp knife.

"As do I," Gentle Dove said.

Silver Moon had a youthful glow to her skin, the clear complexion enhanced by the wind and sun of the plains. Gentle Dove had often thought that Heammawihio, the Great Spirit and Wise One Above, had worked extra hard when he fashioned Silver Moon in her womb. Though the girl resembled Gentle Dove, she was much more beautiful. She had such graceful lines in her features, heightened by flashing but soft black eyes...and her black hair was a wavy mass that cascaded to the middle of her back.

"Mother," said Silver Moon, "what will happen if Father and the other chiefs are unhappy with the treaty the whites have prepared?"

Gentle Dove continued to stir the venison stew in the cast-iron kettle. She looked down at the earthen floor of the tepee, then met her daughter's searching gaze. "I do not want to think about it," she said quietly. "It will mean more fighting and bloodshed."

"Why does there have to be fighting and killing? Why did not the white men stay on faraway shores where they lived before?"

"Do you not remember what George Bent told us? They came to the East from across a wide lake called Atlantic because someone in their homeland was persecuting them for their faith. Only it seems that when they arrived on the eastern shore, some of them decided to come this way. When they saw our land, they coveted it and decided to take it from us. There would not be fighting and killing if we did not resist them."

"But why are they so greedy? Why—"

"Mother!" came the voice of Silver Moon's twelve-year-old brother, Sky Eagle. The flap opened and Sky Eagle stuck his head inside. "Mother! Father is back!"

Black Kettle's family stepped out into the cold wind just as the chief dismounted and a young warrior took his horse toward the rope corral. Instantly Black Kettle was surrounded by his people, asking how the peace treaty meeting had gone. Black Kettle told them it went well. He would call for a meeting and tell them about it after he had eaten supper with his family.

The chief and his family sat on the earthen floor of the tepee, and before eating, thanked Heammawihio for the food.

Sky Eagle, who wore the headband of a youth who anticipated being a great warrior and hunter when he became a man, looked at his father by the flickering light of the fire and said, "Will you tell us now, Father? We are your family."

Black Kettle smiled. "Yes. I can tell my family now."

While they ate and drank, Black Kettle told Gentle Dove and their children the wording of the treaty, and of the move they must make south to Sand Creek.

There was silence in the tepee for a brief moment, then Gentle Dove said, "My husband, it does not bother me to move to Sand Creek, but I am bothered about having to give up most of our firearms to the army."

Black Kettle ran his gaze over their faces. "It will be all right. We will be left with enough weapons to hunt and kill game. And should whites or other Indian tribes bring us trouble, we will have Major Edward Wynkoop's troops to protect us."

A worried expression etched itself on Silver Moon's features. "Father, please excuse your daughter's youth and lack of experience, but how do you know you can trust the white men? I do not mean Major Wynkoop...but the others."

"If we were only dealing with Colonel John Chivington, I would not feel secure in the treaty. But I believe Governor John Evans would not deceive us. And best of all, Major Wynkoop was there observing, and his signature is also on the treaty papers."

"This is good," Gentle Dove said. "My heart is happy that Major Wynkoop will be the army leader we will deal with."

"Yes." The chief nodded. "This is good. I trust Major Wynkoop completely. He is our friend."

"May I ask," said Gentle Dove, "since the army will make us move to Sand Creek, and since they will take most of our firearms...will they also restrict our hunting ground?"

"Nothing was said about such a restriction," Black Kettle said. "Therefore, I must say that there is no restriction. We can hunt wherever we please. You should know also that Colonel Chivington was going to take the weapons from us before we make the journey to Sand Creek, but Major Wynkoop told him he was not, and Chivington did not argue. He is a much larger man, but he seems to have respect for our friend Major Wynkoop."

After the meal, several campfires illuminated the faces of the Cheyenne people as they listened to their chief explain the terms of the peace treaty. Some were skeptical, but since Black Kettle believed that all was well, they accepted it.

3

BY THE END OF THE FIRST WEEK of October, Black Kettle and his six hundred Cheyenne people arrived at the designated spot on the banks of Sand Creek, escorted by Major Edward Wynkoop and a dozen men, including Captain Nate Wyman.

The entire area around the Sand Creek spot was rugged, rolling country, dividing the foothills of the Rocky Mountains to the west from the vast level plains that stretched eastward toward Kansas. It was a sterile wasteland, covered with monotonous clusters of soapweed, sagebrush, and tumbleweed. There was enough grass, however, to feed their horses in spring, summer, and fall. Major Wynkoop had promised hay from Fort Lyon to feed their horses through the coming winter.

While the Indians looked the area over, scanning the lay of the land, Wynkoop took Black Kettle down the steep slope that led to the bank of the creek and showed him the three-foot depth of water. Black Kettle was glad to see it, and was happy when told that in the late spring and summer it was even deeper. The village would have plenty of water.

Wynkoop then pointed southwest across the windswept prairie and said, "Chief, Fort Lyon is that direction. If you ever need me, I'm there to help. I'll come by and check on you often. Please feel free to come to the fort and visit us."

Black Kettle shook hands Indian style with the major and

said, "Thank you, Major Edward Wynkoop, for being friend to Black Kettle and his people."

Gentle Dove and her children, who were standing close by, stepped up to the major, and Gentle Dove said, "We are thankful to Heammawihio for giving us such a good friend, Major."

Silver Moon smiled at the major and said, "Thank you, sir, for all you have done for us. I have prayed that Heammawihio will make your paths smooth."

Wynkoop smiled and thanked them. Then, turning to Nate Wyman, he said, "Well, Captain, we need to head for the fort."

The Indians looked on as the men in blue mounted and rode southwest. When they had gone about a hundred yards, Major Wynkoop turned. The Cheyennes lifted their hands in farewell, and the major waved back.

Black Kettle then turned to his family and said, "We must choose the place for our tepee. Silver Moon…Sky Eagle…you choose it."

Cheyenne custom decreed that the chief's tepee must be centralized in the village. Once the spot was chosen, all other tepees would be erected around it.

A few days after Black Kettle and his people had settled at Sand Creek, they were pleasantly surprised to see Cheyenne Chief War Bonnet and the elderly Chief White Antelope ride in with a few braves, squaws, and children from their villages.

Silver Moon was especially pleased, for in White Antelope's village was a Cheyenne youth named Bear Paw, the son of subchief Snake Killer and his squaw, Jessie Small Hands. Snake Killer was in line to become chief when White Antelope grew too old to lead the people.

Bear Paw was a year older than Silver Moon. They had first

noticed each other two years ago when the Cheyenne villages had a powwow at Black Kettle's village on the Smoky Hill River. They had seen each other only three times since then, and their mutual attachment had grown stronger each time. On the most recent occasion, which had been almost three months before, they had declared to each other their feelings. Though they were too young for marriage, they had received sanction from their parents to be promised to each other.

Silver Moon stood with her parents as the visiting Cheyenne dismounted. Bear Paw's gaze immediately settled on the lovely girl, and she smiled at him.

There was the usual greeting among the Indians, with Bear Paw staying next to his parents until the greeting period was fulfilled. He then turned to Snake Killer and said, "Father, I ask permission now to go to Silver Moon."

Snake Killer's lips curved slightly in a smile, and he looked at Jessie Small Hands, then said, "You may go to her."

Black Kettle and Gentle Dove watched as Bear Paw talked to his father. They smiled at each other and glanced at Silver Moon, whose eyes were riveted on the handsome young man who was now headed her way.

Sky Eagle said, "Oh, look, Silver Moon! Bear Paw is coming to see me! Maybe he wants to try fishing with me in the creek."

Silver Moon elbowed him in the ribs. "He is not coming to see *you*, little brother. He is coming to see the woman he loves!"

"Woman!" he said, snorting. "You are just a girl, my sister. A mere child."

"The child in this family is Sky Eagle. A mere twelve grasses."

Sky Eagle was trying to think of a retort when Bear Paw drew up before Black Kettle and Gentle Dove.

"My greeting to Chief Black Kettle and his beautiful squaw," said Bear Paw.

"It is good to see Bear Paw," said the chief.

"Yes," said Gentle Dove, nodding.

Sky Eagle stepped past his sister and said, "Hello, Bear Paw. You came to see me! Would you like to go fishing in the creek? I have caught many fish there already."

Bear Paw looked at the younger boy with a slight smile and said, "I am always happy to see Sky Eagle…but I must be honest. I did not come to see Sky Eagle." His gaze swung past the boy. "I came to see Silver Moon."

The girl's features tinted slightly and she smiled.

Sky Eagle turned his mouth down and made his lower lip quiver. "I am hurt. I thought Bear Paw came to see me."

"Maybe someday I will come and fish in the creek with you," said Bear Paw, "but not this day. Chief Black Kettle, I ask your permission to take a walk with your daughter down to the creek."

"You have my permission."

"Thank you," said Bear Paw. Then to Silver Moon he said, "I must go and stake out my horse with the others. I will return shortly."

"I will wait here, Bear Paw," Silver Moon said.

Bear Paw hurried away, and Black Kettle and Gentle Dove headed toward War Bonnet and his squaw. Sky Eagle remained beside his sister.

Silver Moon looked at her brother with a scowl and said, "Have you not some friends among our visitors you need to see?"

"Later," he said with a sly grin. "I will first walk to the creek with my sister and Bear Paw. She needs my protection."

"I do not need your protection, little brother. Go find some of your friends."

Sky Eagle pointed at Bear Paw, who had stopped to speak

to one of the girls of his village, a niece of White Antelope. "Look, sister! That is the girl Bear Paw really loves."

Silver Moon let out a little squeal and pinched her brother's ear. Sky Eagle howled and bent his head toward the hand that was giving him pain.

"You are a mean little brother, Sky Eagle! Bear Paw is promised to *me*...not to Little Flower! She is too young for Bear Paw. She is only twelve grasses!" With that, she let go of his ear.

"If you ever pinch my ear again, I will tell Bear Paw that you snore at night and keep the rest of the village awake!"

Silver Moon giggled, took hold of his ear again, and said, "Go ahead and tell him. He won't believe you!"

Sky Eagle howled, sucking air through his teeth, and said, "That hurts!"

"It won't hurt anymore if I let go," Silver Moon said calmly. "And I will let go if you promise to find someone else to bother."

"Ow! Yes! I promise!"

At the creek bank the sweethearts, clad in their fur-lined coats, sat at arm's length on large round rocks. The sun was shining, but the wind coming across the land from the snowcapped Rockies was cold.

They talked of Silver Moon's new home at Sand Creek and of the good that would come from peace with the white man's army. Then they grew quiet and just looked into each other's eyes from time to time while watching the sunlight dance on the rippling surface of the creek.

A jackrabbit popped out of a hole in the side of the creek bank and bounded away.

"He is probably going after food for his family," said Bear

41

Paw. "That is a man's responsibility."

Silver Moon smiled. "Yes."

Bear Paw wanted to hold her hand but dared not. Looking her in the eye, he said, "I will be very happy when it is my responsibility to provide food for you. My heart reaches for you every hour, Silver Moon."

"And mine for you," she said softly above the gurgling of the creek.

Bear Paw was quiet for a moment, then said, "In just two more grasses I will be old enough to qualify as a hunter and warrior. I will then ask your father for Silver Moon's hand in marriage."

Happy tears welled up in Silver Moon's eyes. "The love in my heart for Bear Paw grows stronger as each moon passes. I will be very pleased and honored to be your squaw."

Bear Paw's eyes grew tender as he looked at her and said, "Silver Moon will be the most beautiful bride there ever was."

The girl blushed as she favored him with a shy smile. In her heart, she thanked Heammawihio, the Great Spirit and Wise One Above, for putting love for her in the heart of Bear Paw.

On October 20, the relentless prairie wind was whipping between the buildings of Fort Lyon when a knock came at the door of Major Edward Wynkoop's office. It was midmorning, and Wynkoop was stoking the fire in the potbellied stove. "Yes?" he called. "Come in!"

The door opened, and Captain Nate Wyman stepped inside, his hat pulled low and his collar turned up against the cold.

"You have some visitors, sir," said Wyman. "Arapaho Chiefs Left Hand and Little Raven, along with a dozen braves from each of their villages, have come as a gesture of friendship. One of the braves speaks English and has come to interpret."

A smile spread across the major's face. "Well, great! It's obvious I can't pack twenty-six men in this small cubicle. Do you
know the interpreter's name?"

"Yes, sir. It's Lone Coyote."

"All right. Bring the chiefs and Lone Coyote to me, and if
the braves want to get in out of the wind, take them to the
mess hall."

"Yes, sir," said Wyman.

Wynkoop placed three straight-backed chairs in front of his
desk, then set a pot of coffee on the potbellied stove to heat up.

Moments later, Nate Wyman returned. As he ushered Left
Hand, Little Raven, and Lone Coyote into the office, he said,
"Major, the braves say they are dressed warm enough. They
will wait out in the compound while you and the chiefs have
your visit."

"All right," said Wynkoop. "At least give them some hot
coffee."

"Yes, sir."

Wynkoop shook hands Indian style with all three visitors,
telling Lone Coyote he was glad he'd come along, and asked
him to begin interpreting immediately.

"You men honor me," the major said to Left Hand and
Little Raven. "Please, sit down. I've got some coffee heating up
here on the stove."

The chiefs talked of the relief they felt at having the peace
treaty between themselves, the United States Army, and
Governor John Evans. Their hunting was going well in spite of
having fewer rifles.

Wynkoop had just said how glad he was their people were
thriving when he was interrupted by the sound of loud voices
outside.

Shoving back his chair, he said, "Excuse me, gentlemen. There's something going on out here that I—"

There was a sudden knock at the office door. When the major opened it, Captain Wyman stood there.

"Major," he said breathlessly, "we've got more company out here. General George Shoup and his Third Colorado Cavalry Regiment just rode in. Colonel Shoup would like to see you in your office."

"I'll see him outside," said Wynkoop, reaching to the coat-rack next to the door. He donned his campaign hat, shouldered into his heavy coat, and said, "Left Hand…Little Raven… Lone Coyote…you stay comfortable where you are. I'll be back shortly."

Wynkoop knew of Colonel George L. Shoup and his half-trained, largely undisciplined regiment from the streets of Denver's saloon district. He stepped out to find the entire regiment of three hundred men sitting their horses and glaring at the Arapaho who stood nearby.

The major had never seen Shoup before, but he was aware the man was an ambitious, Indian-hating ex-politician from Denver. Shoup was already off his horse and heading straight for Wynkoop, who met him halfway.

"You're Major Wynkoop, I take it, " gruffed Shoup.

"Yes, sir."

"And you know who I am…and who these men with me are."

"Yes. Captain Wyman told me."

"We're on our way back to Camp Weld from Pueblo, where we were sent by Colonel Chivington to handle some Hopi Indians who had drifted in from New Mexico. Thought we'd stop by and take a look at your fort."

"I assume you were able to bring about a peaceful solution

to the problems," Wynkoop said.

"Yep. They gave us a tussle, so we sent them to their happy hunting ground."

"I see. Big bunch of them?"

"No. Only twenty-three. But when it comes to Indians, Major, I'm a no-nonsense man. Indians give me trouble, they die." Shoup threw a thumb over his shoulder. "What're these filthy Arapaho doing inside this United States Army fort? I understand from the guards at the gate that you've got their chiefs in your office. What's going on here?"

"I take offense at your use of the word *filthy*, Colonel Shoup, and as for what's going on here, I happen to be responsible for those two Arapaho villages. I've been able to develop a good relationship with the chiefs. Does that satisfy your curiosity... sir?"

A slow wave of color spread over Shoup's face. "You're to make sure these bloody savages obey the treaty, Major, but you're not supposed to get chummy with them! Any man in this army who is sympathetic with these barbarian devils had better get out!"

Wynkoop seldom raised his voice, but he could no longer keep his anger in check. "They're not barbarians, and they're not devils, Shoup! It's your kind of attitude that breeds war and hatred between these people and the whites who've stolen their land!"

Shoup's eyes bulged and his entire body shook. "Do you know who you're yelling at, Wynkoop? Do you? In case you haven't noticed...I outrank you! You want to face a court-martial?"

"You don't frighten me, Shoup! You come in here flashing your rank, reaming me out for doing the job I've been assigned to do. Don't threaten me with court-martial! The gate that let you in here will let you out." With that, Wynkoop wheeled and headed for his office while his men—who outnumbered the Third Cavalry Regiment almost two to one—applauded.

Shoup glared at Wynkoop's back, then pivoted with a grunt and headed for his horse. As Shoup settled in the saddle, he glanced back to see Wynkoop pause at his office door and look at him. Shoup gave the major a bitter glance, then kicked his horse's sides and rode away, leading his men through the gate.

The major stepped inside his office to find the chiefs and the interpreter at the window.

"We saw and heard it all, Major Wynkoop," said Lone Coyote. "I told the chiefs what was said."

Wynkoop looked at Left Hand and Little Raven, then said, "Tell them I apologize for the colonel's sharp tongue, Lone Coyote."

When Lone Coyote translated the words into Arapaho, both chiefs spoke in return.

Lone Coyote smiled. "Chief Left Hand and Chief Little Raven say that I should tell you they appreciate the major's kind attitude toward them and our people. They also thank you for defending us...and want you to know they will visit Fort Lyon again soon."

Edward Wynkoop laid a hand on the shoulders of the chiefs and said, "You are welcome anytime."

On November 4, two weeks after Colonel Shoup visited Fort Lyon, Major Wynkoop was in the fort's infirmary, checking on a soldier who was down with pneumonia. He was about to leave when the door opened and Sergeant Ralph Werner entered.

"Major," said Werner, "we've got the Third Colorado

Cavalry Regiment out here again."

"Is Shoup leading them?"

"Yes, sir. He wants to see you immediately."

Wynkoop looked back at the fort physician, who stood beside the patient, and said, "I appreciate what you're doing for him, Doc. Lanny, you concentrate on getting well, okay?"

"Yes, sir," said the young private in a weak voice.

Werner kept pace with the major as he walked briskly toward the center of the parade ground, where he could see the Third Cavalry sitting their horses. Colonel Shoup stood in front of them, his feet planted wide apart, as he watched the approaching major and sergeant. Wynkoop noticed a tall, slender officer standing next to Shoup and wondered who he was.

"You wanted to see me, Colonel?" Wynkoop said.

"Yes," replied Shoup. "This is Major Scott Anthony."

Wynkoop offered his hand, and Anthony met it with the word, "Major," and a solemn-faced nod.

Shoup produced a brown envelope from his coat pocket and handed it to Wynkoop. "Read this, Major."

Wynkoop looked into the colonel's eyes as he took the envelope from his hand. He broke the seal on the envelope and pulled out an official-looking document from the War Department in Washington, D.C.

October 28, 1864
Major Edward Wynkoop
Fort Lyon, Colorado Territory

Sir, this is to notify you that as of the date this paper is placed in your hands, you are hereby relieved of your commission as commandant of Fort Lyon and are being replaced by Major Scott Anthony.

You are ordered to vacate the premises immediately and report to Colonel John Chivington at Camp Weld, Colorado, within two days for further orders.

Signed: James P. Weddel, U.S. Secretary of War
        Henry W. Halleck, General-in-Chief, U.S. Army
  cc: John Evans, Governor, Colorado Territory;
       Denver, Colorado
  cc: Colonel John M. Chivington, Commander,
       Military District of Colorado

The major's voice was tight as he fixed cold eyes on Shoup and said, "I would blame you for this, but I know where it stems from. My guess would be that Major Anthony here is also a close friend of Colonel Chivington."

"As a matter of fact I am," Anthony said. "I served with him at Glorieta Pass."

Wynkoop nodded. "Figures." Then to Shoup he said, "Mark my word, Colonel. If the pattern I've set with these villages and their chiefs is changed, and the treaty is violated, there will be bloodshed."

Anthony stepped forward and faced Wynkoop. "I believe, Major, that you have orders to vacate these premises immediately. As commandant of this fort, I am ordering you to leave. *Now.*"

Twenty minutes later, Major Edward Wynkoop was on his horse with his field gear tied behind the saddle. The soldiers had started to gather around to tell him good-bye.

"You men!" snapped Anthony. "Back to your duties! Major Wynkoop must be on his way. He has only forty-eight hours to report in at Camp Weld."

Wynkoop nudged his horse toward the gate and didn't look

back as he passed through to the windswept prairie.

When the gate was closed, Major Anthony turned to Captain Wyman and said, "I want to meet with all the men on the parade in exactly one hour. We have much planning to do and much to accomplish."

"Yes, sir," said Wyman.

As Wyman walked away, Anthony turned to Shoup and said, "Well, Colonel, this fort is secured. You can be on your way."

"Yeah. That's what we'll do, Major. We'll be on our way. We've got some heathen savages to deal with."

4

THE DAY AFTER MAJOR EDWARD WYNKOOP had been relieved as commandant of Fort Lyon, Chief Left Hand had visitors. As he walked with Lone Coyote, he said in their native tongue, "I do not understand. What is this you are telling me?"

"I am simply repeating what the bluecoat major said, Chief, that he is now commandant of Fort Lyon. Major Wynkoop is being sent somewhere else by the army chiefs in Washington."

"This is news that touches me deeply," said Left Hand as they rounded a group of tepees and the army unit of some sixty soldiers came into view. A large number of the village people stood looking on.

Left Hand noted the tall, slender figure who stood in front of the mounted soldiers. As he stopped before the officer, he spoke in Arapaho, saying, "I am Chief Left Hand. Where has Major Edward Wynkoop gone?"

Lone Coyote translated his chief's words and waited to interpret the white man's reply.

"Major Wynkoop is on his way to Camp Weld," said the officer. "He will be sent to another fort. I don't have any idea where. I'm Major Scott Anthony, his replacement."

"And what is the reason for your visit, Major Scott Anthony?" asked Left Hand.

"We are here to take all of your firearms."

When the interpreted words met his ears, Left Hand's eyes widened. "I do not understand," he said. "The agreement was that we could keep enough firearms to hunt game for our food. If you take the remainder of our firearms, we cannot hunt. We will starve to death."

"You'll be fed rations provided by the army," came Anthony's cold reply.

"But this breaks the peace treaty," argued Left Hand. "Major Wynkoop would never have done this. Why are you breaking the treaty?"

Chief Left Hand's warriors were gathered close by, listening. Vexation showed on their faces.

"Since I was not commandant at Fort Lyon when the treaty was signed, I am not responsible for what Wynkoop agreed to."

Left Hand's heavy brows drew together. He gazed at the major narrowly and leaned forward a little, seeming to probe the very soul of the man as he said, "You do not make sense, Major. It was not just Major Wynkoop who signed the treaty. So did Governor John Evans and Colonel John Chivington."

"They don't have to deal with you like I do!" snapped Anthony. "Let me make it plain, Chief. I don't trust Indians. This village is under my jurisdiction, so I'm taking your weapons. If you try to hide some and keep them from me, you will be punished severely!"

Left Hand looked on in disbelief as the soldiers raised their rifles, cocking the hammers. By the gleam in Anthony's eye, it was obvious that he was itching to give the order to fire.

"It appears I have no choice but to let you take our guns," Left Hand said, "but I will say, once again the white man has proven he speaks with forked tongue."

✦

The next day, White Antelope and many of his people were visiting Black Kettle's village. Dressed warmly against the cold, Bear Paw and Silver Moon were sitting at their favorite spot at the bottom of the eight-foot embankment beside sluggish Sand Creek, which was edged with ice.

"Soon winter will come with the heavy snows," said Bear Paw. "We will not be able to visit."

"I know," said Silver Moon. "This makes me sad. I will not see you until the warmth of spring."

The sound of voices drifted toward them. Bear Paw stood on a rock to look back toward the village. "More visitors. Chiefs Left Hand and Little Raven have arrived, along with a few braves from their villages. They seem upset. We must go and see what is wrong."

Bear Paw wanted to take Silver Moon's hand to help her climb the steep embankment, but he knew he must not. When they reached the top, they hurried and joined the crowd gathering around the Arapaho chiefs and their braves.

As Chiefs Black Kettle and White Antelope faced Chiefs Left Hand and Little Raven in the center of the circle, Left Hand told them the new commandant from Fort Lyon—Major Scott Anthony—and his soldiers had come to his village the day before and taken all of their firearms. Little Raven told them Anthony and his bluecoats had come to his village and taken all of their firearms too.

"What has happened to Major Edward Wynkoop?" Black Kettle said.

"He is on his way to Camp Weld," Left Hand answered. "Major Anthony said Major Wynkoop will be sent to some other fort. He does not know which one."

"How can this be?" said Black Kettle, his face flushed. "We have a treaty!"

"I said this to him," said Little Raven, "as did Left Hand. Major Scott Anthony said he is not responsible to abide by the treaty because he was not commandant at Fort Lyon when it was signed. He also told both of us he does not trust Indians."

"But the treaty was also signed by Governor John Evans and Colonel John Chivington," said White Antelope.

"Yes," said Left Hand. "When I said this to Major Scott Anthony, he said they do not have to deal with the Indians as he does. Our villages are under his authority. So with their guns pointed at us, the bluecoats took all of our firearms."

Black Kettle's breath came quickly as he said, "And you are supposed to starve to death? How are your braves supposed to hunt game to feed their families?"

"We were told the army would provide us rations for our food," said Little Raven.

"Rations? This is what kind of food?"

Little Raven shrugged and looked at Left Hand.

"I do not know," said Left Hand.

Black Kettle turned to White Antelope. "I wonder if the major and his bluecoats are going to come to our villages…and the others that were represented at the peace treaty meeting. Will they also take our guns and feed us with these rations?"

"It would not surprise me," said the silver-haired chief.

"I cannot allow this to happen. I will ride to Denver and talk to Governor John Evans. He is a man of honor. He will overrule this wicked Major Scott Anthony. He will make Major Scott Anthony abide by the treaty and will make him give Left Hand and Little Raven their weapons back."

✦

Black Kettle had planned his trip to Denver carefully and estimated that he would return to his village on Wednesday, November 9. Several braves from his village and some from White Antelope's traveled with him.

On November 8, White Antelope came to Black Kettle's village, as did Little Raven and Left Hand. They and the braves with them stayed the night in tepees provided by the people of the village.

It was almost noon on November 9 when Black Kettle and his braves were seen in the distance, riding toward the village on an inch-deep blanket of snow that had fallen the night before. Within a few minutes they rode into the village, and a crowd gathered around their chief, with White Antelope, Left Hand, and Little Raven in the innermost circle.

Black Kettle's features were stoic as he ran his dark gaze over their faces and said, "I was not able to see Governor John Evans. He is in the East where white man's capital lies. He will not return for many moons. I was promised by his office workers that when he returns, they will tell him Black Kettle was there to see him and still needs to do so. And that it is very important that I see him.

"They said Governor John Evans will send a message over white man's talking wire to Fort Lyon. Someone from there will come and bring me Governor John Evans's message, telling me when I can meet with him in Denver. I must wait until then."

The disappointment among his people was palpable.

Black Kettle then said, "Left Hand...Little Raven...you have received rations from Major Scott Anthony?"

Both chiefs said they had but that the food was almost tasteless and the amount provided every third day was insufficient to feed their people.

Black Kettle rubbed his chin. "None of this would have happened if Major Edward Wynkoop had not been sent away. I would lend my Arapaho brothers our guns to hunt with, but it is best I do not. If Major Scott Anthony should find you with guns, it could mean the shedding of your blood. Instead, my braves will bring meat to you. It will be delivered late at night so no spying bluecoats can see."

Little Raven managed a smile. "This is very much appreciated, Black Kettle."

"We thank you," added Left Hand.

"Do not despair, my brothers," said Black Kettle. "When I see Governor Evans, you will get your firearms back. I believe him to be a man of his word, as it seems so few white men are. He will abide by the peace treaty."

On Friday, November 25, Governor Evans was going over mail that had stacked up in his absence when he heard a light tap at his office door. Recognizing his secretary's knock, he called, "Yes, Esther?"

The door opened, and Evans could see the impressive form of John Chivington behind his secretary. "Colonel Chivington is here to see you, sir. I told him you were awfully busy, but he insists—"

"It's all right," Evans said, smiling. "Let him come in."

Chivington gave the middle-aged secretary an insolent look as he moved past her. She bored holes in the back of his head with blazing eyes and closed the door, leaving them alone.

"So," said Chivington as he sat down in front of Evans's desk, "how did it go in Washington?"

"Very well. Time I got through talking to Jim Weddel and Henry Halleck, they were convinced there's no other solution with the Indians than to crowd them onto reservations. They agreed that if any of them give resistance, they'll have to be gunned down. I've got them and the other military brass in Washington believing that the Cheyenne and Arapaho who signed the treaty have broken it already and are giving Major Anthony real trouble. I drew an especially sordid picture of Black Kettle. So, when we proceed as planned before I left, nobody will ask any questions."

Chivington grinned. "Good! We'll wipe out his whole village and make buzzard meat outta Black Kettle."

Evans nodded. "He was here to see me, you know. While I was gone."

"Black Kettle? Did he say what about?"

"No, but you and I both know it has to be about those Arapaho guns and putting his pals on rations. You know... Anthony breaking the treaty. You said Black Kettle would be more upset by our doing this to his friends than if we'd taken *his* guns. I think you were right."

"So what about seeing him? You gonna do it?"

"Naw. My people here told him I'd send a wire to Fort Lyon, and somebody from there would take it to him so he'd know when to come and see me." Evans laughed. "Ol' Black Kettle's gonna be surprised when he gets a message from you instead of from me!"

"Well, that's all I need to know. I can attack Black Kettle's village with a thousand men and take no prisoners."

"Yep. And after the foundation I laid in Washington, they'll not be surprised when they hear about it."

The colonel slapped his leg and said, "Great! So what day do you want it done?"

"I've been thinking about next Tuesday, the twenty-ninth. How's that sound to you?"

"My scouts have been keeping an eye on the village. The creek has high, steep slopes up to ground level on both sides. Makes it easy for them to get in close and watch and listen. Right now, Black Kettle's got company."

"Oh? Who?"

"Left Hand and Little Raven, and about fifty men, women, and children from their villages. White Antelope's there too. 'Bout a dozen of his people with him. I think Black Kettle is putting on a feed for those Arapaho. I'm hoping they'll still be there—along with White Antelope and his bunch—come Tuesday. If they are, we'll get us more dead Indians than we thought."

"Well, just don't underestimate those savages, John," said the governor. "You'll have a thousand men, but those Cheyenne still have guns, and they're fierce fighters."

Chivington chuckled. "Well, John, let me tell you about the little added bonus. My scouts were able to pick up that Black Kettle is sending two hundred of his warriors on a hunting trip on Sunday. Seems they're providing meat to their Arapaho friends."

"Why doesn't that surprise me?" said Evans.

"Those warriors are gonna be gone about five days. So when I show up with my seven hundred First Colorado Cavalry and three hundred of Shoup's Third Colorado Cavalry, it'll be a picnic. And we won't have to tell Washington anything except that Black Kettle's warriors started the trouble when we rode in and told them they were gonna have to move to Wyoming and be put on a reservation."

Evans slapped his hands together. "Well, this couldn't have worked out better. It's settled then. Attack the village at dawn on Tuesday."

"Will do," said Chivington. "We're gonna make a whole bunch of *good* Indians Tuesday morning!"

It was midday on Monday, November 28, when Black Kettle was in his large tepee with White Antelope, Little Raven, and Left Hand. A fire burned in the center of the tepee, sending its smoke out the air vent at the top. On one side, Gentle Dove and the squaws of the Arapaho chiefs were talking in low tones as they cleaned up the tin plates and utensils from the meal the group had just eaten.

Sky Eagle sat with the men and listened intently to their discussion about the warriors from Black Kettle's village who had gone into the Rocky Mountains, where deer and elk were plentiful. They would come back with plenty of meat to be dried and salted, which would get the Arapaho and the Cheyenne through the winter.

Suddenly everyone inside the tepee heard clapping hands outside the tepee. Sky Eagle leaped to his feet and opened the flap.

"Oh! Hello, Mr. George Bent!" said the boy. "Please, come in."

Every eye went to the man dressed in buckskins and wearing a coat with fur collar and fur-skinned cap.

"I suppose I'm too late for lunch?" said Bent, looking at Gentle Dove.

"I fear so," she replied as her husband got to his feet to welcome his longtime friend. "But if you will stay for supper, you can take your fill."

"I think I'll do just that!" said George as he reached out to shake hands Indian style with Black Kettle. Bent knew everyone in the tepee. He greeted the women, shook hands with the chiefs, then hugged Sky Eagle.

"How did you find us, my friend?" asked Black Kettle.

"I stopped at Chief Crooked Neck's village to say hello, and he told me about the army moving you down here. I needed to go to Pa's trading post, so I thought I'd stop and see you. Crooked Neck also told me about the treaty. I think that's wonderful!"

No one reacted to his comment.

"Uh-oh," he said. "What's wrong?"

George was invited to sit down, and Black Kettle filled him in on what the new commandant at Fort Lyon had done to the Arapaho. He also told him he was expecting a message from Governor John Evans, inviting him to come to Denver and discuss what had happened.

Black Kettle then said, "Would you be able to stay the night with us, George Bent? The squaws will prepare a delicious meal this evening and a good breakfast in the morning before you head for the trading post. I will provide you a private tepee if you will stay."

"That sounds good to me," said Bent. "I'll do it."

"Maybe you could teach these Arapaho English tonight, Mr. George Bent," said Sky Eagle.

George laughed. "Well, my friend, it would take me a little longer than one evening to do that. Of course, with help from you and your sis—" He looked around. "Hey, where's Silver Moon?"

"She is out walking with her intended," said Gentle Dove.

"*Intended?* But she's too young! She's—"

"Fifteen grasses," Black Kettle said. "Nearly sixteen. The young buck is from White Antelope's village. Fine boy. His name is Bear Paw."

George shook his head. "My, my! Where does the time go? Seems like Silver Moon should still be a little girl. She's—"

Bent's words were cut short by a hand clap outside the tepee.

Sky Eagle hurried to the opening. "Father!" he said over his shoulder. "We have more friends here!"

Black Kettle was pleasantly surprised when he saw the bearded faces of fur traders Edmund Guerrier and J. W. Smith, whom he had known for several years. He welcomed them into the tepee.

Introductions were made, and the fur traders were happy to meet George Bent. They had done much business with George's father at Bent's Fort Trading Post.

"We're on our way to the Rockies for more furs," said Smith. "Someone at a trading post just inside the Kansas line, near the Smoky Hill River where Black Kettle's village stood for so long, told us of the move to Sand Creek. They also told us about the peace treaty. Mighty glad to hear about it."

Black Kettle's face was glum as he told the white men of Major Scott Anthony, Fort Lyon's new commandant, and his refusal to honor the treaty. "He and his soldiers took all the guns from the Arapaho villages. They did not leave even one. Most of my warriors are on a hunting trip to provide meat for our village and the villages of our Arapaho brothers."

Smith and Guerrier looked stunned at Black Kettle's words. Then the chief said, "Everything will be all right, my friends, after I meet with Governor John Evans."

The fur traders were invited to stay the night in their own private tepee and gladly accepted.

At the same time Edmund Guerrier and J. W. Smith were being welcomed at Black Kettle's tepee, Major Anthony was called to the gate at Fort Lyon. A massive column of U.S. Army cavalry was approaching the fort from the north. Captains Wyman and Axton joined Anthony.

"What do you make of this, Major?" asked Wyman.

"I don't know. They're still too far out to tell who's in the lead, but I'd say from the size of the man out front, it's probably Colonel Chivington."

"It is, Major," called the sentry in the tower as he lowered his binoculars. "Must be a million of 'em! The column is double wide and has to be ten miles long!"

Captain Wyman chuckled and said, "Now, Corporal Berry, haven't I told you a billion times not to exaggerate?"

Berry and those nearby laughed, but Anthony had his eyes and mind fixed on the cavalry unit, wondering what Chivington was doing so far from Camp Weld with so many men.

Soon the galloping column drew near, horses blowing vapor from their distended nostrils. The breath of each rider could be seen in small puffs on the cold air. Chivington raised a hand, signaling the column to halt, and slid from his saddle.

"Hello, Colonel," said Anthony. "What on earth are you doing out here with all these men? You going to start a war?"

Chivington laughed. "You might say that, Major."

Anthony ran his gaze along the lengthy column. "You must have nearly a thousand men here."

"*Exactly* a thousand. Well, a thousand and one, including me. Three hundred of them are Shoup's Third Cavalry."

"Oh, yes. I see him back there. So what's going on?"

"We're going to wipe out Black Kettle's village tomorrow morning."

"That sounds like something I'd like to be in on, Colonel," said Anthony. "How about me coming along with my troops?"

"Sure, why not? We all need a little fun making good Indians out of bad ones!"

Nate Wyman's eyes flashed angrily. "Wait a minute,

Colonel! Why are you going to attack Black Kettle's village? What have they done?"

Chivington looked at him coldly. "You ask me what they've done, Captain? They've been filthy savages all their lives. That's what they've done."

"What about the treaty and the promise of protection for those people?"

Chivington laughed as Colonel Shoup drew up.

"We got a problem here, Colonel Chivington?" Shoup asked, lancing Wyman with piercing eyes.

"Little objection from the captain about us having a good time at the Sand Creek village tomorrow. Nothing serious."

"Nothing serious?" said Wyman. "You made a treaty with Black Kettle, Colonel Chivington. So did Governor Evans and Major Wynkoop."

Anthony laid a restraining hand on Nate Wyman's shoulder. "Captain," he said, "don't interfere."

"Major, are you blind? There's about to be a violation of the peace treaty! Black Kettle signed it because he trusts us."

"Look, Captain," said Shoup, "maybe you've had your head in the sand. If you only knew the kind of atrocities the Cheyenne and Arapaho have done to white people, you'd be as eager to kill them as we are!"

Wyman's face was flushed, and his breath came out harshly. "And this planned sneak attack of yours *isn't* an atrocity? You signed the treaty, Colonel Chivington. It was done in the name of the U.S. Army. The breaking of the treaty makes every man who takes part in it a truce breaker and a liar!"

Chivington regarded Wyman with malice. "The governor has ordered this attack. He feels, as I do, that Black Kettle is a potential problem. Best thing to do is eliminate the problem before it starts."

Wyman wheeled and faced Anthony. "Major, I want no part of this! If you take men with you on this attack, I will not go!"

Captain Axton voiced the same feeling. "I can't go into combat because of my bad leg, Major Anthony, but even if I were able, I'd refuse to go!"

Suddenly there were many voices among the men of the fort who refused to take part in the attack.

Major Anthony raised his hands to quell the dissent and said, "All right! All right! Be quiet!"

When the voices subsided to a murmur, Anthony said, "Any of you men who do not wish to go along will not be ordered to do so. The rest of us will join Colonels Chivington and Shoup and do our part to make this territory safe for decent white people." He paused, then turned to address Chivington. "You can see there isn't room inside the fort for all of you," he said. "Have your men pitch their tents just outside the fort, and we'll welcome you as our guests for tonight."

5

AFTER THE EVENING MEAL at the Sand Creek village, Bear Paw moved among the tepees by the light of the three-quarter moon and stopped in front of Black Kettle's tepee. He clapped his hands once.

When Silver Moon's little brother appeared, Bear Paw said, "Hello, Sky Eagle. I would like to speak to your father, please."

Although there was much conversation inside the tepee, Black Kettle heard Bear Paw's voice and appeared behind his son. "Yes, Bear Paw?"

"Chief, sir, I asked your daughter if she would go for a moonlight walk with me if you approved. She said she would. May she walk with me, sir?"

"Of course," said Black Kettle. "It would be better, though, if you stay within the village and not go down to the creek, since it is night."

Bear Paw could see Silver Moon putting on her coat and fur cap near the fire. "Yes, sir," he said. "We will be back soon."

As the Indian couple strolled together to the south edge of the village, Bear Paw yearned to take her in his arms, but it was out of the question. When they stopped, she looked up at him, and the light of the moon shone in her black, expressive eyes.

When Bear Paw spoke, his breath hung as a vapor in the

cold air. "My heart reaches for you tonight, Silver Moon. It will always reach for you, even when our grandchildren play about our tepee."

Silver Moon smiled. "Bear Paw, you say such beautiful things. I know that my heart will always reach for you, too, even when we journey on the Hanging Road toward Heammawihio in the sky."

It was Bear Paw's turn to smile. "Those words warm my heart, Silver Moon. I know the day will come when together or apart we must walk the Hanging Road, but I am looking forward to our journey of life together in this world. I will be so proud when you are my squaw and the other young bucks envy me."

Silver Moon giggled. "Oh, Bear Paw, you embarrass me."

"Only because you do not seem to know how very beautiful and full of wonder you are." He paused, then said, "I would like to pray to Heammawihio right now and thank him for the love he has given us for each other, and for the wonderful future we have before us."

Both young people looked toward the heavens as Bear Paw offered his prayer of thanks. Silver Moon blinked at the warm tears welling up in her eyes, then let them spill freely down her cheeks.

Midnight claimed the Colorado prairie as the long column of horsemen pulled away from Fort Lyon and headed northeast to the sound of squeaking saddles and blowing horses. An arctic wind swept across the land beneath the ice-chip brilliance of the starry sky.

Major Scott Anthony led 125 of the fort's garrison at the tail end of the column.

At five o' clock in the morning, a slight hint of dawn hugged the ground when the column, moving eight abreast, topped a rise and looked down the slope. There, stretched along the bend of the nearly frozen creek, lay the Cheyenne village a quarter-mile away, peacefully slumbering.

Chivington rose in his stirrups and gazed over the mounted troops. "All right, men...you know your positions. All units take your places. We'll attack the village from every direction as planned. When dawn gives us enough light, I'll give the signal, and everybody goes at the same time. Remember, we take no prisoners. Understand? This should be short, sweet, and simple."

No one spoke through the strained hush of anticipation, but heads nodded all along the line.

Medicine woman Red Leaf stepped outside her tepee as dawn grayed the eastern sky. She spotted the mounted soldiers against the skyline and saw others moving off the hill in three directions. She was stunned to see such a large number of cavalrymen.

Red Leaf's heart pounded as she rushed to the adjacent tepee and called, "Mr. George Bent! Mr. George Bent!"

The tepee next to Bent's was occupied by Edmund Guerrier and J. W. Smith. The Frenchman was just pulling on his boots, but Smith, who was already dressed, stepped out of the tepee and looked toward Red Leaf. "What's wrong?"

She pointed at the horsemen on the hill. "Army!" she cried.

Smith's jaw slackened at the sight. Bent and Guerrier emerged from their tepees at almost the same time, their line of sight going immediately to the cavalry on the hill and the others who were slowly descending it and spreading out.

"I'll get Black Kettle!" said Guerrier, and broke into a run toward the village's main tepee.

Red Leaf hurried away, stopping at tepees occupied by warriors who had not gone on the hunting trip, calling to them that the bluecoats were there in great numbers. Little by little, men appeared and hurried toward the spot where Smith and Bent stood.

"What do you think this means, Smith?" asked Bent.

"Bloodshed."

"You mean an *attack?*"

"Why else would they come with so many and start spreading out?"

"But there's a peace treaty! They can't do this!"

"Looks like they're going to."

Black Kettle and Edmund Guerrier hurried past the warriors who were gathering and drew up to Smith and Bent. The chief was carrying the U.S. flag and the white flag, and he hurried to the tall pole on the creek side of the village. More Cheyenne came out of their tepees while Black Kettle ran up the flags.

Gentle Dove and her children waited with the others for Black Kettle to rejoin them. When he returned, he looked toward the cavalry on the hill and said, "They can easily see the flags now. Everything will be all right."

"Chief," said Smith, "I don't think those flags will stop them. They're going to attack."

"No!" cried Black Kettle. "We have a treaty!" Looking around at his people, he said, "Do not be afraid. The flags are in place. The bluecoats will not harm us!"

Some of the women began to whimper. Gentle Dove spoke to them, telling them not to fear. Her husband had raised the flags, and the soldiers would not harm them.

Silver Moon moved close to the chief and said, "Father, if they mean us no harm, why are there so many of them, and why do those on the hill just look at us?"

"I cannot tell you, my daughter. It seems that for some reason the bluecoats have come to look at our village."

"But why do some of them ride in a circle as if to surround us?" asked Sky Eagle.

"I do not know," Black Kettle said, "but it cannot be to harm us. We have the treaty."

The Arapaho chiefs and White Antelope were the last to join the group, having spent the night in tepees at the far end of the village.

Bear Paw threaded his way through the crowd to Silver Moon. When he saw the fear on her face, he said softly, "It will be all right, Silver Moon. Your father says we have nothing to fear."

"But I do not trust the white men as Father does," she said in a whisper. "I have been fearful ever since Major Edward Wynkoop was taken from us."

J. W. Smith took off running and halted at the edge of the tepees, waving his arms. "Hey!" he shouted. "White men! There are white men here! Two others besides myself!"

As Colonel John Chivington watched the Indians gather in a cluster, he flicked glances at Shoup's regiment and Anthony's troops, along with many of his First Cavalry, who were forming a circle around the village. A dozen or so of Anthony's men veered off toward the rope corral where the Cheyenne pony herd was kept, on the south side of the creek.

Suddenly Chivington's attention was drawn to a figure running to the edge of the village, waving his arms.

"You see him, sir?" asked one of Chivington's lieutenants.

"Yes. I see him, but I can't make out what he's saying."

"I think he's got it figured out that we're going to attack, and he wants us to know there's a white man in the village."

Chivington shrugged. "If he's fool enough to be so friendly with those devil savages, he deserves to die with them."

"Wait a minute, sir!" said the lieutenant, squinting. "I see two other white men there!"

"Well, too bad for them. The sun's about to put in an appearance. It's time to wipe this bunch of red devils and their white pals off the face of the earth."

As he spoke, the colonel drew his revolver.

J. W. Smith's shouts were cut off as the army leader on the hill-top raised his revolver above his head and fired into the air, then led his riders down the slope toward the village at a full gallop.

"No! No!" cried Smith, running toward them. "Don't fire on the village! There are white men here!"

On came the thundering cavalry. Smith turned and ran.

Terror washed over the village as Black Kettle cried, "Warriors, get your weapons! Everyone else run! Hide!"

The chief turned to his family and said, "Go to the creek! Hide in the embankments!" With that, he bolted for the tepee to get his revolver.

While the warriors and the three white men went for their guns, the ancient men, wrinkled faces frozen with fear, stood motionless, watching the thundering horsemen bear down on the village.

Three companies of the First Colorado Cavalry bounded through the iced-over pools along the creek bed, then splashed through the creek and circled the village to the east and north sides. On the west side were the wild, shouting, eager members of Shoup's Third Regiment.

Suddenly, shots were flying everywhere. Bullets struck tepee walls, bushes, rocks, and sod, scattering dirt and rock shards, some ricocheting off into space, whining like angry hornets.

There was chaos and noise everywhere. Women and children were screaming and wailing, not knowing what to do or where to run. All over the village, warriors were shouting advice to each other and firing their revolvers at the men on horseback.

Gentle Dove and her children had started toward the creek when they heard Black Kettle shout, "Chivington!" They turned and saw Black Kettle pointing at the man leading the soldiers.

Silver Moon had heard that Colonel John Chivington was a huge man, but she had wondered how true that report was. In the brief moment she set eyes on him astride his horse, she decided he was the biggest man she had ever seen.

Gentle Dove led her children toward the creek but halted when she saw the creek bed swarming with soldiers. They turned back and ran amongst the tepees, hunkering down. They caught a glimpse of Black Kettle, who was in the midst of his men, firing at the attacking enemy with his revolver.

In the first deadly volley of army guns, many old men, women, and children went down. Some of the warriors who ran with the women and children to protect them as they tried to find hiding places were cut down by cavalry bullets.

Guerrier and Bent stood in the middle of the battle, firing at the men in blue. Cheyenne warriors fought alongside them, sending hot lead at their attackers.

J. W. Smith had worked his way to the slope of the creek embankment, looking for a spot to help the women and children hide, when a soldier on horseback came thundering at him, raising his gun to fire. Before Smith could bring his gun to bear, the rider was struck with a bullet and knocked out of the saddle. Smith looked back to see who had saved his life—George Bent. Smith waved, then ran and picked up the dead soldier's gun.

In the village, Bear Paw had found a revolver and was firing at soldiers when he saw Gentle Dove, Silver Moon, and Sky Eagle run between the tepees and hunker down behind a bush. The din of the battle roared in his ears. He must protect Black Kettle's family!

Suddenly there were Indians and soldiers in hand-to-hand combat between Bear Paw and Black Kettle's family. As he waited for an opening to go to them, he saw White Antelope standing in front of a tepee. The chief had no gun but was wielding a broken tree limb, swinging at a soldier on horseback. The soldier cursed the old man and fired at him point-blank.

Bear Paw's stomach turned over when he saw his beloved chief fall. He wanted to go to White Antelope but knew the man was already dead. He looked back to where Silver Moon, her mother, and brother were crouched in the brush and picked his way through the combatants, hurrying toward the girl he loved.

Some of the Cheyenne, unnoticed by the soldiers, had made their way down the slopes to the creek bed, quickly finding hiding places below the overhangs of the tall embankments. Some carried revolvers.

The troops shot from every direction as they moved amongst the tepees, sometimes even catching each other in crossfire.

Bear Paw worked his way toward Black Kettle's family, hampered again by men fighting directly in his path. Suddenly he froze when he saw the man identified as Chivington ride his horse to where Silver Moon, Gentle Dove, and Sky Eagle were crouched.

Gentle Dove and her children looked up to see the colonel, revolver in hand, looking down on them. A leer twisted his face when he saw the terror in their eyes.

Suddenly there were two men on horseback directly behind Chivington, swinging at Cheyenne warriors with empty revolvers, trying to fight them off. When Chivington turned his head to look at them, Sky Eagle jumped up and seized the colonel's revolver by the barrel with both hands, attempting to twist it out of his grasp.

Gentle Dove and Silver Moon looked on with horror as man and boy struggled briefly for control. The gun went off. Sky Eagle jerked and fell.

Gentle Dove screamed, then ran toward her son. Chivington's gun roared again, and Gentle Dove went down.

Silver Moon, eyes wild, screamed at him and bent down to pick up a jagged rock.

Chivington snapped back the hammer of his revolver and was bringing it to bear on her when one of the army horses bumped his horse. The gun roared, but the bullet whizzed angrily past Silver Moon's ear. She jerked back and fell.

Chivington struggled to get his startled horse under control at the same time he was drawing a bead on Silver Moon as she scrambled to get up. Just as the colonel fired, Bear Paw dashed forward, putting himself between Chivington and Silver Moon. As Bear Paw fell, the last voice he heard was Silver Moon's, crying his name.

Chivington swore at the girl, aimed his gun, and squeezed the trigger. The hammer made a hollow *click* as it slammed down on an empty cartridge.

Silver Moon hurled the rock she still had in her hand at the colonel as hard as she could. The rock struck him in the forehead, snapping his head back. He reeled in the saddle, grasping the saddle horn to keep from falling.

Silver Moon quickly knelt at her mother's side. Gentle Dove was dead. Silver Moon's heart was in her throat as she hurried to Sky Eagle and found that he was also dead.

She heard another curse and looked up to see Chivington struggling to reload his revolver. The rock had torn a gash in his forehead, and blood was streaming into his eyes. Silver Moon wheeled and made a mad dash between tepees, running as fast as she could.

Silver Moon suddenly came upon her father in combat with a soldier on foot. Neither man had a weapon. The soldier was a much larger man than Black Kettle and was getting the better of him. A solid punch put Black Kettle on the ground. The soldier stood over him, ready to drive a foot into his face.

Silver Moon ran up behind the soldier, leaped on his back, and dug her fingernails into his eyes. The soldier howled, clawing at her hands, then threw her over his shoulder. Silver Moon hit the ground hard, and the wind was knocked out of her.

J. W. Smith and Edmund Guerrier had just come on the scene. Smith cracked the soldier on the head with the barrel of his revolver, and the man fell, unconscious. Quickly, Smith helped Black Kettle to his feet, while the Frenchman lifted Silver Moon.

"Black Kettle, where are Gentle Dove and Sky Eagle?" asked Smith.

Silver Moon said, "My mother and brother are both dead, Mr. Smith. That wicked Chivington killed them!"

Black Kettle gasped and he looked as if his legs would crumple once more.

Silver Moon took hold of her father's hand. "I am sorry, Father. Bear Paw is dead too. Chivington was going to shoot me, but Bear Paw jumped in front of me."

Black Kettle could only close his eyes in sorrow.

"We've got to hide you two," said Guerrier. "Those blood-hungry soldiers won't be satisfied till they've killed the chief. C'mon!"

By this time there were no soldiers in the creek bed. Smith and Guerrier, guiding father and daughter, got them down the steep slope, urged them to a run, and moved down the creek for more than a mile before hiding them in a deep indenture in the embankment.

A stream of Indians, mostly women and children, dazed and wounded, crawled and scrambled along the creek bed toward the west, leaving the dead Cheyenne and Arapaho behind them.

At the place where the two white men hid Black Kettle and Silver Moon—guns ready for action—many of the Cheyenne took refuge, pressing themselves into the protective overhang of the embankment.

By nine o'clock that morning, what would become known as the "Sand Creek Massacre" was over.

George Bent had found a hiding place beneath a collapsed tepee and watched many of the soldiers moving amongst the bodies of slain Indians, making sure they were all dead. Others were picking up wounded soldiers or draping the bodies of dead soldiers over the backs of their horses.

Bent saw John Chivington, with a bandanna wrapped around his head, coming his way accompanied by George Shoup. They stopped about twenty feet from where Bent was hiding, and Chivington swore, saying, "Where could he be?"

"He's probably hiding with those who went down the creek bed, John," said Shoup. "If I was the chief of this village, that's what I'd do. You want to go after him?"

"Too dangerous. One of my men told me he saw some of the Indians press themselves into the embankment. Couple of privates went after them and got themselves shot. Too easy for those savages to hide in there and pick us off. Guess I'll just have to be satisfied, knowing we've wiped this village off the map. What few still live will have to go elsewhere for help. When those hunters come back and find their wives and children dead, they'll no doubt move on somewhere else."

"You're gonna write this thing up big in your report, aren't you?" asked Shoup.

"I'll not only report that we killed those two Arapaho chiefs and White Antelope, I'll say we killed Black Kettle too."

"But what about when he surfaces, alive?"

"Well, he might never stick his face up where white folks can see it again, but if he does, I'll just say we *thought* we killed him. Chances are pretty good he'll stay hidden and die in exile somewhere. We'll be the heroes of the Sand Creek Battle."

Shoup let his gaze sweep over what remained of the village. "More like the Sand Creek Massacre, John, only in reverse. Usually when there's a massacre, it's the Indians who slaughter the whites. What did we lose...fifteen or sixteen men?"

"Nineteen dead. Thirty-eight wounded."

"And how many dead Indians?"

"Looks like better than three hundred. I'll report it as over five hundred. Long as we're gonna bask in glory, George, we might as well bask *big!*"

6

GEORGE BENT WATCHED the cavalry ride out toward Denver. He stayed in his hiding place till they were out of sight, then headed for the creek bed, where he knew many of the Indians had escaped.

As he rose to his feet, Bent ran his gaze over the scattered bodies of the Indians but could not find Black Kettle's body, nor Silver Moon's, nor the bodies of the other two white men. He hoped they were still alive.

As Bent skidded his way down the steep embankment, he saw all around him the bodies of Cheyenne and Arapaho. Many had been shot down in the early part of the attack when some of the soldiers caught them trying to escape. Others had tumbled and rolled down the embankment wounded and had died while attempting to find hiding places.

Bent had walked for nearly a mile along the bank of the creek when he saw Indians come out of their hiding places and look his way. He was relieved when he found Black Kettle, Silver Moon, Smith, and Guerrier alive and unharmed.

The Cheyenne carried their wounded back to the village and made them as comfortable as possible. Then they stood with their chief, his daughter, and the white men, weeping as they gazed in sorrow at the bodies of friends and loved ones.

Cheyenne and Arapaho custom was to place the bodies of their dead on scaffolds and leave them there for a few days, giving their souls time to depart and make their way up the Hanging Road—which the white men called the Milky Way—to the abode of Heammawihio.

Because there were so many dead, Black Kettle and his few remaining people could only place the bodies on the ground faceup and pray for Heammawihio to take the souls to him. There were only two medicine men and one medicine woman left. When they and Black Kettle decided the souls had all departed, a mass burial would take place.

That evening, before everyone retired to their tepees for the night, Silver Moon told the story of how Colonel Chivington had killed her mother and brother...and Bear Paw. She wanted everyone to know of Sky Eagle's courageous attempt to disarm the wicked colonel, of Gentle Dove's grief in seeing her son shot down, and of Bear Paw's act of giving his own life to save hers.

At the end of the story, Silver Moon broke down and wept. Black Kettle tried to comfort her but was deep in his own grief, and could do little. Red Leaf took Silver Moon into her tepee and held her for a long time, speaking words of comfort.

When everyone was getting ready to retire for the night, Red Leaf came to Black Kettle's tepee, where George Bent was talking to him, and said, "Chief Black Kettle, Silver Moon cried herself to sleep in my arms. I have her on my pallet. Since she is sleeping soundly, may I keep her with me for the night?"

The grieving chief gave Red Leaf an appreciative look and said, "Yes, of course. It is good of you to care for her like this."

When Red Leaf was gone, Bent said, "Chief, I know your heart is aching. Would you like for me to sleep here in the tepee nearby?"

"That would be good, my friend and Cheyenne brother. Kindness and love shown by a friend and brother at a time like this is greatly appreciated."

During the night, Red Leaf was awakened three times by Silver Moon crying out in her sleep. When awakened the third time, Red Leaf took Silver Moon in her arms and held her until dawn.

The next day, the girl was unable to eat or drink. Red Leaf kept her inside the tepee, doing everything she knew to try to help her. At times, Silver Moon wailed and sobbed. At other times, Red Leaf could understand Silver Moon's words as she cried over the loss of her mother and brother and Bear Paw.

In Denver, the populace was celebrating what they'd been led to believe was a great military victory. The headlines of Denver's new newspaper, the *Rocky Mountain News,* trumpeted the exciting story in its December 5 issue:

GREAT BATTLE WITH INDIANS!
THE SAVAGES DISPERSED!
500 INDIANS KILLED!
ARMY'S LOSS 19 KILLED, 38 WOUNDED

Under a smaller headline—"Full Particulars"—the paper gave an account of the battle. The article explained that the primary source of the news was a report by Colonel John M. Chivington, former minister of Denver's Broadway Methodist Church, hero of the famous Battle of Glorieta Pass, and now commander of the Military District of Colorado.

In the report, Chivington said that Black Kettle and his "heartless savage warriors" had been attacking white settlements and shedding the blood of whites all over eastern Colorado. He had no choice but to go after them with his troops. He led his First Colorado Cavalry Regiment and the Third Regiment—under the command of Colonel George L. Shoup—out of Camp Weld on November 26 and joined with a small number of troops from Fort Lyon, led by Major Scott Anthony, on November 28.

The newspaper quoted Chivington: "At dawn on November 29, I led the attack on Black Kettle's Cheyenne village, which happened to have several hundred Arapaho warriors visiting at the time. I know now that they were meeting to plan more fierce attacks on white settlements.

"In the village were nine hundred to one thousand warriors strong. We killed troublesome Cheyenne Chiefs Black Kettle and White Antelope, and Arapaho Chiefs Little Raven and Left Hand. In a fierce battle, we also killed between four and five hundred warriors. There are not enough warriors left among Black Kettle's people to cause white settlers any more trouble.

"I mourn the loss of those nineteen gallant men, and pray for the speedy recovery of our wounded. All of our men did nobly in the face of such vicious fighters as the Cheyenne and Arapaho warriors."

At the close of the account, there was a note from the *Rocky Mountain News* chief editor, stating that Colonels Chivington and Shoup would bring a number of their men into Denver on Friday afternoon, December 9, for a parade, and they would be displaying mementos from the battle in public places that night.

The parade took place as scheduled, with thousands of people lining the streets, in spite of the freezing weather, to give praise to their heroes. A military band from Camp Weld rode a hay wagon ahead of the two hundred cavalrymen led by Chivington and Shoup, their rousing songs adding to the excitement.

That night, between acts of a theater performance, soldiers showed off Indian scalps and described their brave deeds to loud cheers and applause. Other scalps were displayed at saloons, where the victorious men in blue were hailed as protectors of the white people who had come west to be part of the great frontier.

While the people of Denver were celebrating Chivington's great victory, Black Kettle's hunting party returned to Sand Creek a few days later than planned. There they found a virtual burial ground where the village had once stood. The few braves who had survived Chivington's attack and stayed to wait for the hunters to return, told the grieving warriors that Chief War Bonnet had taken the survivors to his village, including Black Kettle, Silver Moon, George Bent, and the white fur traders, J. W. Smith and Edmund Guerrier.

One of the hunters, Crow Feather—whose widowed mother had been killed—had fire in his eyes as he said, "Let us go to Camp Weld and kill this Colonel John Chivington!"

The surviving warrior who had done most of the speaking was Spotted Calf. Shaking his head, he said, "No, Crow Feather. To try this would only bring our deaths. There were many hundreds of soldiers with Chivington. They are at Camp Weld. The few of us would not stand a chance."

"But he must pay for his deed!" Crow Feather said.

Spotted Calf let a faint smile curve his lips. "George Bent, J. W. Smith, and Edmund Guerrier are on their way to Denver right now. They are going to meet with Governor John Evans and tell him of the attack. They will make it known that Chivington broke the treaty, and that when he and his men attacked us, they killed our women and children. Chief Black Kettle says that when Governor Evans learns this, he will see that Chivington is properly punished."

"The only proper punishment is death!" said Crow Feather.

"We have no way to make that happen," Spotted Calf said, "but at least Governor John Evans will learn of the horrible deeds Chivington and his men did here."

When night fell at War Bonnet's village, Chief Black Kettle appeared at the chief's tepee, where his squaw, Painted Flower, was cooking supper.

War Bonnet met Black Kettle at the flap and looked beyond him, saying, "Silver Moon is not with you?"

"She is coming. Silver Moon has been spending time with Red Leaf at the tepee you provided for her. Red Leaf is helping her with her heavy heart."

When Black Kettle stepped inside the tepee, Painted Flower said, "This is good that Silver Moon has Red Leaf. As her father, you can help much, but she also needs to be with a woman. Red Leaf can help her in place of her mother."

War Bonnet and Black Kettle sat cross-legged on the earthen floor, talking in low tones about Chivington's attack. War Bonnet was saying that he hoped Bent, Guerrier, and Smith would be able to convince Governor Evans of the truth when Painted Flower turned from the boiling pot at the fire and said, "Our meal is ready, but Silver Moon is not here."

Black Kettle's brow furrowed. "I will go to Red Leaf's tepee and fetch her," he said, rising to his feet. "In her sorrow, she may not have her mind on eating, and does not realize the time."

When Black Kettle arrived at Red Leaf's tepee and clapped his hands for attention, the flap opened and the medicine woman said, "There is something I can do for you, Chief?"

"Silver Moon is late for supper at War Bonnet's tepee."

Red Leaf's face twisted in puzzlement. "But she left in plenty of time to have been there by now."

"She did not say she was stopping at some other tepee along the way?"

"No. She left without saying anything. She has been very quiet all day."

"I must find her."

"I will help you," said the medicine woman, taking her coat from the small table that stood to one side of the tepee.

With Red Leaf at his side, Black Kettle returned to War Bonnet's tepee, telling the chief and Painted Flower that he would have to miss the meal to look for Silver Moon. War Bonnet said he would help look for her, and Painted Flower pulled the steaming pot from the fire and joined them.

Spreading out, they went from tepee to tepee, asking if anyone had seen Silver Moon. When the entire village had been covered and still Black Kettle's daughter had not been found, men and women volunteered to search. Torches were lit, and better than two hundred Indians began searching for Silver Moon. Less than a quarter-hour later, a loud voice came from the woods. A warrior and his squaw had found the girl.

People hurried toward the spot, with Black Kettle in the lead. Silver Moon was sitting on a fallen log clad in her coat and fur cap, hands folded. Black Kettle knelt before her.

"My daughter," he said, "you have caused your father's heart to fear for your safety."

Silver Moon brushed tears from her eyes. "I am sorry, Father. I did not intend to make you afraid for me. I...I was on my way to Chief War Bonnet's tepee, and—" She sniffled and took a deep breath, then said with quavering voice, "I was hurting so much in my heart, I just wanted to be alone. My father, I miss Mother and Sky Eagle so terribly. And Bear Paw. My heart is so much in pain I cannot stand it."

Red Leaf moved to Black Kettle's side and knelt beside him, taking Silver Moon's hands in her own. "Please, child," she said in a tender tone, "do not worry your father in this way. He is grieving also."

"I am truly sorry," said Silver Moon. "In my grief I have not considered my father as I should." She looked at Black Kettle through her tears. "Please forgive me, Father."

"It is all right," Black Kettle replied softly, stroking her cheek.

"Silver Moon," said Painted Flower, "Red Leaf tells me you have not been eating properly. I have wild turkey stew in the pot, getting cold. Will you come and help me heat it up again? You must eat to keep up your strength."

"Yes...I will come."

Black Kettle, his own heart bleeding, took his daughter by the hand and walked with her back to the village.

On Monday, December 12, George Bent, Edmund Guerrier, and J. W. Smith walked down the hall of the territorial Capitol building in Denver at 10:30 A.M. When they reached the door of the governor's outer office, they found it open. Sunshine was flooding the room through two windows on the south side. The secretary's desk was unoccupied. The three men stepped into the room and removed their coats.

"The secretary's probably in the governor's office," said Smith. "Should be out in a minute or so."

Bent tiptoed to the door of the inner office, leaned his head close, and said, "No voices."

A lady who was passing down the hall saw the three men standing in the outer office. Stepping up to the open door, she said, "Are you gentlemen looking for Esther Norland?"

"If that's Governor Evans's secretary, we are, ma'am," said Guerrier.

"Yes, that's her. I saw her in another office down the hall. She might be there a few minutes. You can sit down and wait, if you wish."

"Thank you, ma'am," said Guerrier. "We'll just do that."

There were four wooden chairs set around a small table with newspapers lying on it. Each man picked himself a chair and sat down. George Bent let his gaze stray to the newspapers and soon saw they were daily editions of the *Rocky Mountain News*. He picked up the issue on top and sucked in his breath as he read the headlines.

Edmund Guerrier looked at him and said, "What's that?"

"Last Monday's paper. Look!"

Bent held it up so the other two men could see the bold headlines.

Smith scowled. "Great battle? Where'd they get that?"

"Five hundred Indians killed?" said Bent. "They killed better than three hundred, but not five. They must have gotten their information from Chivington."

Guerrier turned the front page so he could see it. His gaze ran down to the smaller headline at the middle of the page. "They did," he said. "Says here the primary source for their information was a report made by Chivington. Says he was minister of the Broadway Methodist Church here in Denver once, and brags him up as the hero of the Battle of Glorieta Pass."

"A preacher, eh?" said Bent, sneering. "I can't picture those straitlaced Methodists having a bloody beast like him for a pastor."

"Maybe that's why he *used to* be pastor there," suggested Smith. "Maybe something happened to show them what he really is, and they turned him out."

Guerrier's eyes scanned the columns. "Listen to this, fellas. Chivington says Black Kettle and his 'heartless savage warriors' have been attacking white settlements and killing whites all over eastern Colorado. He had no choice but to go after them."

"Dirty liar," muttered Bent.

"And more lies," said Guerrier. "Chivington reported that he found out the Arapaho were at Black Kettle's village because they were planning more fierce attacks on white settlements. He said there were nine hundred to a thousand *warriors* in the village, and they killed between four and five hundred of them, including Black Kettle, White Antelope, Little Raven, and Left Hand."

"I wonder what the lying skunk will say when Black Kettle is seen still breathing," said Bent.

"Yeah," said Smith. "Be sorta hard to explain, won't it? And while lying about all those warriors who were in the village and the four to five hundred they killed, the paper says nothing about all those helpless old men and the women and children they shot down in cold blood."

"Not a word," said the Frenchman. "And down here at the bottom it says that Chivington and some of his men were going to be in a parade on Friday and would display mementos from the battle in public places that night."

"A parade, of all things," said Bent. "Parade of lowdown murderers."

"Any guess as to what the mementos were?" Smith asked, eyebrows arched.

"Scalps, no doubt," Guerrier said.

"Makes me so mad I could eat a rock," said Bent. "Or better yet, stuff one down Chivington's lying throat. Governor Evans has to be told the truth. We—"

Bent noticed a woman standing at the open door to the hall. He wondered how long she had been there.

"May I help you, gentlemen?" she asked. "I'm Esther Norland, Governor Evans's secretary."

All three men rose to their feet. "Yes, ma'am," said Bent. "This is Edmund Guerrier and J. W. Smith. I am George Bent. We've come to see Governor Evans. You see...we were at Black Kettle's village on November 29, when Chivington and his troops launched their attack." He picked up the edition of the *Rocky Mountain News* they had been discussing and said, "This report of Chivington is a pack of lies, ma'am. They slaughtered Indians, all right, but most of them were old men, women, and children. We saw it all and had to fight them in order to save our own lives. We want to see Governor Evans. He's got to know what really happened out there."

Esther felt her mouth go dry. "Well, I'm sorry, gentlemen. Governor Evans is at home. He's very sick with a cold and will not be available for probably at least a week. His doctor fears pneumonia could set in and has told him to stay out of the cold."

"I'm sorry to hear that, ma'am," said Bent. Then to his friends, he said, "Guess we'll have to take our story to the *Rocky Mountain News*, guys."

Guerrier and Smith nodded.

"Sorry to have bothered you, ma'am," Bent said, picking up his coat.

"Oh, it was no bother, Mr. Bent. I'm just sorry the governor wasn't here to receive you."

Esther Norland wrung her hands as the three men passed through the door and closed it behind them. She waited a few moments, then rushed to the door and opened it quietly, peering down the hall. The men were just passing through the door to the street.

Esther hurried to a small closet, took out her hat and coat, and quickly put them on. She then locked the office door and hung a small sign, giving notice that the governor's office was temporarily closed.

Dan Baker, the editor-in-chief of the *Rocky Mountain News,* looked across his desk at the three men and said hoarsely, "Gentlemen, I am shocked to hear this story. From what you've just told me, Black Kettle is alive and well, and you could bring him to Denver to face Chivington and show him to be a liar."

"That's right, Mr. Baker," said George Bent. "You set up the time and place...get Chivington there without knowing what he's about to face. We'll bring Black Kettle, and you bring your cameras."

Baker rubbed his forehead, then gave the men a piercing look as he said, "And this whole story you've just told me... would you be willing to swear to it before a judge in court?"

All three nodded and gave verbal assent.

"Then I'll set it up today. Come back in the morning at nine o'clock, and by swearing to this before a judge, you will put a heavy hammer in my hand to use against Chivington, Shoup, and Anthony."

At ten o'clock the next morning, George Bent, Edmund Guerrier, and J. W. Smith stood before Colorado Territory Superior Judge Emmett Wakefield and several witnesses—including Dan Baker—and gave sworn testimony of what they had seen and heard at the Cheyenne village on Sand Creek on November 29, 1864.

The testimony included their refutation of Colonel John M. Chivington's report that his troops had killed Cheyenne Chief Black Kettle and their offer to bring the chief to face Chivington. It also included refutation of the colonel's facts and figures about the number of warriors they had battled at Sand Creek and the number of warriors they had killed. There was also testimony of the number of elderly men they had slaughtered, as well as defenseless women and children, including tiny infants.

Bent, Smith, and Guerrier then signed the affidavit before a stunned Judge Wakefield and all the others in the courtroom.

Dan Baker asked permission to speak, then stood before the court and said, "Judge Wakefield, I realize that since you have no jurisdiction over the United States Army, your hands are tied. But mine are not. As editor-in-chief of the newspaper that printed Colonel Chivington's report, I'm going to Camp Weld with the information I have and allow Colonel Chivington to make a statement. I'll print what he says in the *Rocky Mountain News*."

"Mr. Baker," said the judge, "that's fair enough. If there are charges to be made against Colonel Chivington and his men, let the U.S. Army do it. All you're doing is reporting the facts."

"Yes, sir," said Baker with gravel in his voice. "Something that wasn't done when the *News* published the report Colonel Chivington turned in to the army authorities in Washington."

7

JOHN CHIVINGTON WAS CROSSING the parade at Camp Weld on Monday afternoon, December 12, when a rider came thundering in from the west. As the rider passed the flagpole and the two sentries standing beside it, he cried, "Colonel Chivington! Colonel Chivington!"

Chivington halted and pivoted his large frame, motioning to the sentries that it was all right, and waited for the rider to rein in. He recognized Dean Ford, Governor Evans's main messenger.

Ford skidded the horse to a stop. "Sir, I have a message for you from Governor Evans." As he spoke, Ford opened a saddlebag, drawing out a brown envelope. Handing it to Chivington, he added, "The governor said I was to get it to you as fast as possible, sir."

"All right," said Chivington with a nod, accepting the envelope. "Does the governor want you to wait for a reply?"

"No, sir. He's sick in bed with a bad cold. He said you'll know what to do."

The colonel nodded again. "Thank you."

Ford wheeled his puffing mount and trotted off the compound, heading back to Denver. Chivington wondered what could be so urgent, but his curiosity would have to wait till he was inside his office. Too many eyes were upon him now.

Moments later, he closed his office door and laid the envelope on the desk. He removed his hat and coat and hung them on the coatrack, then eased his bulky frame into his desk chair and used a letter opener to cut the envelope.

His face turned pale as he read Evans's hastily written message. When he had finished, he took a deep breath, let it out slowly, and wiped a shaky hand across his eyes.

On the afternoon of the next day, Dan Baker drove his buggy to Camp Weld and was met by two corporals who stood near the flagpole. Hauling up, Baker said, "Gentlemen, I am Daniel G. Baker, editor-in-chief of the *Rocky Mountain News*. I need to see Colonel Chivington. It's very important."

"The colonel isn't here, sir," said one of the sentries.

"Oh? When do you expect him back?"

The corporals exchanged glances, then the one who had spoken before said, "Maybe we'd better let you talk to Colonel Shoup, Mr. Baker."

"Colonel Shoup? He can't help me. I need to see Colonel Chivington as soon as possible."

"That's *why* you'd better talk to Colonel Shoup, sir. He's in charge of the camp at present."

"All right. Can you take me to him?"

"Yes, sir. Follow me."

Colonel Shoup had seen them coming, and opened the door.

"Sir, this is Mr. Daniel G. Baker, editor-in-chief of the *Rocky Mountain News*. He was asking to see Colonel Chivington. I told him he should talk to you."

"All right, Corporal, thank you." Shoup waited for the corporal to leave, then said, "Colonel Chivington isn't here, Mr. Baker, and he'll be gone for an undetermined amount of time. Is there something I can do for you?"

Baker squinted at the officer standing before him. "Colonel Shoup, are you saying that Colonel Chivington has left the area?"

"Yes. He suddenly had to make a trip to his home state of Ohio. I don't know what it's about, but he put me in charge, saying he had no idea when he might be back. He's on an east-bound train right now."

The special edition of the *Rocky Mountain News* came off the press the next Tuesday, December 19. The week before, Dan Baker had George Bent, Edmund Guerrier, and J. W. Smith take him and a cameraman to War Bonnet's village. There Baker had a photograph taken of himself and Black Kettle with the three men who had given testimony of the events at Sand Creek.

The special edition told it all. The long article exposed John Chivington's atrocities at Sand Creek and the lies in his report. The headlines called the November 29 attack a treacherous massacre of peaceful Indians, by far the larger number of them women and children. The photograph was printed on the front page under screaming headlines, and readers were reminded that Chivington had reported having killed Chief Black Kettle.

Baker's story said Chief Black Kettle was a leader for peace in the Cheyenne nation, and it included facts about the peace treaty Black Kettle and the other chiefs had signed with Governor John Evans and Colonel John Chivington.

The story spread fast, shocking the territory of Colorado. Eastern newspapers and those on the Pacific coast had at first printed the story hailing the Sand Creek battle as a notable victory for the U.S. Army. Their front pages now gave the facts Baker cited in his special edition. Many of the papers sent wires, asking for the photograph of Baker with Chief Black Kettle and the three eyewitnesses.

Army reports contained the news that a few officers and men who had been with Chivington at Sand Creek had written letters to General-in-Chief Henry W. Halleck in Washington, saying they were in anguish over the part they played in the attack. The letters confirmed that Dan Baker's special edition told the truth.

Newspapers all over the country picked up on it, telling the gruesome story. The nation reacted with shock and revulsion.

While a great stir was going on in Washington over the Sand Creek Massacre, the Plains Indians called a war council on the Smoky Hill River in eastern Colorado. Black Kettle and the surviving chiefs who had gone with him to the peace treaty meeting were in attendance, along with other Cheyenne, Arapaho, and Sioux chiefs.

Black Kettle was asked to speak to the crowd of angry chiefs. But instead of a call for the shedding of white men's blood, he said, "My friends and brothers, as you all know, my squaw and son were killed by Chivington and his troops at Sand Creek. Indeed, I am deeply angry over this, as well as over the loss of so many other people of my village. But I must consider all my other Cheyenne brothers and sisters, as well as my Arapaho and Sioux brothers and sisters. I fear that if we retaliate, the destiny of our tribes on these plains is ultimate extinction. Our only hope of survival is to remain friendly with the whites. They have more soldiers than we have warriors, and they have weapons we cannot match. I beg of you, do not retaliate."

A Cheyenne chief named Crow Dog stepped forth and said in a loud voice, "Black Kettle, you are correct. We *are* brothers and sisters. What was done at your village affects us all. What have we to live for? The white men have taken our land and killed our game. But they were not satisfied with that. They killed our squaws and children at Sand Creek. Now there will be no peace. I say we raise our battle ax until death!"

Cheers greeted Crow Dog's brief speech. Black Kettle's Cheyenne, Arapaho, and Sioux brothers would not rest until they made the whites pay for Sand Creek.

By mid-December, over two thousand Cheyenne, Arapaho, and Sioux warriors went on the warpath—in spite of the snow and freezing weather on the plains. Their cry was "Death to the whites!"

While the frontier trembled, Henry W. Halleck wired Governor John Evans from Washington, reminding him that as territorial governor he had authority over Chivington. Evans was to order Chivington to take a train to Washington immediately to face court-martial charges. Evans's return message told Halleck that Chivington had resigned from military service and was beyond the army's reach, and he was no longer in Colorado.

Halleck took the issue to President Abraham Lincoln, and Lincoln called for a thorough investigation of the Sand Creek Massacre, which resulted in a dual investigation.

America's newspapers began carrying official announcements from Halleck that the Sand Creek affair would be the subject of investigations by the United States Congress and the army. The charges: Chivington and his men had murdered

Indians who thought they were under army protection; most of the dead were women and children; and Indian bodies had been scalped and mutilated.

On a warm day in early June 1865, John Chivington finished cleaning the big printing press where he was employed at the *Columbus Daily News,* threw the rags he had been using in the trash barrel nearby, and glanced at the clock on the wall. It was five o'clock. Quitting time.

Chivington headed for the glassed-in office. Pausing at the open office door, he smiled at his employer and said, "The press is all cleaned up for tomorrow morning's run, Mr. Campbell. See you at five-thirty."

"All right, John," said elderly Oscar Campbell with a smile. "Get yourself a good night's rest. Too bad you don't have yourself a little woman at your house to cook for you."

"Maybe someday, sir, but I'm just not hunting for a wife yet."

"Still afraid no woman'll have you because of all the stink in the papers, eh?"

"Something like that. I'm still amazed you employ me when you have to print all that stuff that comes out of Washington and good old Columbus."

"Well, like I've told you before," said Campbell, tilting his head down and looking at Chivington over his half-moon spectacles, "those bloody Cheyenne massacred my son, daughter-in-law, and three grandchildren in that wagon train back in '59. I think the government should've pinned a medal on you for what you did. Let the bleeding hearts cry about it. You've got a job here as long as you want it. And when the day comes that I can't run this paper anymore, I'll sell it to you if you're interested."

"Sure do appreciate your attitude, sir," said John. "See you in the morning."

The sun was lowering toward the horizon as Chivington rounded the corner on his street. The buggy parked in front of his small house caught his eye immediately. He could tell there were two people in the buggy, and one was definitely a man, but he couldn't make out the other person.

As he drew near, he realized both were men as they stepped out and moved onto the boardwalk and halted in his path, eyeing him. One looked to be in his sixties, and the other was in his fifties and carried a briefcase.

"Good evening, Mr. Chivington," said the older man. "Do you remember me?"

"Seems like I should know you, sir," he said, "but to be honest, I can't say who you are."

"The name's Cletus Borden, Mr. Chivington. *Bishop* Cletus Borden."

"Yes, of course I remember you. You sat on my ordination council…Cincinnati, May of 1845."

Borden gave him a frosty look. "I was pastor of First Methodist Church across the Ohio River in Florence, Kentucky, at the time. And I'm now on the board of directing bishops of the Methodist Church, U.S.A. This is Reverend Martin Yarbro, my assistant."

Yarbro did not offer his hand. Neither did Chivington.

"It took us a while to locate you, Mr. Chivington," said Borden. "May we come inside and talk to you?"

"Sure. Come on in."

The two men sat together in the small parlor facing Chivington.

"Mr. Chivington," Borden said, "we have stayed abreast of what the newspapers have been reporting about the incident at

Sand Creek in Colorado last November. What do you have to say about it all?"

"What's to say?" said Chivington. "The newspapers are biased. For some reason they insist on taking the Indians' part."

"Are you saying they shouldn't? From everything I've read, what took place that day was wholesale slaughter of innocent women and children. Does the fact that they have a red tincture to their skin make it all right to slaughter them?"

Chivington eyed him for a long moment, then said, "Why don't you get to your point, Bishop?"

Borden opened his hand toward his assistant, and Yarbro placed a handful of newspaper clippings in it. The bishop spread the clippings in his hand and said, "Let's see what we have here, Mr. Chivington. Just to note a few...Senator James Doolittle, head of the Senate Committee on Indian Affairs, told the *Washington Post* that during the investigation of the Sand Creek affair by Congress, he learned things that made his 'blood chill and freeze with horror.' And this one, General Ulysses S. Grant—busy cleaning up after the Civil War—takes time to comment in a public meeting: 'Sand Creek was nothing less than a murder by federal troops of trusting Indians who thought they were under the protection of the army.' And this from the *Boston Globe*: 'General Nelson A. Miles says the Sand Creek Massacre is perhaps the foulest and most unjustifiable crime in the annals of America.'"

Chivington met their questioning looks with a stony stare.

Borden shuffled the clippings, lifted a large one, and said, "*Washington Post*. It tells here that on May 30, Congress's Joint Committee on the Conduct of War, headed by Senator Ben Wade of Ohio—*your* state, sir—issued a scathing report, calling the incident at Sand Creek 'the scene of murder and barbarity of the most revolting character.' The article goes on to quote Senator Wade as saying, 'John M. Chivington is denounced by this Committee, and has disgraced the veriest savage. The massacre at Sand Creek, November 29, 1864, scarcely has its parallel in Indian barbarity. Men, women, and children were tortured, murdered, and scalped in a way which would put to shame the savages of interior Africa.'"

Martin Yarbro eyed Chivington with disdain. "What do you have to say about this, Mr. Chivington?"

"I say I've heard enough."

"Let me give you just one more," said the bishop. "You need to hear this one. Again... *Washington Post*. It says that when the investigations were completed in early spring, Joseph Holt, Judge Advocate General of the United States Army, branded Chivington's actions at Sand Creek 'a cowardly and cold-blooded slaughter, sufficient to cover its perpetrators with indelible infamy, and the face of every American with shame and indignation.' The article continues, 'Though Chivington—who is somewhere in Ohio—has resigned from military service and is beyond the army's reach, the Committee calls for the prompt removal from military service those others responsible for the massacre that has now resulted in hundreds of deaths of whites at the hands of Cheyenne, Arapaho, and Sioux tribes in retaliation.'"

"Do you see what you caused, Mr. Chivington?" Yarbro said. "Hundreds of innocent white people have been killed by Indians since the first of this year because of what you did at Sand Creek."

Chivington fought the emotions that stirred within him as Borden said, "Here's an article from the *Rocky Mountain News*. It says that George Shoup and Scott Anthony have been dishonorably discharged from the army in shame and disgrace. And the investigations of both Congress and the army uncovered the guilt of John Evans in conspiring with you in the massacre. When the facts were presented to President Andrew Johnson, he immediately called for Evans's resignation as governor of Colorado Territory."

The bishop shuffled clippings again. "Judge Holt called the incident at Sand Creek 'a cowardly and cold-blooded slaughter, sufficient to cover its perpetrators with *indelible* infamy....' You aren't going to live this down, sir. Scripture says in Numbers 32:23, 'Be sure your sin will find you out.' Your infamy is indeed indelible, Mr. Chivington."

"All right, you've had your say, Bishop Borden." Chivington rose from his chair. "I hope you feel better now."

Borden handed the clippings back to Yarbro. While the assistant began stuffing them in the briefcase, Borden stood up and said, "One more thing, Mr. Chivington. The day you were ordained in Cincinnati, you were given ordination papers by the council. In the name of the Methodist Church, U.S.A., I demand their return."

"I have no idea where they are. Haven't seen them since I left the church in Denver."

"Mm-hmm. Well, I figured as much. Martin…"

Yarbro already had an official-looking paper in his hand and was on his feet. He ceremoniously handed it to the bishop.

Borden said, "Since I figured you might not have the ordination papers available, I had this document drawn up. It is simply a statement I wish you to sign, abdicating your revered position as an ordained Methodist minister. It also states that because of your part in the massacre of innocent women and children at Sand Creek, you understand that your membership as a Methodist is rescinded."

"I don't have a pen," Chivington said, fixing Borden with cold eyes.

"Martin has a pencil," said Borden. "It will do."

The paper was signed, and the two ministers left without further comment. John Chivington closed the door behind them, then walked to the parlor window to watch them climb into the buggy and drive away.

Wheeling about, he smashed a fist into his palm and swore. He'd read over and over about the three white men who had lived through the massacre and told their story to the *Rocky Mountain News*. "If only those three had been killed that day," he said aloud, "none of the rest of this would've happened." Chivington shook his head, swung a fist through the air, and growled, "I should've put bullets in all three of them!"

He went to the kitchen and built a fire in the stove. While he was preparing supper, his mind again went back to the scene of the battle. One scene in particular he had relived many times: when he had shot at and missed the Indian girl...the one who had thrown the rock that struck him in the forehead. That wild, crazed look in her eyes still haunted him. Sometimes when he woke up in the night, he would see those eyes...those big black eyes...full of terror and fury. The image chilled him.

8

"SILVER MOON! Wake up, child! Wake up!"

Silver Moon felt strong hands on her shoulders and opened her eyes. Moonlight streamed through the opening of the tepee and revealed the face of Little Sparrow, the widowed squaw of Eagle Wing, who had been killed at Sand Creek.

"Oh, Little Sparrow!" gasped Silver Moon. "I was having the nightmare again!"

"I know, dear. You were calling Bear Paw's name when I first heard you, then you started screaming."

Silver Moon usually slept in Red Leaf's tepee, but for the past few days Red Leaf had been treating a very sick elderly man, and Little Sparrow had invited Silver Moon to stay with her.

Silver Moon brushed back her disheveled hair and said, "I am so sorry to have awakened you."

Little Sparrow wrapped her arms around Silver Moon and held her close. "You do not have to apologize, my sweet one. Only Heammawihio knows the suffering you have gone through. I am sure the nightmares will go away in time."

Silver Moon was quiet for a moment, then said, "The nightmares may go away, Little Sparrow, but the need for justice will not go away until John Chivington is dead."

Little Sparrow pulled back and looked at the young girl.

"Justice? You mean for your family and Bear Paw?"

"Yes. John Chivington took their lives, yet he still walks the earth in a place called Ohio. This is not right. Justice must be served. There needs to be a grave dug for him, and his wretched body placed in it for the worms to eat."

Little Sparrow blinked in amazement. "Silver Moon, I've never heard you talk this way. What has made you suddenly desire vengeance on this man?"

"It is not so sudden. For so long I have felt nothing but grief since that wicked man murdered my mother, my brother, and Bear Paw. They have walked the Hanging Road, but it has come to me that their spirits will have no rest until justice is done to John Chivington, who took them out of this world before their natural time. As this knowledge has grown in my mind, it has put a restlessness in my spirit and a hatred for that man in my heart. For the sake of Mother, Sky Eagle, and Bear Paw, I must see complete and final justice done."

Little Sparrow glanced toward the tepee opening, where a small night creature skittered by, then said, "Have you talked to your father about this restlessness in your spirit?"

"No. Father still carries much grief. He does not need to hear of what is inside me."

"But your father cares about you very much, Silver Moon. You must share this with him. It is unusual for such a young one to feel as you do."

"I know you have carried your own grief over Two Arrows, yet you have been so kind to my father in trying to help him with his grief. You are truly a remarkable woman, Little Sparrow. Thank you for what you have done for Father...and for me."

"It is my pleasure, child," said Little Sparrow. "But I...must ask you something."

"Yes?"

"This complete and final justice you need on John Chivington, you say it will not be served until he is dead."

"That is right."

"What does this mean?"

Silver Moon drew a deep breath and said, "This means I must find him and kill him."

Little Sparrow frowned. "You?"

"The army has let him get away with murder, and the government has done nothing to bring him to justice. My father's grief has not turned into a need for vengeance, but mine has. So it is up to me."

Little Sparrow took hold of the girl's shoulders and looked her square in the eye. "You will promise me one thing."

"What is that?"

"Tomorrow morning you will talk to Black Kettle about this."

Silver Moon studied Little Sparrow's face for a long moment. "All right," she said. "I promise."

"But my daughter, it is not for you to bring justice to John Chivington!" said Black Kettle as he paced his tepee.

Silver Moon and Little Sparrow stood side by side, their backs to the opening and the early morning sun.

"Then who will, my father? The army has done nothing. The white man's government has exposed him as a murderer, and they do nothing."

"Silver Moon may recall the white missionary and his wife who stayed a night in our village on Smoky Hill River."

"Yes, Father."

"The missionary spoke of evil men, and how his God has

designed life that the evil man's own wickedness will be his downfall. How did he say it is worded in white man's sacred Book? 'The man who digs a pit shall fall into it.' Would not our own Heammawihio feel the same way? John Chivington has dug his own pit. We must let him fall into it."

"But what would be wrong if I gave him a push, Father?"

Little Sparrow covered the smile that came to her lips.

Black Kettle rubbed the back of his neck, then looked intently at his daughter. "Silver Moon, the man is in Ohio. Do you have any idea how far away that is? A girl of sixteen grasses could never make it. And that is only part of it. John Chivington is a large man, very powerful. You are a small girl. How would you ever be able to give him the push you speak of?"

"I will figure a way," Silver Moon said bitterly.

Black Kettle gently gripped her shoulders and looked into her eyes "My daughter, you must drive this desire from your mind. There is nothing you can do."

"But I know the spirits of my mother, my brother, and Bear Paw will not rest until their murderer has been brought to justice."

"My daughter, we must leave Chivington to Heammawihio." Squeezing her shoulders, he said, "Silver Moon, there is no other choice."

The girl bit down on her lower lip and blinked back the tears welling up in her eyes, then nodded. "All right, Father. All right. But I must pray that Heammawihio will somehow let me know when Chivington has fallen into his pit. Until I know I cannot rest, because I will not know that Mother, Sky Eagle, and Bear Paw are at rest."

Black Kettle let go of her and sighed. "I will pray the same way, my daughter."

In the summer of 1865, the Cheyenne people of the late White Antelope's village were in a quandary. Snake Killer, who was to follow White Antelope as chief, was also dead. They had no other man of sufficient age and wisdom to lead them. They went to Black Kettle and asked to join his remnant. Black Kettle agreed, and they placed themselves under him as their chief.

In August, Black Kettle moved his people to a spot some twenty miles due east of Cheyenne City, Wyoming, and established a village there. He remained at peace with the whites, doing all he could to show them a friendly spirit. This proved to be difficult at times, when other Cheyenne and their Arapaho and Sioux brothers, attacked white settlements, wagon trains, and stagecoaches.

Chief War Bonnet, also striving to keep peace with the whites, moved his village to a spot ten miles farther east of Black Kettle's village, just west of the Nebraska-Wyoming border.

The winter of 1865–1866 was extremely severe. Black Kettle decided that come fall, he would move his people south to Oklahoma Indian Territory, where the winters were milder. They would camp for the winter on the Washita River, then return to their Wyoming location in early spring.

In late summer of 1866, Black Kettle wed Little Sparrow. Silver Moon was pleased, for she loved Little Sparrow very much and was happy to see both her father and the lovely widow no longer lonely.

As time passed, Silver Moon matured and became even more beautiful. She still experienced nightmares, reliving the Sand Creek Massacre, but not as frequently. But she clung to the memory of Bear Paw and yearned for her mother and her brother, and with each nightmare her flame of hatred toward John Chivington was kindled anew. She prayed daily to Heammawihio, asking for justice to be served and that somehow she would learn of it when the vile man fell into his pit.

In early September 1868, as had now become their custom, Black Kettle led his people south for the winter to the Washita River in Oklahoma Territory. The day after they arrived and set up their village on the banks of the river, Little Sparrow and Silver Moon were repairing a rip in the side of the girl's tepee, which Black Kettle had given Silver Moon when he and Little Sparrow married.

The stepmother noticed that Silver Moon had seemed preoccupied all morning. Smiling at her as they worked together, she said, "Silver Moon is upset about something. You have had another nightmare?"

"Yes, Little Sparrow. I saw the faces of Mother, Sky Eagle, and Bear Paw. They were very unhappy. I know their murderer is still alive. Heammawihio has not answered my prayers."

"That is because Heammawihio will work in his own time to let John Chivington fall into his pit."

Silver Moon shook her head. "No. Heammawihio has not answered my prayers because he wants *me* to push John Chivington into his pit. I must kill him, Little Sparrow."

The older woman's brow furrowed. "This cannot be, child. Your father told you so when you spoke of this three grasses ago."

"I am no longer a girl," Silver Moon said, pointing to the headband she now wore as a sign of coming into womanhood. "I am nineteen grasses. I am a woman."

"But you are still no match for a man who was once a soldier, Silver Moon. I understand how you feel, but you simply must leave John Chivington to Heammawihio. You must forget trying to exact justice on the man yourself."

Silver Moon closed her eyes and again saw Sky Eagle collapse before the mounted Chivington and the smoking gun in the big man's hand. She saw Gentle Dove run to him and take Chivington's bullet in her heart…and she saw Bear Paw throw his body in the path of the bullet meant for her. Tears streamed down Silver Moon's cheeks.

"I cannot forget, Little Sparrow. I cannot!"

Little Sparrow reached to her stepdaughter, caressed her soft cheek, and said, "In time, your need to punish the man will ease, Silver Moon. You will see."

The night was warm and clear on the banks of the Washita River as the village slept. By candlelight, inside her tepee, Silver Moon packed her belongings in a knapsack. She cradled the .45 caliber revolver she'd found on the ground the day after the massacre at Sand Creek. It was fully loaded.

Tears misted Silver Moon's eyes as she used a pencil stub to write a note to her father on a slip of paper. Weighting the paper on her pallet with a rock, she blew out the candle. With the knapsack tied to her back, she stuck her head out the opening of the tepee and looked around. All was still.

She slipped silently through the opening and headed northeast. She didn't know how far Ohio might be, but she knew it was in that general direction.

The next morning, Black Kettle had the fire going outside the big tepee and was in conversation with a few braves nearby when Little Sparrow approached him, apologized for interrupting, and said, "You must come with me to Silver Moon's tepee."

As they walked together, Black Kettle said, "What is wrong?"

"It is best that you see for yourself."

They reached Silver Moon's tepee, and Little Sparrow paused at the opening and said, "Please enter ahead of me, my husband."

Black Kettle stepped inside and saw that the usual arrangement of Silver Moon's things was different; then his eyes fell to her pallet and the slip of paper under the rock. His hand trembled as he held the message and read it silently:

My Father—
    I must do what I must do. When it is done, I will
return. Please understand. Your daughter loves her
father and stepmother very much.
Silver Moon

The chief set worried eyes on his squaw. "Silver Moon has suffered much since Gentle Dove, Sky Eagle, and Bear Paw were murdered by John Chivington. I wish there was some way I could reach down into her heart and take away the pain, but I cannot."

"You have done all that is possible, my husband."

He cast a glance through the tepee opening. "I could go after her and bring her back by force, but she would only keep trying until she finally got away from me." He folded the paper. "My heart is heavy for Silver Moon. So great is her hatred toward John Chivington and so strong is her need to bring him to justice, that she has not allowed herself to fall in love with a young Cheyenne brave, though many have shown great interest in her."

"I have had the same thoughts. I have talked to her about it when she and I have been alone."

"What did she say?"

"Only that until the spirit of Bear Paw was at rest, she could not let her heart reach for another young man."

As Silver Moon walked, staying on the well-traveled roads as much as possible, she found people along the way who were willing to give her rides in wagons and buggies. Many shared food with her and gave her lodging. On each segment of the journey, people were kind enough to steer her to the proper roads that would carry her toward Ohio.

In late October, as she walked the main road between Joplin and Springfield, Missouri, a string of freight wagons came up behind her, all of one company. The lead wagon was driven by the owner. He offered her a ride and asked where she was headed. When she told him Ohio, he said they were going to Indianapolis, Indiana, to reload their wagons. She could ride that far with the train.

During the trip to Indianapolis, she overheard two men talking. One man mentioned Dayton, Ohio. A day or two later, when the owner of the wagons asked her where in Ohio she was headed, she named "Dayton" as her destination.

Upon arriving in Indianapolis, Silver Moon was given directions to the road that led across the border to Dayton, a hundred miles due east.

She reached Dayton on Thursday, November 26, and decided that since Chivington's name had been in the papers a great deal in the West, the best place to find someone who might know where in the state John Chivington lived was a newspaper.

Though the citizens walking Dayton's city streets eyed her cautiously, they were friendly enough in an aloof sort of way.

When Silver Moon came upon a man dressed in blue, wearing a badge, she knew he must be a lawman, though he dressed differently than any lawman she had ever seen in the West. He directed her to the newspaper office.

Inside the office of the *Dayton Herald*, Louise Pitkin looked up from her desk to see a lovely dark-skinned young woman. The girl carried a canvas knapsack on her back and wore a crude-looking coat. Eyeing Silver Moon's headband as she approached the desk, Louise said, "Good afternoon, miss. May I help you?"

"I hope you can. I am Silver Moon of the Southern Cheyenne. I have traveled a long way to locate a man you probably know about."

Louise cocked her head and smiled. "You speak English quite well, Miss Silver Moon."

"I was taught by a man named George Bent, ma'am."

"He certainly taught you well. Would you like to remove your coat and sit down?"

"Yes. Thank you."

Silver Moon eased the knapsack onto the floor, slipped out of her coat, and sat down on the chair that faced the desk.

Louise ran her gaze over Silver Moon's buckskin blouse and skirt. "How lovely!" she said. "And I suppose you made your clothes yourself."

"This one was made by my stepmother, but I do have others I made myself."

"Let's see, now. You were going to ask about a man..."

"Yes. His name is John Chivington. He—"

"*Colonel* John Chivington? Well, I guess I should say ex-Colonel John Chivington."

"That is him. Would you know where in Ohio I might be able to locate him?"

"Well, I assume he's in Columbus, but I can't say for sure. He *was* there. Columbus is the state capital. Mr. Chivington owned a newspaper there—the *Columbus Daily News*—up until a few months ago. He ran for the Ohio legislature last year but didn't make it." Louise paused. "Since you're from out West, you may know about the Sand Creek Massacre in Colorado."

"Yes. I know about it."

"You probably know that Chivington was charged with killing innocent women and children at Sand Creek."

"I know about that, yes."

"Well, Miss Silver Moon, the incident seems to have followed Chivington ever since. He lost his bid for the legislature because so many politicians spoke out against him for what he did at Sand Creek. And public opinion became so strong against him that people stopped advertising in his newspaper and actually quit buying it. He went broke."

"Broke? I am not acquainted with the use of the word in the way you have used it."

"Oh. He…ah…lost all his money. He had to sell the paper to someone else. It's doing fine, now, I understand."

"But you think Mr. Chivington still lives in Columbus?"

"Last I knew, he did. Can't say for sure now."

Silver Moon rose from the chair and picked up her coat, saying, "Thank you for your help, ma'am. How far is Columbus from here?"

"About seventy-five miles. How are you traveling?"

"I am walking."

"*Walking?*"

"Yes."

"You *walked* all the way from out West?"

"Only part of the way. Many people were kind enough to let me ride in their wagons and buggies."

"I see. Well, there's a carriage that transports passengers between here and there, Miss Silver Moon. It leaves Dayton at five-thirty in the morning. Arrives in Columbus late in the afternoon."

Silver Moon nodded. "I have no money, ma'am. Perhaps I will be able to find someone along the road who will let me ride with them."

Louise tilted her head to one side, frowning. "If you have no money, where will you sleep tonight?"

"I will find a spot somewhere. Thank you for your kindness."

"You will find a spot, all right," said Louise. "At my house. I'm a widow, and I have a spare bedroom. The carriage fare is a dollar, and I also have a spare one of those."

The sun was low and the air turning colder when Silver Moon arrived in Columbus. Louise had given her an extra two dollars with which to rent a hotel room and buy supper that evening and breakfast the next morning.

She was surprised to see the *Columbus Daily News* sign as the carriage slowed to a stop. The newspaper office was half a block from the hotel. Alighting from the carriage, Silver Moon immediately headed for the newspaper building.

As she hurried past some stores, she saw an elderly man come out of the newspaper office and close the door behind him. He was locking it as Silver Moon moved up beside him and said, "Excuse me, sir…"

The old man's eyes bulged as he beheld her headband and strange clothing. "Yes, ma'am?"

"I need to talk to the person who owns the newspaper."

"He won't be here till mornin', ma'am. Are…are you goin' to a costume party or somethin'?"

"I am Silver Moon of the Southern Cheyenne tribe in Wyoming."

"Oh. A real live Injun, eh?"

"What time will the owner be here in the morning?"

"Mr. Musgrave always gets here 'fore anybody else. He'll be in 'bout six-thirty. Rest of us don't come in till seven-thirty. Is there anythin' I can help you with?"

"Well, possibly. Are you acquainted with Mr. John Chivington, the man who used to own the paper?"

"Yes'm. He hired me as janitor here 'bout three months 'fore he had to sell out. Mr. Musgrave kept me on, bless him."

"Could you tell me where he lives?"

"Mr. Musgrave?"

"No. Mr. Chivington."

"Well, let me think. I was there a coupla times. Mmm. Oh, yes. Just a couple blocks down thataway. Fourth Street. Turn right. His house is the second—no, the third house from the corner on the right-hand side. Can't miss it. It's the house with black shutters on the winders."

"Is he married?"

"Nope."

"So no one else lives in the house with him?"

"Nope. Lives alone."

Silver Moon thanked the man and hurried down the street. As she turned the corner, her heart picked up pace. A buggy passed by, the sound of the horse's hooves echoing between the houses.

The sun was touching the western horizon, throwing its orange beams on the third house from the corner on her right...the one with the black shutters.

Silver Moon hung the knapsack on her right shoulder and placed her hand inside. Her fingers closed around the butt of the gun as she stepped up onto the porch.

She knocked on the door with her left hand, keeping her right hand inside the knapsack.

She heard heavy footsteps inside the house...the footsteps of a big man. Her heart thudded against her rib cage when she saw a shadow behind the thin curtains covering the window on the door.

Silver Moon cocked the hammer inside the knapsack as the door swung open and the massive man focused on her face.

9

SILVER MOON SMOTHERED a sudden catch of breath as she saw the silver hair and the leathered face of an old man. Indeed, he was as large as Chivington, if not larger, but at least thirty years older.

Inside the knapsack, her tense fingers relaxed as he said, "What can I do for you, little lady?" His voice was a deep rumble.

A small white-haired woman stepped up beside him, studying Silver Moon's face and clothing.

"I...I must have the wrong house. I am looking for Mr. John Chivington. I'm sorry, I—"

The white-haired man looked at her curiously. "You've got the right house but the wrong man. We bought the house from Chivington in August."

"Oh. I see. C-could you tell me where he lives now?"

"Don't have the slightest idea."

"I'm sorry to have disturbed you, sir," Silver Moon said, taking her hand out of the knapsack and turning to leave.

The man said no more as Silver Moon stepped off the porch, but before he closed the door, she heard him mumble something to his wife about Indians.

Silver Moon checked into the hotel, and while eating supper at the restaurant, she told herself she would return in the morning to the office of the *Columbus Daily News*.

Clarence Musgrave chuckled as he looked at the young Indian woman across his desk. "Well, Miss Silver Moon," he said, "ol' Eddie is in his own little world a lot of the time. I told him Chivington doesn't live in that house anymore, but I guess it didn't register. He still does a good job as janitor, so I keep him on."

The sound of the big press running in a glassed-in room across the hall filled the place.

"Then, sir, can you tell me where Mr. Chivington lives at present?"

"Somewhere west of the Missouri River. That's all I can tell you. When he left here, he said he was going back out west. I don't know how well you know Chivington, but the last time I saw him, he was a broken man. He appeared as if his whole world had fallen down around him. Do you know about his failure in politics?"

"Yes. I know about that."

"When I bought this newspaper from him, it was about to go bankrupt. The entire thing—his bid for the state legislature and the failure of the newspaper—went back to that incident in Colorado in 1864. You know about Sand Creek, I'm sure."

"Yes. I know about it."

"There was a lot said about Chivington and Sand Creek by the time Congress and the army finished their investigations. One statement in particular haunted him...a statement by Judge Holt. He said that what Chivington did at Sand Creek was a cowardly, cold-blooded slaughter, and it covered him with indelible infamy." Musgrave pointed toward the door of his office. "Those were the last words he muttered as he went out that door: 'indelible infamy.'"

The rumble of the big press grew louder for an instant when a small, slender man, wearing a visor cap, came out of the press room and closed the door behind him. He was carrying a newspaper in his hand.

"So Mr. Chivington made no comments on just where in the West he was planning on going?" Silver Moon asked.

"None. I'm sorry I can't give you any more information. I assume your need to contact him is quite important."

"Yes, sir."

The slender man stepped up to the desk and said, "Excuse me, Mr. Musgrave. Here's the first copy of this morning's edition."

"Thanks, Mack," said Musgrave, laying the newspaper on his desk with the front page exposed.

Silver Moon's line of sight fell on the headlines, and though they were upside down to her, she instantly caught the words: *SEVENTH CAVALRY IN BATTLE ON WASHITA*

"What is this news, Mr. Musgrave?" she asked.

"We received a wire late yesterday about a battle led by Colonel George Armstrong Custer and his Seventh Cavalry against a village of Cheyenne Indians on the Washita River in Oklahoma. In fact, the chief of the village was Black Kettle. You might recall that it was his village that Chivington attacked at Sand Creek."

Silver Moon jumped to her feet, spun the paper around, and began reading the article.

"What's wrong, miss?" asked Musgrave. "Are you Cheyenne?"

Silver Moon's eyes took in the lines that said Black Kettle

and his squaw were killed, along with a few hundred other Cheyenne. Others had escaped Custer's guns. Silver Moon's eyes flooded with tears, and her hand went to her mouth as she ejected a tiny squeal.

Clarence Musgrave's face pinched in concern. "What is it, Miss Silver Moon? Did you know the people of that village?"

"More than that!" she said, choking out the words. "That was *my* village. Black Kettle was my father!"

"What? I thought you said you were from Wyoming."

"We live most of the time in Wyoming. But Father has taken us south into Oklahoma Indian Territory for the past couple of years to avoid the severe winters in Wyoming." As she spoke, Silver Moon's knees gave way, and she sat down on the chair. Overcome with grief, she let out a mournful sob and bent double, weeping brokenheartedly.

Musgrave rushed to a back room and returned with a woman about his own age. As they moved together toward the weeping Indian girl, the woman said, "What's her name, Clarence?"

"Silver Moon."

The woman touched Silver Moon's shoulder and bent close, saying, "I'm Lila Musgrave. Is there anything I can do for you?"

Silver Moon looked up, tears shining on her cheeks. "There is nothing anyone can do. The pain in my heart is too great and too deep."

Lila took her in her arms. "Well, at least here's a shoulder to cry on."

When Silver Moon's weeping subsided, Clarence Musgrave asked her how she had come to Ohio. He and his wife were stunned to hear that she had walked except for the occasional rides people had given her.

"Will you still try to find Mr. Chivington?" asked Clarence.

"The West is too large for me to attempt a search."

"Where will you go, dear?" Lila asked. "I mean, since your father's village has been destroyed."

"Chief War Bonnet and my father were very close friends," said Silver Moon. "His village is several miles east of Cheyenne City, Wyoming. I have many friends in the village. War Bonnet will give me a home."

"Do you want to return right away?" asked Lila.

"Yes."

"Well, we're not going to let you walk this time. Clarence and I will take you to the railroad station and buy your tickets."

After being fed a good meal by the Musgraves, Silver Moon stood in the Columbus depot with the couple, tickets in hand. She would ride from Columbus to Kansas City, Missouri. At Kansas City, she would board a train for Cheyenne City.

The train bound for Kansas City was beginning to fill up and would leave in ten minutes. Silver Moon's eyes misted as she said, "I do not have the words to thank you for what you have done for me."

"No need," said Clarence. "It is our joy and pleasure."

"Silver Moon…" said Lila.

"Yes?"

"I'm curious. How do you know John Chivington? Why do you want to find him?"

A grim look hardened the young woman's features. "The man murdered my mother, my brother, and Bear Paw, the young man to whom I was promised. I saw him do it with my own eyes the day the army attacked our village at Sand Creek. For four years I have lived with the horrible scene in my mind and have had nightmares about it. I will not deny it. I came here to make him pay for what he did that day."

The conductor called for all the passengers to board. Silver Moon thanked the couple again, embracing Lila and shaking hands with Clarence, then boarded the train.

John Chivington had arrived in Denver in late August. His attempts to find a job had been futile. The label "indelible infamy" stuck to him.

In mid-September, Chivington learned that Denver County Sheriff Tom Decker was looking for a deputy. He applied for the job.

Decker admitted he really needed a man with Chivington's experience, and wished he could hire him, but his hands were tied. Hiring Chivington would bring too much trouble from the people he served.

Chivington walked away from the sheriff's office a bitter and beaten man. Heavy of heart, he rode west into the Rocky Mountains, figuring he could possibly get a job with a gold mining outfit. He was big and strong. He could wield a pick and shovel, and he could do the work of two smaller men.

He was turned down flat by the mine owners when they learned his identity.

Chivington became increasingly despondent. With little money in his pockets, he decided to try panning for gold on his own. He'd heard there was gold in small creeks that flowed into the Fraser River, high in the mountains, near Granby.

He rode into the town and saw an assayer's office next door to a miner's supply shop. When purchasing his panning equipment, Chivington asked the proprietor if he knew of any cabins in town for rent and was told that an old prospector named Luke Demarest had died a few days ago. His body had been found beside a nearby creek and carried into town to the undertaker. Luke was a bachelor and had no family, so no one had claimed the cabin yet. The store owner gave directions to the place located just south of Granby on the river.

Chivington found the cabin just as the store owner had said. There was also an old shed and a small corral to keep his horse. Luke Demarest's cooking utensils and panning equipment were still there. Apparently no one had even entered the cabin.

The very next day, Chivington began panning for gold in a nearby creek and was pleased at what he found in only a day's work. That evening, while repairing a loose board in the cabin's floor, he found a cache of gold dust beneath the floor. For the first time in months, John M. Chivington had a reason to smile.

Day after day, Chivington lived the hermit's life, away from a world that condemned him for what happened at Sand Creek—deeds for which he felt no repentance.

As time passed, however, he began to have nightmares about the massacre, and he began to rethink what he had done. Often he awakened in the deep of night and found himself sitting up in bed in a cold sweat. The nightmares were vividly real. He would see the women and children in Black Kettle's village as they tried to run from the bullets cutting them down. He would see the bodies and hear the screams over and over again. And the girl with the dark, wild eyes still haunted him.

As the years passed, Chivington often wondered if the haunting would stay with him the way the label "indelible infamy" had. Was he destined to endure both until the day he died?

It was Wednesday, September 4, 1872. Chief United States Marshal John Brockman stepped up to the witness stand in the main courtroom of the Federal Building in Denver, Colorado Territory. The courtroom was about half full, and every eye was fixed on the tall, ruggedly handsome Brockman.

Seated at a large table facing the judge's bench and the witness stand was defendant Armand Watts. His greasy, unkempt hair dangled to his shoulders. Sitting next to Watts was his attorney, Hector Dulotte. Standing behind Watts was Denver County Sheriff Curt Langan. Though Langan had handcuffed Watts before bringing him from the jail for the trial, Langan was playing it safe. One false move and he would be on the cold-blooded murderer like a hungry cat on a fat rat.

The court stenographer, with pencil and paper before her, sat at a smaller table a few feet from the defendant.

Judge James Egan glanced at the twelve-man jury as the bailiff stepped up to the tall man in black who occupied the witness stand. "For the court record, sir," said the bailiff, "will you please state your name?"

"John Brockman."

The bailiff then extended a Bible before Brockman and asked him to place his left hand on it and raise his right hand. "In the testimony you are about to give before this court, do you promise to tell the truth, the whole truth, and nothing but the truth, so help you God?"

"I do."

After the judge instructed Brockman to be seated, the federal prosecuting attorney, Darrold Knight, approached Brockman and said, "Chief Brockman, will you please tell the court what you saw on the night of Monday, August 6?"

The chief U.S. marshal told his story. Brockman was in Limon, Colorado, visiting the town marshal on official business. While he was there, a stagecoach from Goodland, Kansas, rolled into town about noon, carrying a dead man. Brockman and the town marshal heard testimony from the driver, shot-gunner, and three female passengers that Armand Watts had stopped the stage to rob it but was resisted by the only male passenger. Watts shot him dead and galloped away.

Watts, who was already wanted by the law for killing two people during bank robberies, had not worn a mask. Since his photograph was on wanted posters all over the territory, the stage crew and passengers had no doubt he was the one.

Brockman had jumped on his horse and gone after the killer. It took him until that evening to track Watts to a small ranch near the Kansas border. Brockman dismounted, drew his gun, and approached the house from the side. Just as he stepped up on the porch, he heard Watts's voice demanding money from the elderly man who lived alone in the house. Watts threatened to kill the man unless he produced it. The old man insisted he had no money and pleaded for his life.

Just as Brockman burst through the door, Watts's gun fired at the old man. Brockman lined his gun on Watts, who stood with the smoking revolver in his hand, and told him to drop it. Watts did as he was told. Brockman handcuffed him to a post on the front porch and hurried to the victim. The old man was dead.

Judge James Egan set his eyes on Watts's attorney. "Mr. Dulotte, you may cross-examine the witness."

Dulotte stood and said, "There is no need, your honor."

Watts looked up at him, eyes wide. "What? How you gonna get me off unless you try to trip this guy up?"

Dulotte sat down and whispered in Watts's ear, "After what I heard, I don't want you loose on society. You lied to me. You said Brockman didn't catch you in the act."

"He's the one who's lyin'!" hissed Watts.

Dulotte sat back in his chair and said, "We'll let the jury decide that."

Judge Egan offered Darrold Knight the opportunity to ask questions of Chief Brockman. Knight declined, saying the jury had heard Brockman's testimony. Nothing else could be added.

When Brockman stepped down from the witness stand, his steel gray eyes locked with the hate-filled gaze of the defendant. Brockman looked beyond him and smiled at Sheriff Curt Langan and then took his seat in the first row.

The judge sent the jury out, and they returned in less than ten minutes. The verdict, announced by the jury foreman: "Guilty of murder in the first degree."

Judge Egan told the defendant to rise. Dulotte rose with him. The judge sentenced Watts to die on the gallows at sunrise on Friday morning, September 6. He banged the gavel on his desk and adjourned the court.

Armand Watts got up from his chair, seething, as Sheriff Langan took hold of his arm and said, "All right, Watts. Let's go."

Watts gave his attorney an ugly sidelong glance, then moved toward the aisle with Langan. When they came close to John Brockman, Watts snarled the words, "I'd like to brace you in a quick draw. I'd love to put you down and walk all over your dead carcass!"

Langan tightened his grip on the killer's arm and chuckled. "You're a fool, Watts. If you faced this man in a quick draw, you'd end up just as dead as you're going to be when you hit the end of that rope Friday morning. Now move!"

When Langan and Watts had passed through the doorway, Judge Egan stepped up to Brockman and said, "John, I want to congratulate you on tracking Watts down so quickly."

Brockman sighed. "I just wish I'd gotten there a few seconds earlier, Judge. If I had, I could've saved that old man's life."

"You're only human, John. I wish the old man hadn't been

killed too, but at least you fixed it so Watts will never kill again."

As they walked toward the door Egan said, "I haven't seen Breanna for a while. She doing all right?"

"She's fine, Judge, thank you."

"Is she still traveling and doing her visiting nurse's work since you got married?"

"Not as much. She's only taken three traveling assignments from Dr. Goodwin since we got married. Two in July, and one the first week of August. Of late, she's been dividing her time between the hospital and Dr. Goodwin's office. I like having her home...especially when *I'm* home. Today, however, she stayed home to catch up on her sewing."

"Probably has to squeeze in some washing and ironing and that kind of thing once in a while too, eh?"

"Yes, sir. And she gets it all done. She's quite something, Judge."

"Let's see, how long have you two been married now?"

John thought for a moment. "Why, three months exactly! We were married on June 4."

"Well, happy anniversary!"

"Thank you."

The office of the United States marshal was inside the Federal Building, and John spent the rest of the day behind his desk. At quitting time he went to the barn behind the Federal Building. As he approached the small corral, his big black gelding bobbed his head and nickered.

"Hello, Ebony. I'm sure you'd rather I'd been riding you today than that desk chair. And believe me, boy, so would I. Paperwork is part of my job, but it gets rather boring at times."

John placed the saddle blanket on Ebony's broad back, then took the saddle from the top rung of the pole fence. He slung it in place, cinched it down, and led the horse out of the corral.

John trotted Ebony through the streets of Denver, waving to people along the way, and soon was galloping westward. The sun was just touching the jagged mountain peaks as he neared his country home at the eastern edge of the foothills. He rode alongside a creek lined with cottonwood trees still full of green leaves. Within six weeks, the tree limbs would be just about bare.

John's heart quickened pace when the white two-story house came into view. It sat on six acres of ground in a grove of cottonwoods and weeping willows. A white picket fence ran across the front of the property and down the sides, all the way to the rear property line and across the back.

The house had large windows upstairs and down, adorned with black shutters. There was a wide wraparound front porch with attractive outdoor furniture and a large porch swing. Breanna had planted flowers all around the house, and he caught a whiff of their sweet scent as he drew nearer. The cottonwoods and willows swayed in the breeze.

Two buggies were parked out front; he recognized both of them. One belonged to Breanna's sister, Dottie Carroll, who was married to Dr. Matthew Carroll, chief administrator of Mile High Hospital. The other belonged to Stefanie Langan, wife of Denver County Sheriff Curt Langan.

When John trotted Ebony into the yard, the front door flew open, and Dottie's two children, James and Molly Kate, bounded across the porch, shouting, "Hi, Uncle John!" On their heels, calling happy greetings, were the Langans' adopted children, Jared, Susan, and Nathan.

Drawing rein, John smiled at the children and said, "To what do we owe the privilege of having all of you at our house?"

Molly Kate giggled and said, "We have to go back to school tomorrow, and Aunt Breanna gave us a back-to-school party this afternoon."

"Well, good!" he said. "Any food left for me?"

Susan Langan grinned. "Nope! We ate all the cookies Miss Breanna baked. Sorry!"

John chuckled, nodding. "Mm-hmm. You *look* sorry! You youngun's wait on the back porch for me, okay? I'll be with you as soon as I put Ebony in the corral and unsaddle him."

John trotted his horse toward the barn and corral. Ebony whinnied, and from behind the barn came the whinnying reply of Breanna's black stallion, Chance. John never laid eyes on Chance without thinking back to the day the big black had saved his life by carrying him out of a deadly forest fire in Montana.

Moments later, John entered the house by the back door, with the children close around him, and was greeted in the kitchen by Dottie and Stefanie, who were preparing to leave.

Breanna was nowhere in sight.

"Howdy, ladies. I'm told by these kids that all the cookies are gone."

"That's right," said Dottie, smiling. "Not even a crumb left."

"That's too bad. I'm in the mood for something sweet."

"How about me?" came Breanna's voice, just before she rounded the door from the hall and entered the kitchen.

John smiled and said, "All *right!*"

The children and their mothers looked on as Breanna took her husband by the hand and led him behind the pantry door.

Molly Kate giggled. "We know what you're doing back there, Uncle John and Aunt Breanna! You're kissing!"

10

BOTH HORSES PRICKED UP THEIR EARS and snorted when they saw the tall man come out the back door of the house and head toward them. The taste of his wife's sweet kisses was still fresh on John's lips as he glanced westward and took in the glory of the sunset over the majestic Rocky Mountains.

A pair of broad-winged eagles sailed the unbroken silence of the wild heights above the jagged peaks. Shadows stretched from the rugged crags, and between the peaks streamed a red-gold light. The sunshine was slowly losing its fire, and already planet Venus twinkled high in the western sky. A soft wind came off the foothills, laden with incense of pine.

The horses nickered as John opened the corral gate. "I figured I'd feed you boys your supper while Breanna's cooking mine," he said, patting their necks.

Chance and Ebony followed John inside the barn and waited patiently while he opened the grain bin and used a small bucket to dip the mixture of oats and barley. He spread generous portions of grain in the manger, and while the horses went to work on that, he climbed up in the loft and forked hay into the manger, saying, "Here, boys. This is your dessert."

John left the barn and pumped water into the stock tank. As he headed back toward the house, he glanced westward again. Venus was now twinkling like a brilliant diamond against a darkening sky, and a few stars had put in an appearance. There was still a faint golden glow above the shadowed peaks.

The sight of it stole the man's breath. Pausing to take it all in, he said, "Lord, You outdid Yourself on this one. What a gorgeous sunset! Just like You outdid Yourself when You made my beautiful Breanna."

Breanna was standing at the stove when she heard the back door open and close. "The boys all right?" she asked.

"Filling their bellies right now, but one of them is having a hard time. He's jealous of me."

"Oh, really?"

John moved up and enfolded her in his arms. "Yep. Chance thinks it ought to be me in the barn and him in here with you."

Breanna's giggle was cut short as John pressed his lips to hers in a long, lingering kiss. When their lips parted, he looked toward the back door and said, "Eat your heart out, Chance. You never got kisses like these!"

This time Breanna laughed outright. "Get washed up, sweetheart. Supper's almost ready."

"I will," he said stubbornly, "after I get a celebration kiss."

"Celebration kiss?"

"Mm-hmm. This is our three-month anniversary."

"Oh, John! It is!"

After they kissed again, John said, "Judge Egan asked me today after the trial how long we'd been married. That's when it struck me. By the way, he said to tell you happy anniversary."

"Thank you, darling," said Breanna, raising up on her tiptoes and kissing him again. "Now, get washed up."

Later, as they were eating, Breanna asked how the trial had gone.

"It went fast. It took the jury all of seven or eight minutes to come to their verdict. Watts will hang at sunrise on Friday."

"I figured your testimony wouldn't leave much room for doubt."

After a few minutes, John said, "It was nice of you to give those kids a back-to-school party."

"I love them, John. All five are special kids."

He looked into her eyes and said, "You're a special lady."

She smiled at him and lifted her coffee cup to take a sip.

It was quiet again for a moment, then John said, "You should've seen Curt in the courtroom today. He hovered over Watts like a hound dog that had cornered a coon."

"I can believe that."

There was silence again.

John mopped the last bit of gravy from his plate with a piece of bread, then set his gray gaze on her and said, "Sweetheart, why do I get the distinct feeling that you're holding something back?"

Breanna gave him an impish grin. "Who? Me?"

John stuck the gravy-laden piece of bread in his mouth and chewed and swallowed it before saying, "There's nobody else in this room that I know of. Come on, out with it."

"You're almost as good at reading me as I am at reading you."

"I'll get better as time goes by."

Breanna's eyes sparkled as she said, "So will I."

"That's what I'm afraid of."

"Well, my dear husband, what I've been holding back is telling you that I'm leaving in the morning on an assignment."

"Oh?"

"Dr. Goodwin sent me a message by Dottie this afternoon. He needs me to take a nursing assignment in Kimball, Nebraska, for about a week."

John gave her a mock scowl. "But who's going to cook my meals?"

"The same person who cooked them the other times I was gone—the chef at the hotel restaurant."

"Well, I guess since we agreed before the wedding that you'd still take travel assignments now and then, I'll have to let you go, and pine away with loneliness."

"Oh, you poor dear," Breanna said, patting his hand. "And what about my loneliness when *you* travel?"

"That's different."

"Oh? Seems to me that what's good for the goose is good for the gander."

"Okay, okay," he said, squeezing her hand. "So what's the assignment?"

"Kimball's only just opened up a new clinic, and the main nurse there has a relative back East who is seriously ill. She needs to go there for a few days."

"Sounds like a real need, honey. What about your train ticket?"

"I told Dottie to tell Dr. Goodwin I would go. He'll get me a ticket on the Cheyenne City train that leaves at nine o'clock in the morning."

The next morning as the train pulled out of Denver's Union Station, Breanna waved through the window at John and threw him a kiss.

Three hours later she boarded an eastbound train out of

Cheyenne City whose ultimate destination was Omaha. Breanna would get off at Kimball. She took a seat next to a window and presently was joined by an elderly woman named Maisie Hull, who was from Philadelphia. Mrs. Hull had been visiting her son, daughter-in-law, and grandchildren in Rawlins, Wyoming, and was on her way home.

Before the train had been out of the depot fifteen minutes, Breanna had learned that Maisie was a Christian. Based on their kinship in the family of God, Maisie and Breanna had much to talk about. They had talked for about an hour about the joy of knowing Jesus and the peace and contentment that only He could give, when suddenly a dozen or more young Indians pulled alongside the train on their ponies, laughing, whooping, and waving to the passengers.

"Oh!" said Maisie with a gasp. "They're going to attack us!"

Breanna smiled at the Indians and waved to them, then said, "No, no. They're not hostile, Maisie. Take a good look. Those are just teenage boys. They like to race white man's Iron Horse."

"Iron horse?"

"The train."

"Oh. Can you tell what tribe they are?"

"They're Cheyenne."

"My son told me the tribes can be identified by something they wear."

"Mm-hmm. It's their headbands and their feathers. Each tribe has its own style. You get to know them when you're around them a lot like I am."

Maisie's hands were still trembling. "Don't they frighten you, Breanna? I mean...after all, they *are* savages."

"They're human beings who know only the traditions and superstitions they've been taught by their ancestors."

"But they scalp white people!"

"It may surprise you, Maisie, but the North American Indians learned to scalp their enemies *from* white people—the Frenchmen who came to this land in the seventeenth century."

"No!" Maisie said, with dropped jaw.

"Yes."

"Well, I didn't know that."

"Anyway, we do have hostile tribes all over the West. But many of the Indians want to dwell in peace with the white invaders. Some of the Cheyenne are like that."

"Like those boys out there?"

"Yes," said Breanna, running her gaze northward. "If I remember correctly, there's a Cheyenne village just over those hills to the north. That's probably where those boys are from. The chief's name is War Bonnet, but he's very friendly toward whites."

Maisie's eyes bulged. *"War Bonnet!* That's a fierce-sounding name. I'm glad I'm going back to Pennsylvania, where I'll be safe from wild Indians."

The young Cheyenne boys were still keeping pace with the train, and other people in the coach were showing fear as the conductor came in. Hearing their comments, he lifted his voice and said, "Relax, folks! Nothing to fear. Those are just boys. They often race the train."

Breanna lifted a hand to get the conductor's attention. "Sir?"

"Yes, young lady."

"Haven't you been on this run for quite a while?"

"Yes'm. 'Bout six years."

"Then you might know. Isn't there a Cheyenne village north of those hills back there? Chief War Bonnet's village?"

"That's right, ma'am. And I'm glad I can say that War

Bonnet and his people are quite friendly toward whites."

Breanna indicated the woman sitting next to her and said, "That's what I was just telling Mrs. Hull. She's from Pennsylvania."

The conductor smiled at Maisie, then said to Breanna, "Are you from these parts?"

"Yes. My home is near Denver."

"Then you're probably familiar with the Sand Creek Massacre that took place a ways south of here eight years ago."

"I am," Breanna said.

"I recall reading about it in the Philadelphia newspapers," Maisie said. "Don't remember much about it, though."

"I remember it distinctly," said Breanna. "I was actually in eastern Kansas at the time, training for my certified medical nurse certificate."

"Oh, you're a nurse!" said the conductor.

"Yes, sir."

Maisie looked at Breanna with admiration as she said, "You hadn't told me that."

"We were too busy talking about the Lord...then the Indians," said Breanna. She looked back at the conductor. "I remember that the village on Sand Creek was led by a chief named Black Kettle and that he was killed in Oklahoma four years later."

The conductor's attention was drawn to the young Cheyenne riders as they veered away from the train and galloped toward the hills to the north. "Looks like the boys are heading home," he said.

Breanna and Maisie watched the Indians for a moment, then Breanna said, "I know there was quite an investigation after the Sand Creek incident. Congress declared it a massacre, publicly denouncing Colonel Chivington, who led the attack.

Chivington and Colorado's Governor Evans conspired against the Indians, in direct opposition to the treaty they had signed with Black Kettle and many other peaceable chiefs."

The conductor grinned. "I'm impressed with your knowledge of the subject, ma'am."

"Well, it isn't that I've done a lot of reading about it, sir," said Breanna. "It's just that in Denver, the people still talk about it. I've learned by simply listening."

"Are you aware that Chief War Bonnet was one of those chiefs who signed the treaty, along with Black Kettle?"

"No, I wasn't. But I've been told by several people that War Bonnet is friendly toward whites."

"It's a wonder," said the conductor, "after the way Chivington and Evans treated him. It might interest you to know that some of the survivors of Sand Creek *and* from the attack in Oklahoma now live in War Bonnet's village."

Breanna glanced to the north. "Poor people. It's a wonder they'll trust *any* white person, the way they've been treated."

The Cheyenne boys topped the first rise after pulling away from the Iron Horse and slowed their horses to a walk as they angled northwest toward their village.

Hungry Dog, their unofficial leader, bragged, "We did well today. Our ponies can run as fast as white man's Iron Horse."

"They just cannot run for as long!" said Spotted Bull with a laugh.

"That is because it is made of iron!" said Owl Feather, who was wiping perspiration from his face.

Little Big Man rode beside Owl Feather. Frowning, he said, "Is Owl Feather sick like Tissewoonatis, Mantoona, and Brown Weasel Woman?"

Owl Feather shook his head. "No. I am fine. Just warm." The boy would not admit it to his friends, but he was afraid that he was coming down with the same sickness that had stricken the elderly Brown Weasel Woman and two younger women in the village. They were running high fevers and had eruptions on their skin. He-Who-Walks-in-Rain, the village's oldest medicine man, told the people he had seen the disease before. It was a white man's disease known as "the small bumps of skin."

In the village of some seven hundred people were ten medicine men and four medicine women. Two of the medicine men also knew about the "small bumps of skin" disease, and like He-Who-Walks-in-Rain, they knew it was often fatal. When the boys had ridden out of the village to rendezvous with the Iron Horse, the medicine men and medicine women were chanting prayers to the healing spirits. Along with the prayers, they were bathing their patients in cool water in an attempt to bring down the fever. They were also using "smudging," a process where stalks of dried sagebrush were tied together and set on fire. The sick ones were laid next to the fire, and the smoke—which was considered a purifier—was steadily fanned on them.

The boys continued walking the pintos, allowing them to recover after the run alongside the train. After some ten minutes of the slow walk, Hungry Dog said, "The ponies are ready to run again."

The pintos kicked up dust as they raced up the side of a hill, topped the rise, and started down the other side. They were about halfway toward the bottom of the slope, where they would begin to climb the next hill, when Owl Feather let the reins slip through his fingers and peeled off the pinto's back, hitting the ground hard.

Little Big Man pulled rein, shouting for the others to stop. He wheeled, trotted his horse back to where Owl Feather had fallen, and slipped from his horse's back.

Quickly, Hungry Dog was beside Little Big Man, saying, "What is wrong?"

Little Big Man had both hands on Owl Feather's sweat-soaked face. "He has the bumps on his face, and his skin is very hot. He bruised his cheekbone in the fall, but otherwise he seems unhurt."

"We must hurry and get him to He-Who-Walks-in-Rain," Hungry Dog said.

Little Big Man nodded. "Let us put him on my horse. I will hold on to him."

In the Cheyenne village there was great concern over the three fevered women, and it became worse when two of War Bonnet's young warriors approached the chief and told him they too were sick.

Next to the smudging fire being used for the young warrior Lone Wolf, gray-haired shaman Essie Bird Woman was giving instructions to two young women who were training as shamans. One was fanning smoke on Lone Wolf while the other bathed him in cool water. Essie Bird Woman was older yet than He-Who-Walks-in-Rain and had been appointed by Chief War Bonnet as the main trainer of female shamans.

Silver Moon, daughter of the late Chief Black Kettle, stood beside Essie Bird Woman, listening and observing. Now twenty-three years of age—and yet unmarried—Silver Moon was training under the shaman. Her great desire was to be a medicine woman that she might help care for her people.

Silver Moon's head whipped around when the rumble of

pounding hooves filled the village, punctuated by shouts from the young riders that Owl Feather was sick.

He-Who-Walks-in-Rain helped lower the feverish boy from Little Big Man's horse and called for Essie Bird Woman to care for him.

While Silver Moon began bathing Owl Feather's body with cool water, Essie Bird Woman bound stalks of dried sagebrush in bunches, placed them next to the boy within a circle of fist-sized rocks, and set them on fire.

Owl Feather's parents and siblings stood close by, joined by many others, including the boys he had been riding with.

Essie Bird Woman used a buffalo hide fan to blow the smoke on the boy and began a prayerful chant. As she had been trained to do, Silver Moon joined in, blending her voice with the shaman's, pleading for the boy's healing. They were offering their prayers to Aktunowihio, the earth god, whom they believed served below as agent of Heammawihio, the Wise One Above.

War Bonnet, his subchiefs, and the medicine men who were not working on patients stood near where all six of the ailing ones were being treated.

War Bonnet's features looked drawn as he said to He-Who-Walks-in-Rain, "How did this white man's disease you call 'small bumps of skin' come to us?"

The leading shaman rubbed his wrinkled brow. "I remind War Bonnet of the white traders who came here ten or eleven moons ago. One of them was fevered while he was here."

"Mmm," said the chief. "This had not come to my thoughts."

"White trader left his sickness behind."

"Mmm. White man has brought us many diseases."

The medicine man nodded as he said, "Killing diseases."

War Bonnet turned his eyes on the patients and let the chants of the shamans fill his ears. He hoped that Aktunowihio would hear their prayers and grant healing to each one.

By the time night fell, seven more Cheyenne had come down with the fever, bearing the skin eruptions on their bodies. All night long Silver Moon worked on Owl Feather alongside her mentor. About an hour before dawn, two medicine men came to them, telling them to go to their tepees and get some rest.

As Essie Bird Woman and Silver Moon walked toward their tepees, a cool wind moaned across the prairie. The wild yelps of coyotes were fading in the distance, and the sky was a wonderful black velvet dome, spangled with dazzling white stars.

The older woman patted Silver Moon's shoulder and said, "You are learning fast, my young friend. I love listening to you pray. You have a very special connection to the spirits. You will be a good shaman."

They drew up in front of Essie Bird Woman's tepee. "Thank you for the kind and encouraging words," Silver Moon said in a soft tone.

"They are *true* words. Now you get some rest." She disappeared into her tepee.

Silver Moon moved on toward her own tepee, thinking that maybe one day the spirits she faithfully served would help her find John Chivington.

Suddenly she saw a dark form in the shadows along the path. The sight of it quickened her pulse and slowed her pace. The form moved into the flickering light of the smudge fires nearby, and she recognized Iron Hawk. He stood in front of her tepee, smiling at her.

Iron Hawk was nearly two years older than Silver Moon.

He wore the headband and single eagle feather, which marked him as a full-fledged warrior. He was quite muscular and ruggedly handsome.

He had been in love with Silver Moon since shortly after she arrived at the village from her Ohio journey four years ago. She was very fond of him, but she had not been willing to let go of the memory of Bear Paw. This, combined with the bitter hatred she held toward John Chivington, had kept her from letting herself fall in love with Iron Hawk.

As Silver Moon drew up to him, Iron Hawk said, "You have been at Owl Feather's side for many hours. I am glad to see you are finally going to get some rest."

"Iron Hawk, it is not yet dawn. What are you doing up at this hour?"

"I have observed you through the night, and I have been asking Heammawihio to give you strength for your task. I waited here so I could see you for a moment before you go inside. It is strong in my heart for me to tell you once again that Iron Hawk's love for you is forever."

Silver Moon afforded him a sweet smile. "Iron Hawk knows I am very fond of him."

"He waits for the day Silver Moon's heart will be more than fond of him. He yearns to hear her say that her heart reaches for him with love."

Tears filled Silver Moon's eyes. "You are such a wonderful man, Iron Hawk. But as I have told you many times before, it is best if you find another Cheyenne woman to love. You know that my heart holds some things that keep me from falling in love with you."

"But I cannot love another woman," he said flatly. "If Silver Moon never loves me, I will live my life without a woman's love."

His words touched her deeply, and she felt a tear slide down her cheek.

"I know Silver Moon carries a pleasant memory of Bear Paw," said Iron Hawk, "and you have told me of the horrible white man who killed him, your mother, and your brother. I understand your hatred toward the man, but you must let him go from your mind. He must not reach out to you from the past and destroy your chance for happiness."

Silver Moon brushed away the tear. "I cannot let him go from my mind, Iron Hawk. Nor do I want to. I have felt of late that if Bear Paw could speak to me, he would say I should fall in love and have happiness with a husband who loves me, but the hatred within my heart for John Chivington can be gone only when I make him pay for what he did. The spirits of Gentle Dove, Sky Eagle, and Bear Paw are not at rest. John Chivington must die for what he did before they will have rest."

Iron Hawk set his jaw. "I only wish I knew where to find this murderer. I would kill him and deliver his lifeless body to you. Justice would be done, and your heart would be emptied of him."

Silver Moon's lips quivered as she said, "If this justice was done, I could allow my heart to reach toward Iron Hawk."

Happy to hear her say that much, Iron Hawk told her to get some sleep then moved away into the shadows.

Lying on the pallet inside her tepee, Silver Moon wept, praying, "O great Heammawihio, please deliver the wicked John Chivington into my hand. Let me make him pay for his crimes, so my heart will be free to love Iron Hawk. You have helped me to know these past few days that Bear Paw would have me to find happiness with Iron Hawk, but I must know Bear Paw is at rest because his murderer has paid for his crimes."

✦

The next day, many more people in the village came down with the fever. All the shamans and their apprentices labored and prayed over the sick ones. Essie Bird Woman and Silver Moon worked on several patients, returning periodically to check on Owl Feather. His condition was not improving.

The next day, Brown Weasel Woman died, and the day after that, both Tissewoonatis and Mantoona died. Two days later, Owl Feather died. Lone Wolf and the other warrior who took sick at the same time were still hanging on to life by a thread.

There was weeping and wailing as the bodies were wrapped in death garments and placed on scaffolds at the edge of the village near the burial ground. High-pitched chanted prayers were offered to Aktunowihio, asking him to release the spirits of the dead very soon that they might rise into the sky and walk the Hanging Road to the land of Heammawihio.

The tepees of the families who had a loved one die of the disease were burned to ensure them a safe journey to the land in the sky. After sufficient time for the souls to begin their journey—five to seven days—the bodies were taken down and placed in graves at the burial ground.

11

↑

DAY AFTER DAY, bodies were raised toward the sky on somber scaffolds as more of War Bonnet's people died. The wailing sounds of the mourners rode the unfeeling wind. Every day more graves were dug while the gravediggers wept over the loss of family members and friends.

The shamans could be heard above the wails and cries of the mourners as they chanted in high-pitched voices, imploring the spirits to give them power to stop the disease before it wiped out the entire village.

As the sun went down on the ninth day since the dread disease had struck, Essie Bird Woman and Silver Moon chanted over White Cloud, an old warrior who had been sick for three days. They fanned smoke on him and bathed him with cool water. His breathing was weak and raspy at best, and since midafternoon he had been unconscious.

The fire cast orange light on the women's faces; all else was in deep shadow. Silver Moon was pressing wet cloths to the sides of White Cloud's neck when she noticed the buffalo hide fan slip from Essie Bird Woman's hand.

The shaman tried to pick it up again but couldn't make her

fingers grasp it. She batted her eyelids and raised a hand to her brow, letting out a moan.

"Essie Bird Woman!" Silver Moon dropped the cloths into the water pail and felt the older woman's moist forehead. "You have the fever!"

She helped her mentor lie down, then called for He-Who-Walks-in-Rain. The old shaman came, with War Bonnet and his subchiefs on his heels.

Silver Moon held Essie Bird Woman's hands in her own as He-Who-Walks-in-Rain knelt beside them. "She has the fever," said Silver Moon, her heart heavy in her breast.

Word spread quickly through the village that even one of their spiritual leaders was down with the disease. Silver Moon and He-Who-Walks-in-Rain teamed up to pray over Essie Bird Woman, fanning smoke on her and bathing her with cool water.

A crowd gathered to look upon Essie Bird Woman. Sitting close by were Spotted Bull and Little Big Man. Both were not feeling well and had shared that fact with each other.

Spotted Bull wiped sweat from his face and said, "I do not understand how the sickness can come to a shaman. They are the messengers of Aktunowihio and Heammawihio. They have special powers with the spirits, yet Essie Bird Woman has the sickness."

"I do not understand it either," said Little Big Man, feeling a strange light-headedness. "I would think the gods would protect their messengers."

"We need to go to white men for help," said Spotted Bull. "They have medicine. If we do not get help very soon, you and I will be lying beside those smudging fires."

"And our bodies will be on scaffolds."

Spotted Bull's gaze fell on Hungry Dog, who was standing

aloof from the group gathered around Essie Bird Woman. His eyes looked dull, and he was wiping moisture from his brow.

"Little Big Man, look." Spotted Bull pointed at their friend and unofficial leader. "Hungry Dog is getting the sickness too!"

Little Big Man looked at Hungry Dog and nodded. "Yes. We must get help before it is too late. Let us go talk to Hungry Dog. He will know what to do."

The boys approached Hungry Dog, who was about to find a place to sit down. Little Big Man kept his voice low and said, "Are you feeling the fever too?"

Hungry Dog nodded.

"We must go to the whites for help, Hungry Dog," said Spotted Bull. "The Cheyenne gods are not answering the prayers of the shamans."

"You are right. Let us talk to our fathers."

The boys found all three of their fathers discussing the situation with a group of men, including He-Who-Walks-in-Rain. They had agreed not to tell their fathers about their own symptoms.

As the boys stood quietly, waiting to be recognized, the medicine man paused and turned toward the trio. "What do you boys want?"

"We want to talk to our fathers," said Hungry Dog.

"What is it, my son?" asked Black Wind.

"We have been discussing the sickness and how it is taking the lives of our people, Father. Someone should ride to the nearest white men's town and ask for help. They have medicine. Since the 'small bumps of skin' sickness is white man's disease, we believe they may have medicine that will stop the disease from spreading and make our sick ones well."

Black Wind and the others looked to He-Who-Walks-in-Rain. The shaman pulled his mouth into a thin line and said,

"This would be unwise, Hungry Dog. By going to white men for help we would offend Heammawihio and Aktunowihio. If we offend our gods, we will suffer their wrath."

"But they have not answered the shamans' prayers," argued Little Big Man. "Must our people die because the gods pay no attention?"

He-Who-Walks-in-Rain blinked at the boy's words.

Little Big Man's father, Falling Stone, spoke up. "Son, you are not to speak to a shaman in this manner! Especially to pass judgment on our gods!"

"I am sorry, Father, but as I see more graves being dug every day, I must be honest. I have lost faith in Heammawihio and Aktunowihio. They have the power to stop the disease, but they do not stop it."

Falling Stone's eyes flashed anger and he started to reprove his son, but He-Who-Walks-in-Rain raised a hand to silence him. "Do not be alarmed at the boy's words. Sometimes you and I feel the same way but are fearful to say it."

The men in the group exchanged guilty looks.

He-Who-Walks-in-Rain said to the three boys, "We are earthly, and at times our faith grows weak, but we must trust our gods to do what is best for us. We must not go to white men for their medicine. This would offend our gods."

Suddenly a middle-aged woman rushed up. "He-Who-Walks-in-Rain! Broken Hand has collapsed! He is very sick with the fever. Chief War Bonnet is with him. He told me to come for you."

As the men rushed away to see about Broken Hand, Little Big Man said to his two friends, "Another of our spiritual leaders has been struck down with the fever. Our gods have forsaken us."

"It seems they have," said Spotted Bull.

"Yes," agreed Hungry Dog. "We must go for help before we are too sick to ride."

"To Kimball?" asked Little Big Man.

"Yes. There is a doctor in Kimball."

"But will a white doctor help three Indian boys?" asked Spotted Bull.

"We can only try. But if the doctor *will* help us, possibly he will also come and help our people."

"We must ride when no one sees us," said Little Big Man. "Our fathers will not let us go if we ask for permission."

"Yes," said Hungry Dog. "We will slip away in the darkness tonight while most of the village sleeps."

A bright morning sun shone in the Nebraska sky as Breanna Baylor Brockman left the Western Union office in Kimball, and Dr. Boyd Castleton helped her into the buggy. "All set," she said, settling on the seat beside Nurse Delia Fields. "Now John will know when to pick me up at Union Station in Denver."

Castleton climbed aboard, took the reins, and put the horse to a trot. Looking past Delia, he said, "Breanna, I can never thank you enough for coming to my aid when I so desperately needed someone to fill in for Delia."

"It was my pleasure, Doctor. And you certainly paid me generously."

"You did a great job. You deserve to be paid generously."

"I'm so sorry I was gone longer than anticipated," said Delia. "I hope your husband isn't upset because you've been away ten days."

"Not at all," said Breanna. "John knows these things happen. I'm just glad your sister is going to be all right."

"Thank you. So am I."

The buggy swung into the parking lot of the depot.

"Your train's already here," said Castleton. "You'll be home this evening, won't you?"

"Yes. I have an hour-and-a-half layover in Cheyenne City between trains. I'll arrive in Denver in time for John to take me out to dinner!"

It was nearly midmorning when Hungry Dog, Spotted Bull, and Little Big Man lay in the grass beside the road that ran between Kimball and Cheyenne City. The pintos grazed nearby, swishing their tails and paying no attention to the band of crows that flitted about them, cawing and flapping their wings.

Perspiration shone on the boys' faces. They had arrived at the road shortly after slipping out of the village in the middle of the night, but were feeling so ill they could go no farther. They had decided to wait for someone to come along the road, hoping they would take pity and get them to a doctor. Or if a train came along first, they hoped the white men who engineered it would stop and carry them to a doctor. The railroad tracks were just across the road.

Little Big Man worked his tongue loose in his dry mouth and said, "I am getting the bumps on my face."

"Me too," said Spotted Bull, lying flat on his back, eyes closed.

"We should have brought water along," said Little Big Man.

Hungry Dog nodded. "Yes, but we didn't know how sick we would be by the time we got to the road. We—"

Hungry Dog's words were cut off by the sound of a train whistle. He raised up on an elbow and looked to the east. On the horizon, black smoke was lifting toward the sky. He swallowed with difficulty and said, "We...we must go over to the tracks so they will see us."

The boys struggled to their feet, their heads spinning.

"We must take the horses with us," said Spotted Bull. "The men who engineer the train will see them a long way off and begin slowing down."

The boys stumbled toward their pintos, picked up the reins, and slowly led the ponies across the road. As Little Big Man began leading his pinto onto the elevated track bed, he suddenly fell to his knees. Spotted Bull, who was in the lead, collapsed right on the tracks. Hungry Dog stumbled toward his friends, his head spinning as he placed his horse on the track bed and ground reined him Indian style.

The train's whistle sounded again, this time much louder.

Little Big Man had managed to get to his feet and had just wrapped a single rein around his pinto's cannon bone below the knee when he lost his balance and fell onto the tracks, passing out. Hungry Dog finished ground reining his friend's horse, then sat down and fought to stay conscious.

Back at the Cheyenne village, two young warriors—Iron Hawk and his cousin, Running Fox—stood before War Bonnet, He-Who-Walks-in-Rain, and the parents of the missing boys.

He-Who-Walks-in-Rain said, "Because of their words last night I feel certain the boys have ridden to Kimball or to Cheyenne City to bring a white doctor and his medicine. Their concern for our people is commendable, but I fear offending Heammawihio and Aktunowihio."

Chief War Bonnet looked at Iron Hawk and Running Fox and said, "You must bring them back before they bring white men here."

Iron Hawk nodded. "We will find them, Chief."

Suddenly a heartrending wail came from the area where the patients were being treated. As the chief and the others looked toward the sound of wailing, Bull Elk, one of the medicine men, came toward War Bonnet.

"Broken Hand has just died," he said. "It is the voice of his squaw that you hear."

This news hit everyone with a jolt. When would Heammawihio and Aktunowihio answer their prayers and stop this horrid disease?

Breanna was reading her Bible when she noticed a change in the rhythmic clicking of the train's wheels. She glanced out the window and recognized the area where the Cheyenne boys had raced the train the day she traveled to Kimball. There was no stopping place between Kimball and Cheyenne City. Why was the train slowing down?

When they chugged to a halt, there was a hubbub of voices in the coach as everyone peered from the windows, trying to see what was going on.

Suddenly the conductor passed by outside Breanna's side of the train, hurrying toward the engine. The man sitting in front of Breanna opened a window and stuck his head out, calling, "Hey, conductor! What're we stopped for?"

The conductor paused, looked over his shoulder, and said, "There're some Indians lying on the tracks! Looks like they're either sick or dead!"

Breanna stepped into the aisle and reached for her overnight bag, setting it on the seat, then removed her black medical bag.

The man who had stuck his head out the window said, "Where are you going, lady?"

"I'm a nurse. If they're sick, I want to help."

"You'd help *Indians?* Savages?"

"Indians are human beings, mister," Breanna said as she brushed past him. "And I've seen my share of white savages too."

She left the man gawking after her as she moved out the door and quickly bounded down the metal steps of the car's platform. She could see the engineer and the fireman lifting two bodies and placing them beside the coal car. The conductor picked up a third Cheyenne boy from off the elevated track.

A few male passengers had arrived on the scene, and three of them led the pintos from the tracks.

Breanna hurried toward the crew. "Gentlemen, I'm a nurse. May I be of help?"

The engineer looked relieved as he said, "Come right ahead, ma'am. These two are out, but this boy here is conscious."

Breanna knelt down and looked into the boy's dull eyes and felt his feverish brow. "Do you speak English, son?" she asked.

"Yes...ma'am," he answered weakly.

"Are you Cheyenne?"

He nodded, licking his dry lips.

Breanna looked up at the crew. "These boys have smallpox."

The engineer took a step back. "Smallpox! And we touched 'em!"

The faces of the fireman and the conductor and the man standing beside the pintos went pale.

"Could one of you gentlemen bring water, please?" asked Breanna.

"I'll get you some, ma'am," said the conductor, "but you shouldn't be touching them, either." He hurried away.

The fireman and the engineer wiped their hands on their pants.

Breanna stroked the boy's hair tenderly. "What is your name?" she asked.

"Hungry Dog."

"Are you from Chief War Bonnet's village?"

"Yes. You...know...of our village?"

"Yes. Why are you boys here?"

Hungry Dog licked his lips. His eyelids drooped and he spoke with effort. "Many...people in village...sick. Some have died. We...were on our way...to Kimb— Kimball...to ask for help...from doctor."

"There is help now, Hungry Dog. I—"

The conductor held a canteen in front of her face and she thanked him before putting it to Hungry Dog's lips. "Here is water," she said. "Take it slowly."

As the boy took small sips of water, Breanna said, "Hungry Dog, I am a nurse. Do you know what a nurse is?"

"You...are like a doctor."

"Yes. I am trained to work with doctors. I've dealt with smallpox before. I'm going to take you and these other boys back to the village and help you and your people."

"Ma'am," said the engineer, "you'll be putting yourself in grave danger if you go to that village. The Cheyenne are hostile toward whites."

"They're not *all* hostile, sir," said Breanna. She elevated Hungry Dog's head to make it easier for him to swallow. "War Bonnet has declared himself and his people to be at peace with us. That's why these boys tried to ride to Kimball and seek help from Dr. Castleton."

"All right, let's say they won't harm you. There's still a problem. How are you going to get the boys to the village? Two of these young bucks are unconscious, and even Hungry Dog here won't be able to sit up on his horse and ride. How are you going to keep them on their horses? And where will *you* ride?"

"I'll have to drape them belly-down on the horses," she said. "And as for me...I'll walk."

"What you want to do is admirable, ma'am," said the fireman, "but like us, you've been exposed to the smallpox. Who's going to take care of *you* if you get sick out there in the village?"

"I've had inoculation for it, sir," said Breanna, still giving Hungry Dog small sips of water. "I assume by your behavior a few moments ago that none of you have been."

They looked at the boy she supported in her arms, fear showing in their eyes, and shook their heads.

"Then you must get this done as soon as you arrive in Cheyenne City. Even if one of you has already contracted it, the inoculation will make your case much lighter."

"Pardon me, ma'am," said the engineer, "but what is your name?"

"Breanna Brockman. *Mrs.* Breanna Brockman."

"Well, Mrs. Brockman, I hate to see you try to do this by yourself. Maybe there's someone on the train who would go along with you."

"I can't ask anyone to do that," she said. "From what I've heard about the village, it's really not too far."

"It is about seven or eight of...white man's miles," said Hungry Dog.

Spotted Bull began to moan. Breanna eased Hungry Dog's head to the ground and rushed to the other boy, who was now rolling his head back and forth and fluttering his eyelids. She glanced at Hungry Dog. "What is this one's name?"

"Spotted Bull."

Breanna called the boy by name and gave him water, assuring him she was his friend.

"I think this other one is about to come around too," said

the conductor. "He's moving his head."

Moments later, Breanna went to Little Big Man. As she held the canteen to his lips, she gave instructions to the crewmen. "I'll need someone to bring my overnight bag to me. And I need a cup to mix water and the salicylic acid powders in my medical bag. After I give a good dose to all three of these boys, I'll need you gentlemen to help me get them on their horses. And I'll need something to tie them on with."

As the men eyed one another, Breanna said, "You can't get exposed any more than you already have been."

"All right," said the engineer. "We'll help you when you're ready. There's some hemp cord in the baggage car. You can use that to tie them on their horses."

"I'll get the cup and your overnight bag for you," said the conductor.

"I could use some more water too," Breanna called after him as both men hurried away.

She noticed that passengers were standing beside the coaches, looking on. The word *smallpox* was on many lips.

As Breanna continued to give Little Big Man small sips of water, she said to the fireman, "I'll need someone to go to the clinic in Cheyenne City and see Dr. James Malcolm. He knows me. I need as much salicylic acid as he can possibly let me have. Someone there will need to ride a fast horse and bring it to me at the village. I can save lives only if I have the salicylic acid. Can you help me?"

"I'll do my best, Mrs. Brockman."

"I have money," said Breanna. "I'll give you sufficient to pay for the medicine and to generously pay the man who brings it to the village."

"I'll see that it's done. I'm sure there will be someone in Cheyenne City who'd like to pick up a few extra dollars." He paused. "Of course, it'll have to be a man who knows War Bonnet's village is friendly to white folks."

"Just about everyone in Cheyenne City knows about War Bonnet's peaceful ways."

"Okay. That'll help."

"Oh. And one more favor."

"Yes, ma'am?"

"I need to send a telegram to my husband in Denver and let him know I won't be arriving this evening as scheduled, and why. I'll give you the money to pay for the telegram, and some extra for your trouble."

"No extra is necessary, Mrs. Brockman. I'm glad to help. What's your husband's name, and what's the address?"

"Just send it to Chief United States Marshal John Brockman at the Federal Building in Denver. He'll get it."

The fireman had produced a pencil stub and a slip of paper from the bib in his overalls. His eyebrows arched. "Your husband is the chief U.S. marshal?"

"Yes, sir."

The engineer appeared out of the crowd at the same time as the conductor. One had a coil of hemp cord in his hand and the other had a cup, Breanna's overnight bag, and another canteen.

As they walked together, the engineer said, "That's some little gal."

The conductor jerked his head in a nod. "I'll say. The kind that makes a perfect nurse…dedicated to helping humanity and willing to sacrifice for others."

Breanna, who was kneeling beside Little Big Man, glanced up and saw the two crewmen approaching, and then she noticed a tall man in an army uniform move out of the crowd. He arrived at her side ahead of the engineer and conductor.

He smiled at Breanna and hunkered down on the other side

of the boy. "I heard you tell them your name, Mrs. Brockman, and the conductor told us a little while ago that you're a nurse."

"Yes," she said.

"My name is Myron Donaldson. I'm the chaplain at Fort Laramie."

"I'm glad to meet you, Chaplain Donaldson. How long have you been chaplain at Fort Laramie?"

"Almost seven years."

"Then you're the one I've been hearing about."

"Oh?"

"A lot of army chaplains only preach a social gospel. But I've been told you preach the real gospel of the Lord Jesus Christ—salvation through His bloodshedding death, burial, and resurrection."

Donaldson smiled again. "You've been told the truth."

"Wonderful!" said Breanna as she eased the canteen away from Little Big Man's mouth.

"You must be a child of God yourself," said the chaplain.

"I sure am."

"I thought you might be."

"And why is that?"

"Oh, you just have that look about you."

Breanna smiled at him. "Well, I'm glad it shows."

"I came over here to offer my help," said Chaplain Donaldson. "I'll go with you to the village and see that these boys don't fall off their horses. We'll put two of them on one horse; that way, you can ride the third one."

"Well, thank you, Chaplain. I really appreciate this. But have you been inoculated for smallp—"

"Indians!" came a shout from the crowd.

Instantly, every eye was fixed on the two young warriors galloping toward the train.

12

THE MEN PASSENGERS who wore side arms touched their revolvers as the Indians rode up. Women and children looked on, wide-eyed and nervous.

When Iron Hawk and Running Fox drew rein, they raised their hands in a sign of peace, then looked down at the three Cheyenne boys stretched out on the ground.

Hungry Dog looked at Breanna and said, "These are warriors from our village."

"I am Iron Hawk," said the huskier of the two. "This is Running Fox. These boys left the village without permission from their fathers or Chief War Bonnet. We were sent to find them and bring them back."

Breanna rose to her feet. "Iron Hawk, my name is Mrs. Breanna Brockman, and I am a nurse. Do you understand what a nurse is?"

The young warrior nodded as he slid from his pinto's back. Running Fox also dismounted.

"Hungry Dog tells me that many are sick in your village with this disease, and some have died."

Iron Hawk's expression was solemn as he said, "Our shamans are bathing the sick in water and using the smudging, as well as offering prayers."

"But our people continue to become ill...and to die," said Hungry Dog. "The prayers of the shamans...are not being answered by our gods. This is why we left the village...and rode this way. We were going to Kimball...to bring doctor."

While the Indians talked, Breanna took the cup from the conductor's hand, poured water into it, and took an envelope of salicylic acid from her medical bag. She poured a measured amount into the cup and began stirring it.

"But you should not have tried to ride when you were becoming ill yourselves," Running Fox said to Hungry Dog.

"We did not know we...were so sick."

Spotted Bull set his dull gaze on Iron Hawk. "Did Essie Bird Woman...die?"

"No. She still lives."

"And does Broken Hand still live?" asked Hungry Dog.

Running Fox's head drooped, and he shut his eyes in sorrow.

Iron Hawk's features looked bleak as he said, "Broken Hand is dead."

Hungry Dog swallowed with difficulty, but he no longer spoke so haltingly. "Heammawihio and Aktunowihio have forsaken us. They even allow a medicine man to die. We must have help from whites, or we all die."

"But He-Who-Walks-in-Rain said if we bring white doctor and his medicine, it will offend our gods," said Iron Hawk.

Hungry Dog's voice increased slightly in volume. "Heammawihio and Aktunowihio do not care about us. Why should we care if we offend them? This nurse woman is making us medicine. She was going to bring us to village. Someone will bring more medicine from Cheyenne City...to help all of our sick ones."

The warriors turned their gaze on Breanna.

"This was my plan," she said.

Iron Hawk and Running Fox exchanged fearful glances, then Iron Hawk said, "Our people do not wish to bring the wrath of our gods by turning from them to white man's medicine."

Breanna held up the cup in her hand and said, "I am offering to come to the village with my medicine, if your chief will let me. Right now, I'm going to give this medicine to these sick boys."

Iron Hawk stiffened. "What will it do?"

"It will lower their fevers. If the fever does not come down, they will die."

Iron Hawk glanced at Running Fox. The latter turned to Breanna and asked, "If you give them the medicine, they will not die?"

"I can't promise that. This disease is deadly, and it's hard to stop. But I can promise you that if their fever doesn't come down, they will die. The medicine I have will do more for them than if I bathe them with cool water. That is necessary too, but only after we get them to the village. The medicine will cool them from the inside."

Breanna went to Spotted Bull, who seemed to be the most ill, and started giving him the mixture.

The engineer pulled out his pocket watch. "Ma'am, we've got to get moving. We're already way behind schedule. If you're going to go on with us, you'll have to finish giving them the medicine in a hurry."

Breanna looked at the two warriors. "Do I get on the train or are you going to take me to your village?"

Iron Hawk looked in the direction of his village, then turned to his cousin and said, "Since Broken Hand died, and possibly Essie Bird Woman will die...perhaps Chief War Bonnet and He-Who-Walks-in-Rain will let Mrs. Brockman give medicine."

Running Fox nodded. "I have been thinking the same."

"Mrs. Brockman," said Iron Hawk, "is Cheyenne City your home?"

"No. I live near Denver. Do you know of it?"

"Yes. It is many miles south of Cheyenne City. We cannot promise that you will be welcome to use your medicine at our village, but we think it is possible. If our chief and the elder shaman do not allow you to treat our people, Running Fox and I will take you to Cheyenne City so you can take a train to Denver."

Breanna nodded, then said, "Do you think there's a good chance they'll allow me to treat the sick?"

"Yes, because our shamans are not able to stop the sickness at all."

Breanna turned to Chaplain Myron Donaldson and said, "You offered to go with me to the village. Instead, will you do me another favor?"

"Of course."

She quickly explained to Donaldson what she had asked the fireman to do and asked if he would be the man to contact Dr. James Malcolm about the salicylic acid and bring it to her at the village.

"I certainly will," said Donaldson.

Breanna asked him to bring as much medicine as possible, and she gave him enough money to purchase a large amount if it was available.

Donaldson asked Iron Hawk for directions to War Bonnet's village, then said to Breanna, "I will also send the wire to your husband. No need for the fireman to do it when I'm going to Cheyenne myself."

Breanna thanked him and expressed her appreciation to the other men for being willing to help her.

When she had finished administering the salicylic acid mixture to the three boys, they were placed aboard their pintos. Breanna would ride with Hungry Dog, and the warriors would ride with the other two. Iron Hawk tied Breanna's luggage on the back of one of the riderless ponies, and they headed north toward the hills as the train pulled away.

Silver Moon had been left to tend to Essie Bird Woman alone. While she bathed her with cool water, Silver Moon prayed earnestly in her heart, O Aktunowihio, gracious god of the earth below, your humble servant begs you to plead with Heammawihio for mercy on my people. The Wise One Above must stop the white man's disease before others die. Essie Bird Woman burns up with fever. She will die if you do not obtain help for her from Heammawihio.

Her prayers were interrupted by the sound of riders coming in from the south. Chief War Bonnet, He-Who-Walks-in-Rain, the subchiefs, and many of the people had gathered to meet them.

Silver Moon rose to her feet to watch. She knew Iron Hawk and Running Fox had gone to find the missing boys and was glad they had been successful, but she saw immediately that the boys were sick. Her eyes fixed on the golden-haired white woman who rode a pinto, holding on to Hungry Dog slumped in front of her.

The parents of the three boys ran to the edge of the village ahead of the others to meet the riders as they reined in.

"The boys have the small bumps of skin disease," said Iron Hawk, then slid from his horse's back and eased Spotted Bull to the ground as his parents closed in. Running Fox dismounted and helped Little Big Man's parents take him off the horse.

Black Wind dashed up to Breanna's pinto and raised his hands to take Hungry Dog. His squaw was at his elbow. As the boys were carried toward the smudge fires, Iron Hawk helped Breanna from the horse and led her toward Chief War Bonnet.

"The man with the chief is the elder shaman of the village, He-Who-Walks-in-Rain," Iron Hawk whispered to Breanna.

She nodded, her pulse quickening.

The faces of the chief and his companion were stoic as they watched Breanna's approach.

"Chief War Bonnet," said Iron Hawk, "this woman is a nurse...a medicine woman among the whites. Her name is Mrs. Breanna Brockman. She has come to offer us help. She knows much about the small bumps of skin disease."

War Bonnet's arms were folded across his chest. He nodded once in greeting, then turned his gaze to Iron Hawk and said, "How did you meet up with Mrs. Breanna Brockman?"

Breanna felt all eyes on her as Iron Hawk explained that the boys were on their way to Kimball to bring the white doctor to the village but had become so ill they could not go on. They had lain by the railroad tracks near the road between Kimball and Cheyenne City until the train stopped and Mrs. Brockman got off to help them.

As Iron Hawk spoke, Breanna let her eyes stray to the bodies on scaffolds at the edge of the village. She counted thirteen of them. Beyond them was the burial ground. Mounds of freshly turned dirt indicated many new graves.

War Bonnet set dark eyes on Breanna and said, "Mrs. Brockman was very kind to help our boys. She is also very kind to come to the village to help us. But she must understand that our shamans are working on the sick and praying to our gods."

"I do understand that, Chief," said Breanna, "but from what Iron Hawk and Running Fox told me, many of your people have died because of the disease. I have already given the boys medicine to bring down their fevers, and I must give them more soon. This must be done, or they will die. I have more of the medicine with me, and I have a friend who is planning to purchase more of this medicine in Cheyenne City and bring it here. I can't promise that I can keep all of your sick ones from dying, but the medicine will help save many lives if I'm allowed to give it to those who are sick."

War Bonnet turned to He-Who-Walks-in-Rain and said something in Cheyenne. The shaman replied, then War Bonnet called for all the shamans and their pupils to gather around.

Iron Hawk spoke in a whisper to Breanna. "Chief War Bonnet is interested in your offer. He wants to tell the spiritual leaders about it and get their opinions."

As a medicine woman in training, Silver Moon came forward and moved up beside Iron Hawk, who smiled at her. She smiled back, then looked closely at the white woman with the lovely blond hair.

When all who had been summoned were gathered, War Bonnet spoke in his native language so that all would understand. He told them the story of the boys' ride toward Kimball, their collapse by the train tracks, and the help given by the woman with "sunshine hair." He told them that Sunshine Hair was a nurse and had already given the boys some of her medicine to bring their fevers down.

Breanna watched the group as War Bonnet spoke, trying to discern from their reactions what he was saying. Most of the Indians looked puzzled, some looked pleased, but one medicine man scowled at her, his fiery gaze piercing her.

During the discussion that followed the chief's narrative, Iron Hawk whispered to Breanna, "The Chief calls you 'Sunshine Hair.'"

Breanna smiled, then glanced at the maiden who stood on the other side of Iron Hawk. The young warrior introduced them.

"I am glad to meet you, Silver Moon," said Breanna, smiling at her. "Such a pretty name...for such a pretty girl."

Silver Moon smiled shyly. "You are very kind."

The trio turned back to the discussion. While Iron Hawk and Silver Moon listened, Breanna watched for reactions. She knew about the Cheyenne religion and understood their dilemma. They feared offending their gods by allowing a white "medicine woman" to treat the sick and dying.

The fiery eyes of the one shaman stayed fixed on Breanna, even when he spoke to the others. If looks could kill, she thought, I'd be dead.

Breanna had been praying all the while, but now she said under her breath, "Dear Lord, I ask You to work in the minds of this chief and his leaders. May they allow me to use the salicylic acid. And please help Chaplain Donaldson to obtain a good supply from Dr. Malcolm...and to get here with it soon." Breanna glanced at the stern-looking shaman once again, and her lips moved with the words, "Lord, please don't let that one get in the way. And please also make it possible for me to inoculate those who haven't yet come down with the smallpox. You know, Lord, that it could wipe out the whole village if it isn't stopped soon."

Suddenly Hungry Dog's father moved up to the fringes of the group and said something. Immediately the discussion stopped and they parted ranks, allowing Black Wind to speak to the chief and the elder shaman.

Iron Hawk leaned close to Breanna and said, "Black Wind is telling them Hungry Dog's fever is way down."

Breanna breathed a word of thanks to her true and living God.

"Now Black Wind is telling them Spotted Bull and Little Big Man are cooler too."

War Bonnet grunted something to Black Wind, then to He-Who-Walks-in-Rain. The three of them headed for the place where the sick lay beside the smudging fires.

War Bonnet watched as He-Who-Walks-in-Rain knelt down and felt Hungry Dog's brow. He went to Spotted Bull next and felt his brow. He did the same with Little Big Man. He then stepped to another victim of the disease, a boy about the age of the other three. He felt the boy's brow, then turned and spoke in Cheyenne to his chief.

There were smiles on every face except for that of the fiery-eyed shaman.

Breanna whispered to Iron Hawk, "Who is the medicine man who scowls at me?"

"He is Bull Elk. He is afraid if War Bonnet allows you to do your work, our gods will be angry and punish us."

War Bonnet approached Breanna with He-Who-Walks-in-Rain beside him and said, "We are pleased to see that Hungry Dog, Spotted Bull, and Little Big Man are much better. For this we thank you."

"I am very glad the boys are better, Chief War Bonnet," said Breanna. "It is important that I give them more medicine very soon so they will continue to improve."

"You have my permission to do that and to begin giving it to the others who are sick."

Suddenly Bull Elk stepped before the chief and the elder shaman, his eyes like a sullen flame, and said, "This is big mistake! Our gods will be furious! We insult them if we allow this white woman to use her medicine on our people! We must look to Heammawihio and Aktunowihio to heal the sick ones among us!"

A low murmur traveled through the crowd.

War Bonnet spoke in a level tone as he replied, "Bull Elk must listen to me. He-Who-Walks-in-Rain and War Bonnet are in agreement that Heammawihio and Aktunowihio have sent woman with sunshine hair to help us. She is their answer to our prayers. In the many moons the sickness has been among us, no fever has been broken like we have seen in Hungry Dog, Spotted Bull, and Little Big Man."

Bull Elk stood in silence. Then he gave Breanna a hard look, walked into the crowd, and joined his squaw.

"My medicine supply is small right now, Chief War Bonnet," Breanna said, "but as I told you, I have a friend who will bring much more as soon as he can."

War Bonnet nodded. "Sunshine Hair already knew that Heammawihio and Aktunowihio were sending her. This is why she told her friend to bring more of the medicine from Cheyenne City. This is good."

"Since my supply is small," Breanna said, "it is best that I give the medicine to those who have been sick the longest."

"The shamans will tell you where they are," said War Bonnet.

"All right, Chief. I'll give medicine to the three boys, because we've started them on the road to recovery. Then I'll start with those who have been sick the longest. I'll make the medicine go as far as I can and then hope that my friend will soon arrive with more. When I've run out of the medicine I'm carrying, I'd like to talk with you. It would be good if the shamans listened in on it, too. I want to tell you how I can stop the rest of you from getting the disease."

War Bonnet looked surprised. "You could do this?"

"Yes."

"Then we will listen."

"Good. Right now I must get to work, and I'll need someone to help me."

"It is best if your helper comes from among the shamans," said He-Who-Walks-in-Rain.

Silver Moon stepped forward and said, "He-Who-Walks-in-Rain knows that I am in training to be a shaman. May I help Sunshine Hair? I can also tell her the order in which the sick ones have fallen ill."

The elder shaman looked to the chief for his approval. War Bonnet smiled and nodded.

He-Who-Walks-in-Rain said, "Yes, Silver Moon. You are to be helper to Sunshine Hair. She is our gift from Heammawihio."

Breanna turned to Silver Moon and said, "I'm very pleased to have you as my helper. Let's begin at once. I'll need water and a bowl to mix the powders in, and a cup to give it to the patients."

"I will see that water is brought to you, Mrs. Br—" Iron Hawk paused. "Would it be all right if I call you Sunshine Hair?"

"Of course. I'm honored that your chief has given me this name."

Iron Hawk nodded his approval. "All right, Sunshine Hair. I will keep you supplied with water from the creek."

"I will bring you the bowl and the cup," said Silver Moon.

Running Fox appeared beside them with Breanna's overnight bag. "I removed this from the horse, Sunshine Hair."

"Oh, thank you, Running Fox." She gave him a warm smile. Then to Silver Moon she said, "I will meet you where the three boys lie. We'll give them more medicine, then begin with the others."

The crowd broke up as Breanna hurried to the three boys.

She felt their foreheads and was pleased their temperatures were so much closer to normal.

The shamans had gone back to work on their patients, adding dried sagebrush to the smudging fires, and were once again bathing their faces, necks, and wrists with cool water as they fanned the smoke on them.

Bull Elk watched Breanna move from patient to patient and speak to the shamans. He began to pray under his breath, "O Heammawihio, great god of the sky, I ask for your forgiveness toward War Bonnet for allowing this white woman to bring her devil brew into our village. Please do not punish us."

Breanna returned to the three boys when she saw Silver Moon coming from among the tepees and Iron Hawk from the creek with two crude buckets filled with water.

As all three converged, Iron Hawk smiled at Silver Moon, then said to Breanna, "I will come and check on you in a little while and bring you more water when it is needed."

"Thank you, Iron Hawk."

"Thank you for caring about my people."

"I love the Cheyenne people," she said.

He nodded. "That is easy to see."

"Well, Silver Moon," Breanna said, "to work."

The dark-eyed young woman watched Breanna pour water into the bowl, then drop a measure of the white powder into the water.

While Breanna used the handle of a knife to mix the powder and water, Silver Moon asked, "What is this medicine called?"

"Salicylic acid."

"Acid? Does not acid burn the skin?"

"Some acids do, but not this kind." Breanna laid the knife aside. "All right. You hold the cup, Silver Moon, and I'll pour."

Since Spotted Bull had been the sickest, Breanna started with him. She elevated his head and let Silver Moon put the cup to his lips. When he had drunk the liquid, they moved to Little Big Man, and from him to Hungry Dog. All the while the parents of the boys stood close by, watching.

When they had finished with the boys Breanna said, "All right, Silver Moon, let's start with the others. Who has been sick the longest?"

"That will be Essie Bird Woman. She is a medicine woman but is very, very sick."

The three sets of parents came to Breanna as she and Silver Moon were mixing more medicine. The prairie breeze toyed with the single eagle feather on the headband of one of the fathers as he said, "Sunshine Hair, I am Falling Stone, father of Little Big Man. This is my squaw, Meadowlark. I speak for these other parents, and for Meadowlark and myself. We wish to thank you for what you have done. We know our gods, Heammawihio and Aktunowihio, are not your gods. But we thank them for sending you to us."

Breanna smiled, her heart heavy for these precious people who did not know the true God. "I can only say, Falling Stone, that I am here as a servant of *my* God, whose Son, Jesus Christ, has put a deep love in my heart for all people, including the Cheyenne. I am very happy that I can be here to help."

Falling Stone smiled. "We welcome you, Sunshine Hair…servant of your God."

Silver Moon had heard of this Jesus Christ. She wondered if His other servants were as pleasant, kind, and loving as Sunshine Hair.

13

AS BREANNA AND SILVER MOON threaded their way among the sick who lay next to smudging fires, Breanna prayed fervently in her heart, Dear Lord, I'm here to help these people. As You give me opportunity and wisdom, I want to sow the seed of the Word in their hearts and give them the gospel. I ask your protection on me, for Satan will do his best to hinder me. You know that Bull Elk is very angry that I am here. Please keep him from stirring up trouble for me. And, Lord, help me with this medicine woman I'm about to deal with. Give me wisdom, please, and keep Your mighty hand on me.

Silver Moon went ahead of Breanna, carrying the cup and bowl in one hand and one of the buckets of water in the other. She knelt beside Essie Bird Woman as Breanna drew up, carrying the other bucket and her medical bag.

The medicine woman opened her eyes and smiled weakly at Silver Moon, then looked at the yellow-haired woman who knelt beside her.

"Essie Bird Woman, have you been awake?" asked Silver Moon.

The woman's brow was moist with perspiration, but her eyes were moderately clear. "Some of the time," she replied weakly.

"Do you know about the white nurse who has come to help us?"

"I heard something about her…" Essie Bird Woman's eyes trailed from Silver Moon's face to Breanna's. "She is the one they call Sunshine Hair."

"Yes," said the girl. "She is here. Can you see her?"

The shaman nodded, meeting Breanna's gaze with a smile.

"Hello, Essie Bird Woman. I have medicine to give you." Breanna looked at Silver Moon. "Does she know about the three boys?"

"I told her, but with the high fever I don't know if she understood, or if she did, that she remembers."

"Yes…" said Essie Bird Woman. "I remember."

"The medicine I have for you is the same as I gave to Hungry Dog, Little Big Man, and Spotted Bull," said Breanna. "It has helped them, and I believe it will help you."

The shaman nodded.

When they had finished giving the mixture to Essie Bird Woman, Breanna took hold of her hand and said, "You rest now. It will take the medicine a while to work, but your fever will go down, I'm sure."

Silver Moon touched the older woman's face with gentle fingers and said, "We will be back to see you later."

As Silver Moon led Breanna to the next patient, a sudden wail pierced the air. A young mother held her dead child—a boy about three years old—beside one of the smudging fires. The father, a warrior, stood beside her and a medicine man, his face drawn and pallid.

Silver Moon went to them and spoke words of condolence to the parents in Cheyenne, then led Breanna to the next patient, an elderly man.

Breanna's gaze found War Bonnet and she prayed silently

once again, asking the Lord to work in his heart—and in those of the shamans—to allow her to give inoculations.

As she and Silver Moon gave the salicylic mixture to the elderly man, Breanna glanced at the bodies on the scaffolds and then at the fresh graves. She was deeply burdened for the souls of these people who had no real hope as they faced eternity.

After leaving the elderly man with shamans, Breanna and Silver Moon went to a teenage girl who was barely conscious. Silver Moon elevated the girl's head, and Breanna got some of the mixture into the girl's mouth.

"What can you do to stop the rest of us from getting the disease?" Silver Moon asked.

"Do you know what inoculation is, Silver Moon?"

"No. What is inoc— How do you say it?"

"Inoculation."

Suddenly there was a deep rumble, like the roll of thunder. Both women looked past the west edge of the village and saw a large number of U.S. Army cavalrymen, weapons held ready for action.

Sudden terror came alive inside Silver Moon, beating through her like the frantic wings of a frightened bird. She let out a tremulous cry, then quickly covered her mouth to stifle it.

"Honey, are you all right?" asked Breanna.

Silver Moon swallowed hard but said nothing.

The Cheyenne people were scattering, and some of the warriors headed toward the rifles that leaned against their tepees. War Bonnet called for them to remain calm, saying that if they were being attacked, the soldiers would already be firing their guns.

Breanna took hold of the trembling girl and said, "Silver Moon, it's all right. The soldiers are not attacking us. Did you hear Chief War Bonnet? He said we are not being attacked."

The troopers galloped to the outskirts of the village and began to spread out, as if expecting a fight from the Indians. Silver Moon and Breanna watched as War Bonnet and his subchiefs went to meet the officer who was flanked by half a dozen men.

War Bonnet halted at the edge of the village and waited for the riders to haul up. The leader's insignia showed him to be a captain, and the two men who stayed closest to him were lieutenants. The captain remained on his horse and looked down at the stone-faced Indian who wore a long headdress.

"Are you Chief War Bonnet?"

"I am."

"I'm Captain Robert Owen out of Fort Laramie. Which way did the Cheyenne war party go?"

"I have not seen a Cheyenne war party."

Owen drew a quick breath, and his eyes turned dark with anger. "We've been chasing a band of Cheyenne who attacked a white settlement near Bear Creek Mountain south of the fort. Those killers came straight this way. They had to have come right by this village within the last half hour. In fact, I'm thinking they're probably *from* this village. Now don't try to fool me, War Bonnet. You know where they are. Which way did they go?"

"The war party you pursue is *not* of this village, Captain, and I say again, I have not seen them."

"You're a liar! You're covering for your own savage killers! Where are they? Are you hiding 'em somewhere?"

War Bonnet's warriors moved slowly to where their guns leaned against the tepees.

War Bonnet held his voice steady as he said, "My people and I have been at peace with the whites for over eight grasses, Captain. Whoever these warriors were, I am telling you they are not of this village. And they have not been near here. We have not seen them."

Robert Owen narrowed his eyes, adjusted his position in the saddle, and said, "If I find out you're lying, War Bonnet, you and your savages are gonna be sorry. *Real* sorry!"

"Captain!" came a sharp female voice.

The captain blinked in surprise as Breanna, her cheeks tinted with anger, threaded her way through the people and drew up before his horse. "Chief War Bonnet is not lying! I have been here for over three hours, and there has been no Cheyenne war party come by or to this village!"

Owen touched the brim of his campaign hat. "Well, now, just who might this little spitfire be? And what is she doing living among the Cheyenne?"

"I'm not a resident here, Captain. I just told you I've been in the village for over three hours. I came here to save lives. My name is Breanna Brockman, for your information. My home is in Colorado, near Denver. I'm a nurse."

Owen lifted his eyebrows and cocked his head. "You're a nurse, you say?"

"Yes."

"And you're in this village to save lives?"

"Just a minute, Captain," said the lieutenant who sat on his left. "I'd like to ask the lady something. I'm Lieutenant Boyce Matthews, ma'am. I know about white people and their relationships with Indians. My father is an Indian agent in Arizona."

"So what is your question, Lieutenant?"

"By what authority are you practicing medicine in this village?"

Breanna's temper rose as she said, "There is no Indian agent overseeing these Cheyenne like there is in Arizona with the Apache. I need nobody's approval."

"Oh? Well, we could report you, you know."

"To whom?"

"How about the U.S. marshal's office that governs this district?"

"And just where is that office, Lieutenant?"

"You said you're from Denver. You ought to know that the U.S. marshal's office overseeing the entire western district is located there."

"Oh, I'm very much aware of it. Tell you what, Lieutenant Matthews, why don't you report me to the *chief* United States marshal?"

"Well, I just might do that."

"Do you know his name?"

"John Brockman."

"And just what law am I breaking that you would report me to Chief Brockman?"

Matthews thought a moment. "Well, I—"

"You know there isn't any such law, Lieutenant," said Captain Owen. "Besides, you'd come out the loser if you tried to get Chief Brockman to prosecute her."

"What do you mean, sir?"

"Didn't you hear the lady's name?"

"Yes. Breanna Brock—"

Breanna gave him a cold smile. "If you'd like to report me to my husband, sir, you better have proof that I've broken some law that's currently on the books. Now, let's see, Captain Owen, before we were interrupted, I believe you were questioning my statement about being in this village to save lives. Take a look over there, Captain." She swung her arm toward the people lying on the grass among the smoking fires. "What we have in this village is an outbreak of smallpox." She then pointed at the scaffolds and said, "You're a soldier, Captain. I assume you know corpses when you see them. Those people died just recently. And if you'll look beyond them, you'll see fresh graves in the burial ground. You do know what smallpox is, don't you, Captain?"

"Why, yes, I—"

"Then you know we've got a deadly plague here. I'm trying to stop the plague; you're interrupting my work. Take your chase somewhere else. Your Cheyenne war party apparently has given you the slip. I am not a liar any more than Chief War Bonnet is, so while you and your men are sitting there on your horses, the Indians who attacked the settlement are getting farther and farther away."

Captain Owen thought he heard a muffled snicker behind him. He turned his head quickly, but every man wore a solemn expression. He straightened in the saddle and was about to reply when Breanna cut him off.

"Captain, have you and your men been inoculated for smallpox?"

"Well, I—"

"Because if you haven't, you're in real danger right now. As a certified medical nurse, I can tell you this disease is contracted not only by physical contact with an infected person, it's also airborne...and you and your men are breathing infected air this very instant!"

Owen clamped his lips shut and wheeled his mount, goading its sides. In a few minutes, the band of soldiers disappeared over a hill, heading east.

The chief gave Breanna an appreciative look and said, "It appears to War Bonnet that Captain Robert Owen wishes he not stop here. Sunshine Hair made him look like a fool."

Many of the Cheyenne raised their voices in approval of War Bonnet's words.

As the cheers faded, a smile worked its way across the chief's face, and he said, "Sunshine Hair have sharp tongue and sharp mind. Maybe she be next chief of this village!"

Breanna chuckled. In the face of all the sadness around them, it felt good. "I don't think I qualify, Chief," she said. "I'm not Cheyenne."

"We make you honorary Cheyenne!" called out one of the women.

Breanna smiled as she looked around the crowd of faces, then said to War Bonnet, "I must get back to work." She turned toward her assistant and said, "Come, Silver Moon."

Bull Elk's gaze followed Breanna as she walked away. He could not help but like the white woman—especially for the way she'd handled the soldiers. But he could not approve what he considered a violation of his gods.

"I did not know your real name until you told it to the soldier coats," Silver Moon said. "I think *Breanna* is a beautiful name."

"Thank you, Silver Moon."

"If…if sometimes I called you Breanna instead of Sunshine Hair, would it be all right?"

"Of course. I call you Silver Moon, don't I?"

"Yes."

"Then you can call me Breanna."

"I would like to hear about your husband."

"I'd love to tell you about him when we have time to just sit and talk."

"Do you have children?"

"Not yet. We've only been married since June."

Silver Moon pointed out the next person in line to receive the salicylic acid mixture, and they went to work.

"Breanna, before the soldiers came, you were telling me about inoc…"

"Inoculation."

"Yes. Inoculation. You used that word to the captain. Tell me about it."

As Breanna poured tiny sips of the mixture down the throat of their half-conscious patient she said, "I can tell by the way you speak English, Silver Moon, that you have been educated to a degree in white man's ways."

"Yes. A man named George Bent, who was educated in a university in the East, came to my father's village many times when I was younger. He taught us to read and write English, and he even gave us some books to read. Mostly they were history books about white man's coming to this land from across the big lake...the Atlantic Ocean."

Breanna paused for a moment before administering the last drops of medicine to the patient. "You haven't mentioned your father before. You called it *his* village. Is your father a chief?"

"He *was* a chief. My father is dead. My entire family is dead."

"Oh, I'm sorry. I didn't know."

"Of course you did not. Please do not feel bad. I...I will tell you about my family when we talk about your husband," Silver Moon said quietly.

"All right. I'd like to hear about them."

They finished with the patient and moved on to an elderly man, whose body was soaked with sweat. Using cloths to dry his face, they began preparing the mixture.

"You were going to tell me about inoculation," said Silver Moon.

"Yes. First, let me explain that smallpox—which has also been called *variola*—was described in Chinese writings over three thousand years ago. Are you acquainted with China?"

"A little. I know it is an ancient land, and the people have yellow skin and narrow eyes. It is far away across many waters."

"That's right. Here," Breanna said, lifting the elderly man's head a bit. "You give it to him."

While Silver Moon held the cup to the patient's mouth, Breanna said, "Many, many years ago there was a sickness called the Black Plague. It was all over the world and killed many thousands of people. During that time, the Black Plague was the worst disease on earth. However, smallpox replaced the Black Plague as the world's greatest killer disease. It snuffed out hundreds of thousands of lives, until about a hundred years ago."

"And we have it right here in our village," said Silver Moon.

Breanna nodded. "The first reasonably effective method of controlling smallpox was discovered by an English physician in about 1762. His name was Dr. Thomas Dimsdale. Do you know about England?"

"Yes. Most of the white people who first set foot on this land that belonged to the red man came from there."

"That's right. Dr. Dimsdale discovered a process that he called 'variolation.' You've seen that every person affected with smallpox has these small bumps on their skin..."

"Yes."

"The small bumps are called pustules."

"I never heard that word before."

"I'm not surprised. There is a yellow-white fluid called *pus* inside each pustule."

Silver Moon nodded.

"Variolation is the process of inserting pus from a smallpox pustule into the bloodstream of a person who does not have smallpox. This is done by scratching the skin deep enough to produce blood, then dipping a pus-tipped needle into the scratch. This is *inoculation*. It keeps the unaffected person from ever getting smallpox."

"Does it always work?"

"Almost every time. There have been a few cases when it didn't work, but very few. There is another inoculation that always works, and that's when medical people can obtain pus from cowpox."

"Cowpox? That sounds like a disease cows get."

"It is. And doctors today have discovered that when people are inoculated with the cowpox pus, they *never* get smallpox."

Silver Moon thought for a moment, then said, "Of course, we do not have any cowpox pus, so if we are going to inoculate our people, it will have to come from these who are sick."

"That's right. And that's what we're going to do if your Chief War Bonnet gives me permission."

Silver Moon spoke in tender tones to the aged Indian man she was giving the mixture to and lovingly patted his head.

Breanna marveled at how good Silver Moon was with the sick. No wonder she wanted to be a shaman. *If only I can give her the gospel and win her to Jesus,* she thought. *Please, Lord. Help me to lead Silver Moon to You.*

"Have you heard of a country called Russia, Silver Moon?" asked Breanna.

"Yes. Like England, it is a part of Europe."

"In 1768, smallpox was running rampant in Russia."

"Running rampant? Does that mean it was killing many people in that country?"

"It does. The top leader in Russia at that time was a woman. Her title was empress. They called her Catherine the Great. The empress sent for Dr. Thomas Dimsdale, asking him to come to Russia and use his inoculation on her family before the disease came on them and killed them all. So he went to Russia. He inoculated Catherine, her family, and everyone who worked in the palace. When the smallpox plague had run its course in Russia and none of those inoculated came down with it, Catherine called Dr. Dimsdale back to her country to honor him. She paid him a great sum of money, promised him that money would be sent to him for the rest of his life, and gave him the rank of baron. This made him an honorary nobleman of Russia."

"That is an interesting story," said Silver Moon. "We Cheyenne know about *honorary*. This is why one of the women used the word, referring to you, when Chief War Bonnet made a joke about you becoming chief one day. You know of the white trader and explorer Jim Bridger?"

"Oh, yes."

"He saved the life of Cheyenne Chief Big Mountain's son. Chief Big Mountain honored Jim Bridger by making him an honorary Cheyenne warrior."

"I see."

Silver Moon pondered the Russian story. "So in Dr. Dimsdale's day, he had no cowpox pus, but used smallpox pus?"

"Yes."

"If none of Catherine's family and palace people got smallpox, maybe it will work that way with our people when we inoculate them."

"I am praying this is so," said Breanna.

"You pray to your God, whose Son is Jesus Christ…is that correct?"

Breanna nodded.

"And I pray to Heammawihio. He has a lesser god here on earth, whose name is Aktunowihio, but he has no son. Since we both are praying, perhaps it will be that everyone who receives the inoculation will not get the smallpox."

Breanna wanted so much to tell Silver Moon about Jesus,

but this was not the time. Instead she said, "The main thing now, Silver Moon, is for me to explain about inoculation to Chief War Bonnet and the shamans, so I can get permission to do it."

"How much of the white powder do you have left?"

"Very little."

"When we run out, you can have your talk with Chief War Bonnet and the shamans."

"That's what I will do, Silver Moon. Now, let's get as many of these fevers as possible under control."

14

WITH SILVER MOON AT HER SIDE, Breanna administered the salicylic acid mixture to as many people as possible until she finally ran out of the powder. When she had given the last drop to a patient, she sighed, "Well, Silver Moon, the others will have to wait till Chaplain Donaldson brings more."

Silver Moon nodded. "I am glad we were able to treat as many as we did."

The shamans continued the smudge fires and bathing their patients with cool water.

Breanna stood and looked around. "Let's check on our patients."

When they approached Hungry Dog, Spotted Bull, and Little Big Man, Breanna's heart seemed to skip a beat. The boys' parents were with them, and all three boys were smiling. Their fevers had broken, and they had some sparkle in their eyes.

"How can we ever thank you properly, Sunshine Hair?" said Black Wind. "If you had not cared for our sons and had not given them your medicine, they probably would have died."

"Just seeing these boys feeling better is enough thanks," she said. "And the reason I care is because of my Lord and Saviour, Jesus Christ. It is His love flowing through my heart that you

see, Black Wind. I praise and thank Him that He has used the
medicine to break the fevers of these boys."

Silver Moon was having a hard time holding back words of
praise for Heammawihio and Aktunowihio, but she felt to
speak out would offend Sunshine Hair. In her heart, she
thanked her gods that the boys were now recovering.

Essie Bird Woman's eyes were clear, and she smiled at the two
women as they drew up and knelt beside her. "I am feeling
much better," she said.

"You look better," said Breanna, laying a palm on her brow.
"And your fever has broken."

"This is wonderful!" exclaimed Silver Moon.

"I am better because of you, Sunshine Hair," said Essie Bird
Woman. "Thank you for coming to us."

"The real thanks goes to Jesus Christ," Breanna said, smiling down at her. "He is the Great Physician."

Silver Moon was stunned when she heard Essie Bird
Woman say, "I have heard of your Jesus Christ, Sunshine Hair,
but I have not heard Him called the Great Physician. Please
thank Him for me, will you?"

The look on Silver Moon's face did not escape Breanna, but
she continued to keep her gaze on the shaman and said, "I will
thank Jesus for you, Essie Bird Woman."

"We must also give thanks to Heammawihio and Aktunowihio, Essie Bird Woman," Silver Moon said.

The aging shaman set her dark eyes on Silver Moon, gave
her the slight hint of a smile, but did not reply.

"Well," said Breanna, taking in Silver Moon's astonishment
at her mentor's silence, "we must hurry, Silver Moon, and
check on the rest of our patients."

Essie Bird Woman thanked Breanna again as they moved away.

The fevers were down in each patient who had been given a dose of salicylic acid an hour or more earlier. Some fevers were already broken.

Breanna looked at Silver Moon and said, "It's time for me to talk with Chief War Bonnet and the shamans. I want to get started with the inoculations right away."

"Breanna," said Silver Moon. "I must ask you something."

"Of course."

"Did you mind me saying that Heammawihio and Aktuno-wihio should be thanked for Essie Bird Woman's recovery?"

Breanna gave her a loving look. "No, I understand how you feel." She wanted to say more but felt a restraint in her spirit and remembered the words of Jesus to be "wise as serpents and harmless as doves."

Silver Moon let out a tiny sigh. "I am glad. Now I must ask you something else."

"Yes?"

"Have you had the inoculation for smallpox?"

"When I first started my nursing career I took the inoculation in case I might be working with smallpox patients."

"I am glad," said Silver Moon. "I certainly would not want you to get sick."

Breanna smiled. "If War Bonnet permits me to do the inoculations, you, Miss Silver Moon, will be the first person inoculated."

They noticed Iron Hawk threading his way among the patients. When he drew up before them, he looked at Silver Moon, then said to Breanna, "It seems your medicine is working, Sunshine Hair. The shamans tell me that some of the sick ones are getting better."

"Yes," said Breanna. Then to Silver Moon she said, "I will go to Chief War Bonnet now."

"I will wait close by," said Silver Moon.

"*We* will wait close by," said Iron Hawk, moving closer to Silver Moon.

Silver Moon felt her heart lift, and she looked at Iron Hawk with a soft expression in her eyes. If only she could be rid of her hatred toward John Chivington and the need to exact revenge on him, she could so easily let herself fall in love with Iron Hawk.

Breanna stood before Chief War Bonnet and the men he had assembled. The male shamans who were unaffected by the sickness were there, as well as six subchiefs.

War Bonnet informed them that Sunshine Hair had a method of preventing those who were yet unaffected by the disease from getting it. She would explain it to them. Before he turned the meeting over to her War Bonnet said, "All of you men know that the medicine Sunshine Hair has given our sick ones is working. Some are out of danger now. Their fevers are broken. We wait for more medicine to be brought from Cheyenne City. It is good that we express our appreciation."

There was a rumble of voices as the Indians spoke their thanks to Breanna, most of them speaking Cheyenne.

Breanna noticed that one shaman did not speak. Bull Elk's face looked as if it had been chiseled out of granite. She felt the pressure of his stern eyes as she carefully but briefly explained the process of inoculation. One subchief spoke in low tones, translating for those in the group who needed it.

"I cannot guarantee the inoculation will work on everyone, Chief War Bonnet. There may be some of the people who are already about to come down with it, but no signs have yet appeared. The inoculation will not work for them. So you can see I must begin immediately to inoculate as many as possible. Silver Moon will help me. But I cannot do it unless I receive permission from you."

The chief turned to face the group and told them he was in favor of allowing Sunshine Hair to begin the inoculation, but he wanted to hear what the shamans had to say.

In a matter of minutes, every shaman except one spoke his approval, and the subchiefs agreed with their chief that Sunshine Hair should begin immediately. Bull Elk stood with arms folded across his chest and a stony expression on his face. War Bonnet now addressed him.

"Bull Elk is the only man who has not spoken his approval. Why is this?"

The shaman set fierce eyes on Breanna and said, "I have no desire to be at odds with my chief and these other men, but this white woman's presence offends our gods. We will be punished if we allow her to do this white man's medicine practice on our people."

"Bull Elk," said the chief, "we have already seen that her medicine has saved lives in this village. It is as I have said: Sunshine Hair was sent to us by Heammawihio. Can Bull Elk argue with this?"

Bull Elk hesitated, then replied, "It is difficult for Bull Elk to believe Heammawihio would send a white woman who does not worship him to deliver us from this sickness."

War Bonnet's countenance darkened. "Since Bull Elk is the only shaman here who has that difficulty, it would be good if he would think about his opinion. The lives of our people are at stake. All of the prayers offered by the shamans have not brought healing directly from the hand of Heammawihio, or even Aktunowihio. But Heammawihio has sent us Sunshine Hair to bring the healing. We must not offend him by refusing to believe that he would send a white woman to save lives and give healing."

Bull Elk's stony face did not change expression as he said in a deep grunt, "I say no more."

War Bonnet turned to Breanna and said, "Sunshine Hair is permitted to do inoculation."

Relief washed over Breanna. "Thank you, Chief." She caught Bull Elk's cold look as she turned and hurried away.

Breanna found Silver Moon and Iron Hawk where she had left them. "Permission granted," she said with a smile.

"Good!" said Silver Moon.

"Is there anything I can do to help?" asked Iron Hawk.

"You could build us a small fire in front of Silver Moon's tepee and keep it going."

"I will do that," said Iron Hawk, and he hurried toward the stack of kindling in the center of the village.

To Silver Moon, Breanna said, "I will need a small bowl to catch the pus. I want to collect a good amount from several of the sick ones. We will not take it from the small children, only the older children and the adults. I will need you to explain in Cheyenne for those who do not know English that there will be slight pain when I puncture the pustules. I'll need you to do the same for the ones we inoculate. Tell them I will have to scratch them enough to draw blood, so there will be some pain."

Silver Moon nodded her understanding.

"I have a long needle in my medical bag that I'll use. Once the pus is in the bowl, we must place it periodically over the fire to keep it warm."

The bowl was produced from Silver Moon's tepee, and the two women moved through the rows of affected ones. When Breanna felt she had a sufficient amount of pus to begin inoculation, she led Silver Moon back to the fire in front of her tepee. Iron Hawk was there, keeping an eye on it.

Breanna held the bowl over the flames and said, "Iron Hawk, I will inoculate Silver Moon first, then you. As soon as I have finished with you, I need you to begin gathering people here at the tent, five or six at a time, and keep them coming."

"I will do that," Iron Hawk assured her.

"All right, Silver Moon, bare whichever arm you want me to scratch."

Silver Moon pulled up the left sleeve of her buckskin dress to the elbow.

"No, honey. Let's go almost to the shoulder. This inoculation is going to leave a permanent scar. It will be small, but still a scar."

Silver Moon nodded, flicked a glance at Iron Hawk, and pulled the sleeve high. She winced slightly when the needle pierced her skin and watched intently as Breanna dipped the tip of the needle in the pus and pressed it into the bleeding scratch.

"There," said Breanna. "All done. All right, Iron Hawk. Get that sleeve up."

The handsome young warrior's features lost some color as he rolled up the left sleeve of his buckskin shirt, and there was a hint of trepidation in his eyes.

Breanna smiled, holding the needle ready. "Men are the same everywhere," she said. "Even the big rough, tough ones cringe at a needle."

"It is true that women bear pain better than men, Breanna," said Silver Moon, pulling her sleeve down.

"My mother used to say it was a good thing God made it so the women had the babies in the family. If the men had the babies, no family would have more than one."

Iron Hawk made up his mind he would show no reaction when the needle dug into his skin. Breanna saw him brace himself, and she pressed the needle slightly harder than necessary. The rugged young warrior winced.

Silver Moon turned away as if hurt to see Iron Hawk in pain, but actually it was to hide the smile on her face.

"All right, Iron Hawk," said Breanna, "you gather them in while I warm up the pus."

The first group of people to be inoculated were the chief and his squaw, followed by the subchiefs and their squaws, then the shamans and their mates. Conspicuously absent was Bull Elk.

While Breanna inoculated War Bonnet she said, "Chief, I have seen Bull Elk with a woman. I assume she is his squaw."

"Yes. Her name is Calf Woman."

"I see that Bull Elk has chosen not to be inoculated, but shouldn't Calf Woman have it if she wants it?"

"She cannot unless Bull Elk gives permission."

"Shouldn't someone try to get it across to him that Calf Woman is in danger if she is not inoculated?"

"He is aware of this, but he fears Heammawihio's punishment more than Calf Woman or himself getting the sickness."

When Breanna had finished working on the first group, Iron Hawk had more people standing ready. As time passed, most of the men, women, and children submitted to the variolation.

At one point, a wail went up among the sick ones when a child died. Only moments later, a middle-aged woman died.

Breanna's heart was heavy for the grieving family members

as the bodies were quickly placed on scaffolds amidst the cries and wails of the survivors. While she worked she prayed silently for God's hand to be on her as she labored to save those who were still alive.

It was late afternoon when an unusually loud, high-pitched chant came from inside a tepee and was heard all over the village. Breanna was reheating pus over the fire as Silver Moon helped a young boy roll up his sleeve. Silver Moon studied the tepees on that side of the village and said, "The chant is coming from Bull Elk's tepee."

Iron Hawk, who had just returned with more wood for the fire, said, "I will go and see why Bull Elk chants so loudly."

Breanna looked at the scene around her and listened to the wailing. A man had just died because she had no salicylic powder to give him. There were better than twenty others burning up with fever, waiting for the relief that could come only from the medicine.

Lord, she prayed, I really need Chaplain Donaldson to get here with the salicylic acid. There are so many more who need it. Please get him here soon.

As Silver Moon continued to explain the process to each person being inoculated, she occasionally glanced toward Iron Hawk, who was standing in front of Bull Elk's tepee with Chief War Bonnet and He-Who-Walks-in-Rain. Suddenly he wheeled and came running back.

"It is Calf Woman," he said. "She has a high fever."

Just then Breanna heard a shout from somewhere on the west side of the village. She turned to Silver Moon. "What is it?"

"A rider is coming from the west."

"Oh, praise the Lord! That'll be Chaplain Donaldson. Iron

Hawk, would you tell Chief War Bonnet that if the man on the horse says he is Chaplain Donaldson to let him come in. He has the salicylic acid."

Iron Hawk found War Bonnet already at the west edge of the village, along with his subchiefs, waiting for the rider. He gave the chief Breanna's message and waited to see if this was indeed the chaplain.

The rider thundered in on a panting, sweaty horse and skidded to a halt. He looked down from the saddle, and his eyes locked on the Indian in full headdress as he said, "I come in peace. You are Chief War Bonnet?"

"I am. And I believe you are Chaplain Donaldson."

"Yes, I am. Mrs. Brockman must have told you I was coming."

"She did. You are bringing medicine."

"Got it right here in my saddlebags. May I dismount?"

"Please do. Sunshine Hair is inoculating our people. We have many more sick ones who need the medicine. War Bonnet thanks you for bringing it."

"It is my pleasure, Chief." Donaldson smiled. "You call Mrs. Brockman 'Sunshine Hair'?"

The chief nodded.

"Well, the name fits her. Not only does she have sunshine hair, she has a sunshine soul."

The chaplain dismounted and unbuckled the saddlebags, placing them over his shoulder. His attention was drawn to the young warrior who stepped toward him from War Bonnet's side and said, "Chaplain Donaldson, I am Iron Hawk. I will take you to Sunshine Hair."

"All right. Let's go."

Breanna had just scratched a small child, resulting in an outburst of tears, when she saw Iron Hawk leading the tall man between the tepees. The parents, having already received their inoculations, hurried away with their crying child.

"Hello, Chaplain. Am I ever glad to see you!"

Donaldson smiled at Breanna and swung the saddlebags from his shoulder, setting them on the ground. "Iron Hawk was just telling me of the good results you've had with the salicylic acid. I'm glad to hear it. There's plenty more right here."

"You'll never know how much I appreciate your doing this, Chaplain," said Breanna. "It's going to save many lives."

He reached inside the leather bags and said, "Where would you like me to put all these envelopes?"

"I have a box," said Silver Moon, dashing into her tepee. When she returned with it, Breanna introduced Donaldson to Silver Moon and helped him unload the handfuls of envelopes into the box.

"This is a good supply," said Breanna. "Ought to be plenty. Was there enough money to cover it, or do I owe you?"

Donaldson pulled out a wad of bills from his pocket. "Your doctor friend donated the medicine, ma'am. Said to tell you he's proud of what you're doing."

"Well, bless his heart!" said Breanna, accepting the money. "I'll have to write him a great big thank-you letter."

Bull Elk's loud wailing filled the air. When Donaldson looked in that direction, Breanna said, "One of the medicine men. His wife just came down with the smallpox."

"I wired your husband, Mrs. Brockman. Gave him your message, explaining where you are."

"Did you take out the money for the wire from here?" she

asked, holding up the wad of bills.

"No, ma'am. The cost of the wire is on me."

"Are you sure?"

"Yes."

"That's awfully nice of you. Thank you."

War Bonnet appeared beside them and said, "Chaplain Donaldson, may we feed you before you make your return ride?"

"Thank you very much, Chief, but I won't have time. I must head back immediately."

Breanna expressed her appreciation for the chaplain's kindness and watched him ride away. Then she had Silver Moon choose a squaw as a helper and started them mixing the salicylic acid with water. Silver Moon would administer the medicine while Breanna continued her inoculations.

By the time darkness fell, two more adults had died. One of the medicine men went to Bull Elk's tepee to inform him of the latest deaths and found the shaman frantically bathing Calf Woman's face and neck with cool water. Her temperature was exceedingly high, and she was on the verge of delirium.

The inoculations were completed, and all the sick ones had been given generous doses of the salicylic mixture. A weary Breanna was washing up at the fire in front of Silver Moon's tepee. The stars shone down from the heavens and the moon put in an appearance on the eastern horizon.

Silver Moon and Iron Hawk had eaten their evening meal with the parents of Spotted Bull, Little Big Man, and Hungry Dog, and were returning along the path. They stopped in front of Silver Moon's tepee and stood over Breanna as she knelt beside the fire, drying her hands.

"Are you ready to eat your supper now?" asked Silver Moon. "They have kept the food hot for you."

"That was awfully nice of them," said Breanna. "I just didn't want to stop until I was done with the inoculations. I'm hungry enough now to eat a bear."

There was movement in the shadows behind Silver Moon and Iron Hawk, and Breanna was surprised to see the face of Bull Elk by the firelight. She rose to her feet, and an indescribable peace came over her.

"Hello, Bull Elk. How is Calf Woman? Iron Hawk told me she has the fever."

Bull Elk cleared his throat and said, "Sunshine Hair, would you allow me to speak with you privately?"

"Silver Moon and I will go for a walk, Bull Elk," said Iron Hawk. "You can talk to Sunshine Hair right here."

When Iron Hawk and Silver Moon were out of earshot, Bull Elk clasped his trembling hands in front of him and said, "I am a vile man who deserves nothing but your wrath…but I am asking for your help."

15

↑

"YOU ARE NOT AN OBJECT of my wrath, Bull Elk." Breanna gave the medicine man a kindly look. "What can I do to help you?"

Bull Elk lowered his head slightly and said, "This foolish man asks your forgiveness. My attitude toward you and your medicine has been wrong. I realize now that Chief War Bonnet was correct when he said Heammawihio sent you to us."

Bull Elk's hands were still clasped in front of him in supplication. Breanna laid her steady hand on top of his and squeezed gently. "I forgive you, Bull Elk. I know Calf Woman is very sick. Do you want me to use my medicine on her?"

Tears misted the shaman's eyes. "Yes. Please. She is very, very sick. And...the thing you do with the needle..."

"Inoculation."

"Yes. Will you do that to me?"

"Of course. I will find Silver Moon and come to your tepee."

Bull Elk nodded, meeting her gaze through tears. "Thank you, Sunshine Hair. Thank you."

"You are quite welcome. You go back to your squaw, and I'll be there shortly."

Breanna found Silver Moon and Iron Hawk kneeling beside

Essie Bird Woman. She explained to them that Bull Elk had asked for her help with Calf Woman and inoculation for himself.

"This is good," said Iron Hawk. "It is not like Bull Elk to humble himself about anything."

"Do you want me to help?" asked Silver Moon.

"Yes. If you will make a mixture and give it to Calf Woman, I will draw more pus from one of the sick ones and inoculate Bull Elk."

"Is there anything I can do?" asked Iron Hawk.

"Not at the moment, but you might stay close by Bull Elk's tepee in case we need you."

Essie Bird Woman spoke. "Sunshine Hair, you were so kind to come to us. If it were not for you, many more would be dead, including this medicine woman. Thank you."

Breanna leaned over and caressed the cool, wrinkled cheek of Essie Bird Woman. "I am glad I could come to you. And it is so good to know you will recover."

A crowd had gathered outside when Breanna and Silver Moon entered Bull Elk's tepee.

A small fire burned in the center of the tepee, giving off sufficient light for the work to be done. With a cup of the salicylic acid mixture in hand, Silver Moon dropped down beside the sweat-soaked Calf Woman.

"Bull Elk, I want to check Calf Woman first, then I will inoculate you," Breanna said, holding bowl and needle.

The somber-faced medicine man nodded.

"This is bad, Breanna," said Silver Moon.

Breanna knelt on Calf Woman's other side and saw the sheen of perspiration on her face. Her teeth were chattering, and her vacant eyes stared unblinking into space. She felt Calf Woman's brow and bit her lower lip.

"She's burning up. We must get the mixture into her quickly."

Bull Elk stood over them anxiously as Breanna squeezed his squaw's cheeks, shook her head gently, and said, "Calf Woman. Can you hear me?"

The vacant eyes turned slowly, attempting to focus on Breanna's face.

"Can you hear me, dear?"

Calf Woman worked her jaw soundlessly for a few seconds, then made a slight grunt and blinked her eyelids lazily.

"Silver Moon has some medicine for you," said Breanna. "You must swallow it for her. Do you understand?"

Calf Woman nodded slightly.

"All right, Silver Moon," said Breanna. "Don't try to give it to her too fast...just steady. Tiny sips."

Silver Moon elevated Calf Woman's head with one hand while holding the cup in the other.

"I'll hold her head for you as soon as I give Bull Elk the inoculation," said Breanna, rising to her feet.

Silver Moon murmured soothing words to Calf Woman as she gave her the mixture.

Breanna took Bull Elk to the far side of the tepee and said in a low tone, "I must be honest with you, Bull Elk. Calf Woman is seriously ill. Her fever is very high. She may die."

Bull Elk's voice broke. "It is my fault. If I...had let you use the needle on her, she would not have come down with the sickness."

"It's possible that she was already coming down with it, but if we could've used this medicine earlier, she wouldn't have become this ill."

"So it is still my fault."

"Well, at least you're allowing us to treat her now. We'll do everything we can to save her life. I need you to roll up one of your sleeves so I can use the needle high up on your arm. There'll be a little pain when I scratch the skin."

When the inoculation was done, Breanna knelt down and supported Calf Woman's head while Silver Moon put the salicylic acid mixture down her throat in small amounts. With her free hand, Breanna mopped perspiration from the sick woman's face. "Bull Elk," she said, "if you would get me a pail of water and some cloths, I'll bathe Calf Woman in the water as soon as she's taken this first cup of medicine."

Bull Elk picked up a wooden pail from next to the thin wall of the tepee. "I will return shortly," he said, rushing out.

Chief War Bonnet was in the crowd that stood outside. He met Bull Elk and said, "I have been told you have asked Sunshine Hair to treat Calf Woman."

"Yes. I must hurry. Sunshine Hair needs water for Calf Woman. I was wrong, Chief. Heammawihio sent her here, as you said."

"I am glad to hear you say this, Bull Elk."

"I have taken the needle, but my delay in calling for help for Calf Woman could mean her death. Sunshine Hair told me her condition is very serious."

"We will talk later," said War Bonnet. "Get the water and take it to Sunshine Hair."

While Silver Moon continued to pour small portions of the mixture into Calf Woman's sagging mouth, she said, "Breanna, is there any hope? Can she live when her fever has gone this high?"

"Not ordinarily."

"But it is possible?"

"It is possible. But only by the hand of her Creator."

Silver Moon paused. "By this you mean the white man's God."

"Silver Moon, the true and living God of heaven and earth is not just white man's God. He is the Creator of all mankind—all of earth and its creatures, and all of the heavens above. He—"

Bull Elk stepped inside the tepee with the pail of water. "I...I was listening before I came in. Sunshine Hair, you were speaking of the Creator, the true and living God...."

"Yes?"

"He is not just white man's God?"

"No. He gave His Son as a gift to all mankind as the way to the Father in heaven. The way to forgiveness of sin."

Silver Moon looked up and said, "Breanna, I have given all the medicine in the cup to Calf Woman."

"All right. Let's begin bathing her with the water. You bathe her wrists, and I'll bathe her neck and temples. We must cool the blood where the veins are most accessible."

Bull Elk set the pail of water beside his squaw and took some cloths out of a basket, handing them to Breanna. As the two women went to work, he stood over them and watched. "She is so very sick," he said, despair in his voice.

Breanna held a wet cloth against the jugular vein on Calf Woman's neck. She looked up at the shaman and said, "Bull Elk, if you will allow it, I will pray right now to the great Creator God through His Son, Jesus Christ, and ask Him to spare Calf Woman's life."

"You may pray to your God," he said, nodding.

Already on her knees, Breanna bowed her head and asked the Lord to spare Calf Woman's life. And she thanked Him for the salvation He offered by grace through faith in His crucifixion and resurrection.

Iron Hawk, who stood among the crowd outside, heard things he had never heard before. Bull Elk stood mesmerized by the white woman's words—by her earnest pleas for Calf Woman's life and the story of the Creator God that was emerging as she spoke.

Silver Moon continued to bathe Calf Woman's wrists, and for a moment she felt that Breanna was talking to the *real* God of the universe. This thought suddenly burned her heart, and she silently prayed for Heammawihio to forgive her for thinking he was not real.

When the villagers had retired to their tepees for the night, Chief War Bonnet and his squaw, Painted Flower, came to the opening of Bull Elk's tepee. Bull Elk invited them in. They found Iron Hawk kneeling beside Silver Moon as she used the cool water on Calf Woman. Breanna had just given the patient her third cup of the salicylic acid mixture.

"Is there any improvement, Sunshine Hair?" asked Painted Flower.

"Not yet, but at least she is no worse."

"Will your Jesus Christ God heal her?" asked War Bonnet.

"I believe He will, Chief. He told me in His Book to ask, and to believe He will give me what I ask for. I believe Calf Woman is going to live."

"Why has He not healed her by now?"

"He does things in His own time. Until He does, I will continue to give her the medicine and bathe her with the water. He expects me to do what I can to help her."

"We must tell you," said Painted Flower, "that the shamans have told He-Who-Walks-in-Rain the medicine is working well on everyone. All the sick ones are becoming cooler."

"I'm very glad to hear that," said Breanna, pulling a cloth from the pail and partially wringing it out. "Most people who die with smallpox die from the fever. Only a few die from the effects of the fever."

Silver Moon dipped cloths in the bucket and sighed.

"You're tired, little lady," said Breanna. "You go on to your tepee and get to bed."

"You are staying here to work on Calf Woman, are you not?"

"All night if I have to."

"Then I will stay with you."

"You are tired, child," Painted Flower said. "You go to your tepee and get some sleep. I will stay and help Sunshine Hair."

"It is not necessary for the squaw of our chief to do this," said Silver Moon. "I will stay."

Breanna patted the young girl's hand. "It is best that you get a good night's rest. I'll need your help in the morning."

"This is wise, Silver Moon," said Painted Flower. "It will not hurt the chief's squaw to stay and help."

Silver Moon rose to her feet. "All right. I will be ready to work again in the morning."

"I will walk you to your tepee, Silver Moon," said Iron Hawk.

She warmed the young man with a smile, then bent and hugged Breanna's neck. "I love you, Breanna," she said sweetly.

The words touched Breanna deeply. "I love you too," she said.

As Iron Hawk and Silver Moon walked down the path toward her tepee, he said, "Do you believe Sunshine Hair's God will heal Calf Woman?"

"If she is healed, I believe it will really be done by Heammawihio."

They drew up in front of her tepee.

"Iron Hawk has worked hard today," she said. "He must rest, too."

"I will. I..."

"Yes?"

"I believe you pleased Sunshine Hair when you told her you love her."

"I hope so. She is a wonderful person. I do love her."

"I am waiting for the day when you will use those words for me."

Silver Moon's smile was visible in the moonlight. "Good night," she said. "Thank you for walking me to my tepee." As she spoke she slipped inside.

The sound of gunfire, shouting men, screaming women and children, and neighing horses thundered in Silver Moon's ears. She was running through the village, her legs feeling heavy as she sought refuge from the man who had murdered her brother, mother, and the man she was to marry. She heard a choking, gasping sound....

Silver Moon raised up on her pallet with the realization that the sound was coming from her. A shudder ran through her as she looked around and saw the shadows on the wall of her tepee.

She covered her face with her hands and sucked in a short breath, muttering, "It is all right, Silver Moon. Just another horrible nightmare."

As she lay down, wiping cold sweat from her face, her hatred for John Chivington surfaced once more. If only I could see him die from a bullet I had put in his heart, she thought. Just so he lived long enough to know it was me who killed him.

↑

Inside Bull Elk's tepee, as the night hours passed, Breanna and Painted Flower continually bathed Calf Woman in cool water and periodically administered the salicylic acid mixture.

Bull Elk kept the small fire burning and sat beside it, cross-legged, arms folded over his chest. He watched the women intently for a moment then closed his eyes and swayed from side to side, his mouth set in a thin line.

When Calf Woman became delirious, tossing her head back and forth and mumbling words in Cheyenne, Painted Flower whispered, "She is speaking like a child."

Breanna nodded. "It's the fever. It's taking her back to her childhood in her mind."

Suddenly Calf Woman raised up and made a gagging sound, then fell back. Her eyes were closed, and she wasn't breathing.

"No!" cried Breanna.

Bull Elk's eyes flew open, and he stopped swaying. He and Painted Flower watched as Breanna desperately massaged Calf Woman's chest and said, "O Lord Jesus, please! Don't let her die!"

After a few seconds, Calf Woman coughed and started breathing again.

"Thank You, Lord!" Breanna said. "Thank You!"

Bull Elk and Painted Flower exchanged wide-eyed glances.

When Calf Woman was breathing normally again, Breanna went back to the bathing process, stopping after a while to let Painted Flower give her another cup of the salicylic acid mixture.

Footsteps were heard outside the tepee, and Bull Elk went to the flap and opened it.

"I am sorry to bother you, Bull Elk," said He-Who-Walks-in-Rain, "but we need Sunshine Hair. Little Star Light has the fever."

Breanna turned toward them. "Who is this?"

"It is daughter of warrior Two Arrows and Fawn Eyes. She is four grasses."

Breanna turned to Painted Flower and said, "Continue the bathing. I'll be back as soon as I can." Taking her medical bag with her, she rushed through the opening to follow the head medicine man.

Nearly an hour had passed when Breanna finally returned to Bull Elk's tepee. It was almost 4:00 A.M.

"How is Calf Woman?" she asked as she moved past Bull Elk, who had opened the flap for her.

"She is still very hot," Painted Flower said, "and has been talking like a child again."

"But she's breathed steadily?"

"Yes."

"How long since you gave her the medicine?"

"Right after you left."

"I'll give her some more."

"Is Star Light very sick?"

"Yes. I inoculated her today, but she was already coming down with the smallpox. She showed no signs of it then. I left some salicylic acid powders with the parents."

Bull Elk was sitting cross-legged again, arms folded. He rocked back and forth while Breanna worked at getting another cup of the mixture down Calf Woman. By the time she finished, there was a slight hint of gray light touching the east wall of the tepee.

Just then Calf Woman said, "Thank you...for...helping me."

Breanna bent over her patient and could see her eyes had

cleared. She laid a palm on the woman's brow and said to the others, "Her fever's broken!" Then she clapped her hands together joyfully and cried, "Thank You, Lord Jesus! Thank You!"

Bull Elk was so elated he forgot himself and said, "Yes! Thank You, Lord Jesus! Thank You…" He flicked a glance at Painted Flower, blushed, then took Calf Woman's hand in his and kept his eyes on her face.

Painted Flower gazed at Bull Elk in amazement, unable to believe her ears. She silently wondered what Heammawihio thought of his outburst.

At sunrise, a bone-tired Breanna was inside Two Arrows's tepee, checking little Star Light. The child's fever had not come down.

Covering a yawn, Breanna said to the parents, "Silver Moon is preparing some breakfast for me. You keep the cool water on Star Light, give her some more medicine, and I'll be back very soon."

In twenty minutes, Breanna and Silver Moon were back at Two Arrows's tepee, working on the fevered child. They had placed her pallet just outside the opening. Star Light was conscious but dull-eyed. As the parents looked on, holding their two older children close to them, Breanna noticed Chief War Bonnet and Bull Elk coming along the path.

"Will the child be all right?" War Bonnet asked.

"She is very sick, Chief. But I've been silently praying to my God, asking Him to make her well. We are doing everything we can for her."

"That is good," said the chief. "I have come to thank you, Sunshine Hair, for the work you have done with our sick ones, and for the sleepless night you spent to save Calf Woman's life."

"Yes," said Bull Elk. "I am here to say thank you again. Calf Woman is resting well now."

"I am so happy she is out of danger." Breanna paused for only a moment, then added, "My wonderful Jesus, the Great Physician, was very good to spare Calf Woman's life."

War Bonnet nodded with a tight smile, but did not comment. He spoke some encouraging words to the parents of little Star Light, then turned and walked away.

Before following his chief, Bull Elk leaned close to Breanna and said, "I would like to hear more about your Great Physician, Sunshine Hair, and so would Calf Woman."

"I will come to your tepee as soon as I can, Bull Elk, and tell both of you more about Him."

Bull Elk nodded, then walked away.

Breanna looked into Silver Moon's dark, expressive eyes that reflected her confusion and dismay. Lord, she prayed silently, please let me lead Silver Moon to You before I leave this village.

She turned to the little four-year-old girl and gave her another dose of the salicylic acid mixture, then instructed her parents to continue bathing her while she and Silver Moon checked on the other patients. For the most part they found a dramatic lessening of fever in those who were sick. Still, a few needed more medicine.

While they worked over a small boy, Silver Moon said, "You were going to tell me about your husband, Breanna."

"Oh my...it's hard to know where to begin. John is the most wonderful man I have ever met."

While they moved from one patient to another, Breanna sang the praises of the man who had been known for so long as the Stranger. She told Silver Moon how they met when John appeared from out of nowhere during a fierce thunderstorm on the Kansas plains and saved her life during a cattle stampede. Then she told the highlights of their courtship, right up to their wedding three months ago.

When Breanna finished her story she said, "Now, what about Silver Moon? She is at least twenty grasses, yet she is not married."

"Twenty-three grasses to be exact."

"I see Iron Hawk around a great deal of the time. Are you promised to each other?"

"I am very fond of Iron Hawk. He is a fine young man. But we are not promised to each other."

"He is in love with you. I see it in his eyes."

"Yes. Iron Hawk has asked me to be his squaw, but I cannot allow myself to fall in love with him."

Breanna eyed her curiously. "Cannot *allow* yourself? What do you mean?"

Silver Moon started to say something, then closed her eyes as if steeling herself against a deep inward pain.

Breanna stopped what she was doing with a patient, touched her new friend's arm, and said, "Someone has hurt you, hasn't he?"

"Not in the way you might think," Silver Moon said, wiping tears from her eyes. "It is not that some young man I was in love with turned away from me and broke my heart."

"Then how did someone hurt you? Who was it?"

Silver Moon pressed a hand to her lips and blinked against more tears as she said, "I will tell you *who* it was. Then I will tell you what he did. I really have been wanting to talk to you about it." Silver Moon took a deep breath and said, "Have you heard of Colonel John Chivington?"

"Yes. I know about him. He was a big hero during the Civil War. And he was a low-down skunk when he attacked the

Cheyenne village at Sand Creek a few years ago."

Silver Moon said shakily, "John Chivington is the man who hurt me, Breanna."

"He is? How?"

"Do you remember the name of the Cheyenne chief whose village Chivington attacked at Sand Creek?"

"I believe it was Black Kettle."

"You asked about my father having a village, and being a chief…"

"Yes?"

"Black Kettle was my father."

16

BREANNA'S FACE BLANCHED and her throat tightened. "You're Black Kettle's daughter?"

"I am."

"Then you were at Sand Creek when Chivington and his troops massacred hundreds of women and children. You saw it all."

"Yes," said Silver Moon, wiping a palm across her eyes.

"You would have been...how old?"

"Fifteen. I was with my mother, Gentle Dove, and my younger brother, Sky Eagle. We were trying to get to a safe place, and Chivington rode up on us, grinning like a devil. It all happened so fast. Before I knew it, he had shot Sky Eagle and my mother, killing them. Chivington fired at me, but somehow he missed. The bullet came so close to my head that it knocked me down. I had a rock in my hand. I don't even remember picking it up. Chivington lined his gun on me again. But Bear Paw—" She closed her eyes and took a deep breath. "Bear Paw, the one I had been promised to, came from somewhere close by. I did not see him until just before he threw himself in front of me and took the bullet. Chivington aimed his gun at me again and pulled the trigger. But the gun was empty. I still had the rock, and I threw it at his head as hard as I could. It struck him in the face. I turned and ran. I remember looking back at him, and his face was bloodied. Later, my father and I ended up hiding along Sand Creek while the soldiers rode away."

"Silver Moon," said Breanna in a hushed voice, "what a horrible nightmare for you to experience! Then to go through almost the same thing again in the Custer attack in Oklahoma. Was Black Kettle's wife who was killed with him on the Washita your stepmother?"

"Yes...Little Sparrow was her name. I loved her very much. But I was not in the village on the Washita River when Custer attacked my people."

"Oh?"

"I was in Ohio." Bitterness rose in Silver Moon's eyes, turning them blacker than ever. "You spoke of the nightmare I lived through at Sand Creek, Breanna. I have relived that nightmare over and over again all these years...awake and asleep. I have awakened in the night countless times in a cold sweat, having watched my loved ones shot down one more time, and—and I have seen the ugly, evil face of John Chivington behind his smoking gun, his devil eyes burning into my mind." Silver Moon took a deep breath and went on. "I went to Ohio for one purpose. Chivington was living there. I went to kill him." Fierce hatred etched itself on Silver Moon's face. "I would like to see George Custer dead for what he did on the Washita... but my greater desire is to see John Chivington dead at my own hand!"

Breanna considered the implications of all she had heard, then said, "You did not find Chivington in Ohio?"

"No. He had already headed back to the West. Justice was not served, Breanna. But somehow...some way...someday I will find him and final justice will be served. Heammawihio will one day deliver him into my hand."

"Silver Moon," Breanna said, "there's no way I can understand your feelings about the Sand Creek Massacre, nor how you feel toward Chivington. But carrying this hatred and bitterness inside you will dry up your soul. You're a sweet and loving young woman. Please don't let this destroy you."

"I will never find peace until I know Chivington is dead. The spirits of my mother, my brother, and Bear Paw will never rest until he has paid for what he did. I know that. Nothing would give me more pleasure than to be the one who ends his life." The bitterness eased slightly as Silver Moon looked into the face of this woman who had shown her people so much love. "Now do you understand why I cannot allow myself to fall in love with Iron Hawk, Breanna? My heart is filled with hatred for Chivington. There is no room in my heart to be in love with Iron Hawk. I have told him this. I have even told him he should find someone else to love and marry, but he says if he does not marry me, he will live his life without a squaw."

"Iron Hawk is a fine young man, Silver Moon. You should not miss a happy life as his squaw to feed your hatred for John Chivington. Your chances of ever finding the man are next to impossible. And believe me, the vengeance you want would not be as sweet as you imagine. Evil men have a way of getting what they deserve. God's Book says, 'Whoso diggeth a pit shall fall therein: and he that rolleth a stone, it will return upon him.'"

The pit. Yes, I would love to be the one to shove Chivington into the pit, and I would love to be the one to give the stone a big push! And it would be sweet…very, very sweet!

Breanna looked up and saw Two Arrows hurrying toward her.

"Sunshine Hair!" he called. "Star Light is getting worse! We need you."

Breanna gave the cup of medicine to Silver Moon, telling her to finish giving the dose to the boy and to continue the bathing process. Moments later, she knelt beside little Star Light and was dismayed to find her fever had gone higher.

Fawn Eyes looked at Breanna with red and swollen eyes. "What can you do, Sunshine Hair? The medicine seems to have no effect on her, and the water does not cool her."

Breanna sighed. "We will keep bathing her with the water, but what she really needs is ice. Her fever has got to come down, or she...her little body needs to be packed in ice."

"Ice?" said Two Arrows. "You are not wanting to say it, but Star Light will die if the fever does not come down, and it will take ice to do it?"

"Yes."

"But we are still in summer," came Fawn Eyes's strained voice. "There will be no ice until many moons have passed. There is no hope for our little Star Light."

Iron Hawk came along the path and stopped. "I was just with Silver Moon," he said. "She told me Star Light is not doing well."

"Sunshine Hair says she will die unless the fever comes down soon, Iron Hawk," said Two Arrows, his countenance drawn. "The water is not cold enough. She needs to be packed in ice."

"Ice? Without ice she will die?"

"Yes," said Breanna. "Nothing we've done has helped her."

"But there is no ice at this time of year."

"Only when it hails," said Breanna.

Fawn Eyes looked toward the sky. "There are only white clouds. No storm clouds. And even when it rains here on the prairie, it does not usually hail."

Breanna ran her gaze over their faces. The Spirit of God

seemed to prod her heart. "It would if the Almighty God of heaven were to make it hail," she said firmly.

"He certainly made Calf Woman's body cool down when you prayed, Sunshine Hair," said Iron Hawk.

"I have prayed the same for Star Light," said Breanna, "but He has not seen fit to answer as He did for Calf Woman. I believe He wants to show His mighty hand in another way."

"You will pray for hail?" asked Two Arrows.

"Do I need War Bonnet's permission this time?"

"You would get it, I am sure," said Two Arrows, "but you have my permission...and you have Fawn Eyes's permission. We are the parents."

Breanna knelt beside Star Light and took hold of her feverish little hand. To her amazement, Iron Hawk knelt with her. The parents went to their knees, too, as their other two children looked on.

Breanna bowed her head and said, "Lord, You said in Your Book, 'Call unto me, and I will answer thee, and shew thee great and mighty things, which thou knowest not.' What we need right now is a hailstorm, Lord. We need a great and mighty thing from You right now. I'll tell it to Your glory before these people, Father. For the sake of this little child's life, I ask in the precious name of Jesus Christ, Your Son and my Saviour...bring a hailstorm. Quickly."

High in the Rocky Mountains of Colorado, John Chivington left the sparkling waters of a small creek that flowed into the Fraser River and headed down the side of the mountain. After a full day of panning, he had a small cloth sack half full of tiny gold nuggets. Not bad for a day's work, he told himself.

Chivington returned to his cabin and stashed the gold

under the floorboard where he had found the original cache, built a fire in the cookstove, and put on the coffeepot. Then he went to the small barn and corral to feed and water his horse.

Back at the cabin Chivington poured coffee into a tin cup. As he turned toward the table, he caught a glimpse of his gaunt, haggard face in the small mirror hanging beside the cupboard. He studied his reflection for a long moment, then shook his head and sighed. He unbuckled his gun belt and wrapped the belt around the holster, then laid the Colt .45 on the table and sat down.

You really should eat, John, said the voice inside his head. If you don't, you won't be able to pan gold. You'll starve to death.

Chivington swallowed a mouthful of the hot liquid and said out loud, "So what would be so bad about starving to death? At least if I was dead, I wouldn't have to live this hermit's life. And I wouldn't have to live with this fear—always looking over my shoulder, always listening for footsteps behind me, always having those horrid nightmares. What would be so bad about that?"

He rose from the table and poured more steaming coffee into his cup. Just as he was moving toward the table, he heard footsteps on the porch. The sound made him jump, and he swore under his breath when the coffee sloshed onto his hand. In one smooth move he set the cup on the table and pulled his gun from its holster.

Chivington kept heavy burlap sacks over the windows for privacy, but he made out the shadow of a man passing the window next to the door. Suddenly there was a loud knock. He held the Colt .45 in a two-handed grip, both hands trembling as he aimed the muzzle at the rough-hewn door and called, "Who is it?"

"Colonel Chivington?" came a familiar voice. But he

couldn't think whose it was. "Sir, it's Scott Anthony! I've come a long way to see you!"

Anthony. Yes, of course. Major Scott Anthony.

"Sir?"

"Coming!" said Chivington, placing the gun back in its holster. He crossed the room, slid back the dead bolt, and opened the door. The lantern light from inside the cabin threw an orange glow on Anthony's face.

Anthony's brow furrowed as he focused on Chivington's haggard features and said, "Sir, it's good to see you!"

A smile crept across Chivington's lips—something rare these days. "Come in, Scott! Come in!"

The old friends shook hands, then Anthony said, "You look pale, sir...and you've lost a lot of weight. I hardly recognized you."

"Yeah, I have lost a little flesh. How about a cup of coffee? Fresh pot over here."

"Sure."

When the coffee was poured and the old friends were sitting across from each other at the table, Chivington said, "I want to know what's been happening with you, Scott, but first...how did you find me?"

"I was passing through Denver a few days ago, and I remembered it used to be your home. You know, when you were with the church. So I started asking around and found a couple of men who used to be under you in the army at Camp Weld. They were corporals back then. Jess Andrews and Darren Rebhorn. Remember 'em?"

Chivington rubbed his temples. "No, can't say as I do."

"Well, anyhow, they'd heard you were living up here in the mountains near Granby."

"I didn't think anybody knew I was here, except the assayer

in town and the folks who run the general store."

Anthony shrugged. "Guess maybe one of them must've told somebody who was passing through. Who knows?"

"Yeah. Who knows."

"Well, I've got a little time on my hands right now, so I decided to rent me a horse and ride up here. See if I could find you. When I got to Granby, I started asking around. I happened onto the assayer, Charlie Fremont. He's the one who told me how to find you."

"Well, Scott, I'm sure glad you did. It's really good to see you again."

"You too, sir. Only I hate to see you looking so pale and thin-faced and all. Have you been sick?"

"No. Not what you'd call sick."

Anthony looked at the gun on the table, then said, "When you opened the door, you looked a little scared. What's wrong, sir?"

Chivington took a gulp of coffee then said, "I live in fear, Scott. All the time."

"From what?"

"Indians. Cheyenne. Survivors of the Sand Creek thing. I have nightmares about them coming after me. I often wake up at night when there's a strange sound, fearful that they've come to torture and kill me." He took a deep breath. "And now I'm even more scared. *You* found me. That means they can too."

"Well, one thing's for sure, Colonel…if it's Indians, you won't hear a sound. You probably heard me walk onto the porch."

"Yeah."

"If it was a vengeful Cheyenne, you wouldn't hear his approach."

"I know that, but my nerves are shot. Besides, living alone

with nobody to talk to is tough on the nerves too."

"The assayer told me you make your living by panning for gold."

"Mm-hmm."

"Isn't there something else you'd rather do? I mean, especially living out here all by yourself with nobody but the birds and the chipmunks to talk to?"

Chivington sighed. "I've tried to get a job as a lawman, but with that black mark Congress and the army put on me, nobody will hire me. I tried to get on as a deputy sheriff in Denver, but I got turned down."

"That's too bad."

Chivington looked at the worn wood of the table and said, "I think I'll let a little more time pass, then try it again in Denver. I see by the newspapers that they've got a new sheriff in Denver County. Fella named Curt Langan. Maybe since he's new, I can get hired when I apply again."

"It's worth a try. I hate to see you living up here all by yourself."

"Well, that's enough about me. What's been happening in Scott Anthony's life since he got kicked out of the army?"

"First thing was…when the shame came, Maryanne left me. Divorced me. Took the children. I have no idea where they are. I've been drifting around, taking odd jobs ever since. It's been pretty rough. Too many people know about Sand Creek and still carry a healthy grudge toward us."

"Yeah. Tell me about it!"

"However, a little good fortune has come my way. I just landed a good job with a friend who's got a big ranch down in Texas. Job won't start for another couple of weeks. That's what I meant when I said I had a little time on my hands. I'll go back to Denver from here and take a train to Austin." Anthony drank the last of his coffee, smacked his lips, and said, "You make pretty good coffee, Colonel. Got any more in that pot?"

When a fresh cup was poured for both, Anthony said, "You know, Colonel, I still remember that day at Sand Creek as if it were yesterday. Indians lying everywhere. You remember when that—"

"Let's don't talk about it. I have nightmares about it 'most every night. I see those bodies strewn and scattered everywhere."

Anthony looked surprised, then frowned. "Colonel, you telling me you're sorry we did it? I thought you said the only good Indian was a dead Indian." He chuckled. "We sure made a lot of good Indians that day!"

Chivington's hands began to tremble. "Scott, I never really saw myself for what I was. Not until those government investigations took place and the ignominy of our actions at Sand Creek was put in print. When I read those reports, I realized what a heartless and bloody man I was. The nightmares have almost driven me out of my mind. Sometimes I see the Cheyenne—women and children especially—crawl up out of their graves, pointing accusing fingers at me. I...I wake up in a cold sweat. I'm afraid I'll never stop dreaming about them. I can't eat, I can't sleep. Some nights I lie awake till dawn, afraid to go to sleep for fear I'll have another nightmare."

"Sir," said Anthony, "I'm sorry to hear this. You need to keep your mind occupied on other things. You need to be with other people...anything to keep your mind off Sand Creek. I'm sorry I brought it up."

"Don't be, Scott. How could you know what's been going on with me?"

Anthony began talking about other things—politics, the weather, the price of gold, his Texas rancher friend and the details about his new job. As it grew late he said, "Well, Colonel, I'd best be going."

"Where you going this time of night?"

"To bed, where you should be going too. I've got a room at the hotel in Granby. I'll head east in the morning."

Both men rose from the table.

"I'd invite you to stay here for the night, but all I have is that bed over there that I sleep on. But I could sleep on the floor and—"

"That's all right, sir. I've already paid for the room."

Chivington stood on the porch and watched his old friend ride away. Soon the dark night swallowed horse and rider. Chivington hurried inside and bolted the door, then went to the cupboard to make some more coffee. With all the talk about Sand Creek, he knew he would have nightmares if he slept.

When he had polished off the final cup of coffee, he turned the lantern down low and eased back in the worn-out, over-stuffed cowhide chair, a legacy from the previous owner. He occupied his mind by thinking about his childhood in Ohio and his growing-up years. Several times his eyes grew heavy, and his head jerked up. Finally, in spite of the coffee and his efforts to stay awake, he fell asleep in the chair....

Chivington led his men as they galloped down the slope toward the Cheyenne village on Sand Creek. Silver-haired Indian men, as well as children and women, fell under the barrage of rifle fire. What few warriors were in the village fired back, while most of the people tried to run away.

Suddenly Chivington was in the scene he had relived so many times. After shooting down the young boy who had tried to wrest the revolver from his hand, Chivington saw the Cheyenne woman running toward the fallen boy. Chivington squeezed the trigger and hit her square in the chest. She fell, facedown.

A teenage girl screamed at him and leaned over to pick up a rock. He fired at her, but his horse moved and spoiled his aim. He snapped the hammer back to take another shot, but a young Cheyenne buck jumped in front of the girl, taking the bullet. The girl wailed, crying out a name Chivington couldn't distinguish. She looked up at him, her face frozen in terror. Every detail of the girl's frightened features was etched into his brain.

He lined the revolver on her again and squeezed the trigger. The hammer dropped on a spent shell. As he started to reload, something struck him on the forehead. Blood was running into his eyes, blinding him. All he could see on the screen of his mind was the terrified face of the Indian girl....

Chivington sat bolt upright in the chair, gasping for breath. Had he heard a wild cry somewhere outside? Or was it just an echo from the nightmare?

He blinked and stared around the one-room cabin, but something obstructed his vision. It was the girl's face. It was as if her face were stamped on his very eyes, and he had to look through her to see the room around him.

Chivington cursed himself for falling asleep. His pulse pounded in his temples. Would he never be able to erase the horror of that face from his mind?

He rose from the chair and moved to the cupboard by the dim light of the lantern. He dipped water from the pail and took several gulps, then replaced the dipper and wiped the excess water from his mouth with his sleeve.

"You've got to stay awake, John," he mumbled. "Stay awake."

He eased himself into the cowhide chair once more and held himself rigid. He closed his eyes and thought about the last week of March 1862. Glorieta Pass. Nobody had done an investigation on the Battle of Glorieta Pass. Oh no. Colonel John M. Chivington was the Union's big hero there. Because of his leadership in that battle, the Confederacy's grand dream of expanding their military might to the Pacific was dissolved once and for all. Glorieta Pass became known as the "Gettsyburg of the West," and what Colonel Joshua L. Chamberlain was to Gettysburg, Colonel John M. Chivington was to Glorieta Pass—the Union's champion.

Chivington's thoughts grew hazy. Soon his head dropped forward onto his chest, and he slept.

17

⬧

SUDDENLY THE HERO of Glorieta Pass found himself in a Cheyenne burial ground. Indians—or at least what had been Indians—were crawling out of graves, their near-skeletal bodies withered and wrinkled. The stench of death was all around, repugnant and overpowering.

On their foreheads, the warriors wore red-and-white head-bands with single eagle feathers standing erect behind their nearly fleshless skulls. The women and children wore head-bands that marked them as Cheyenne, as did the old men, whose silver hair hung in clumps.

Terror prickled Chivington's scalp as the young man who had taken the bullet for the girl emerged from his grave. On either side of him, two more of the living dead were climbing out of graves. Chivington recognized the boy who had attempted to wrest the revolver from his hand and the boy's mother.

The dead Indians walked toward Chivington. Terror made him fight for each breath. He was unable to speak, and when he tried to run, his legs were leaden weights that wouldn't let him move.

As the Indians came closer they wailed: "Chivington! Chivington!" Their hollow eyes were coals of fire, and they pointed accusing fingers at him. "We trusted you! You murdered us! You must join us! Vengeance is ours! We want you! You must di-i-e-e!"

"No-o-o! No-o-o! Please forgive me! I'm sorry! So sorry!"

Suddenly Chivington found himself on the floor of his cabin. He had fallen from the chair and was looking up at the ceiling. The dancing shadows seemed to be the walking dead, come to take him to the grave. He was drenched with perspiration, and he quaked with terror.

He felt a moment of sweet relief when he realized he had been dreaming again. As his heartbeat slowly returned to its normal pace, John Chivington groped his way to the chair and buried his head in his hands. When the shaking wouldn't stop, he began to weep uncontrollably.

Fawn Eyes, Two Arrows, and Iron Hawk remained on their knees while Breanna pleaded with her heavenly Father for hail so that little Star Light might live. Many other Cheyenne stood nearby and wondered at this white woman who had come to help them.

"Lord Jesus," Breanna prayed, holding the little girl's hand, "this precious child deserves to live. Lord, You said, 'Whatsoever ye shall ask in my name, that will I do, that the Father may be glorified in the Son. If ye shall ask anything in my name, I will do it.' Lord Jesus, when You send the hail and this little girl's life is spared because of it, I will tell it to this entire village. I will tell it so that in the eyes of these people, the Father will be glorified in the Son."

Such words Fawn Eyes, Two Arrows, and Iron Hawk had

never heard before, but they felt the power of them. Sunshine Hair had a hold on her God.

And then the three were stunned to feel a cold wind whip across the prairie, flapping the walls of the tepees. They looked toward the sky and saw dark clouds prowling across the plains from the north as if they had been waiting there for orders from Sunshine Hair's God.

The wind smelled of rain.

By the time a tearful Breanna closed her prayer, the sun was covered by heavy black clouds and there was lightning to the north, followed by the distant rumble of thunder.

The trio rose to their feet, as did Breanna. She looked at the sky and said, "Let's take Star Light inside the tepee. It's going to rain and hail."

All of the other patients were carried into tepees as the wind grew stronger and the storm came south.

When Star Light was inside the tepee along with her parents, her siblings, and Iron Hawk, Breanna went back to the opening and looked skyward. "Thank You, Lord," she murmured. "Thank You for being the faithful and true God You are."

She felt shoulders brush her own and turned to see Fawn Eyes on one side and Iron Hawk on the other. Two Arrows stood behind them. They watched in wordless wonder as the swirling black clouds bore down on the village.

After a moment Iron Hawk said, "Sunshine Hair, you are right. There is hail in those clouds."

"Yes, there is. Fawn Eyes, I'm going to need a heavy blanket to put Star Light in when the hail comes. She must be wrapped in it, and we will pack the ice in the blanket with her."

"I have blankets," said the hopeful mother. "I will get one."

"Good. Until there is enough hail to pack her in, we will

continue to bathe her with cool water, and I will also give her another dose of the medicine."

In less than a quarter hour, rain began to fall. Lightning slashed the sky with daggers of white fire. Thunder boomed like cannonade. Before long there were tiny ice crystals mixed with the rain, and soon the rain had turned to hail. It pelted the sides of the tepees and bounced on the ground. Although the ice pellets were small, causing no damage to the tepees, they began to cover the ground and fill up the low places.

Cheers went up all over the village.

Two Arrows reached for a leather pail. "I will go pick up the ice."

"I will go with you," said Iron Hawk. "Do you have another pail?"

Two Arrows produced a second pail, and both men went out into the storm.

When the men returned, dripping wet, Breanna had the sick child lying on the blanket. "Pour it on both sides of her," she said to the men. "And go get more, quickly."

Two Arrows and Iron Hawk went back outside and filled the pails as fast as they could. Suddenly Bull Elk was beside them, and three more warriors arrived with pails. Soon there was plenty of ice to pack around the little girl, and more on the way.

Fawn Eyes held Star Light in her arms while Breanna pressed handfuls of ice to her cheeks and neck. The little girl was barely conscious—hardly aware of the sudden cold that encased her body. Several pails of ice stood ready for use if Breanna needed them.

Suddenly the wind subsided and the hail stopped. It rained for a few minutes; then the clouds broke up.

Some of the people left their tepees and gathered outside

Two Arrows's tepee. As Two Arrows thanked the men who had gathered hail, War Bonnet and He-Who-Walks-in-Rain threaded their way through the press and stopped just in front of the tepee.

"What has happened here?" War Bonnet asked Two Arrows.

"Sunshine Hair told us that unless she could pack ice around Star Light, the fever would only get worse and take her life. Fawn Eyes and I despaired, saying there would be no ice until winter came. And then—" Two Arrows's voice broke. "And then Sunshine Hair told us she would pray to her God and ask Him to send a hailstorm so she would have ice to pack Star Light in."

The crowd stayed close to Two Arrows's tepee, waiting to hear how it went with little Star Light. The child had been ice-packed for an hour when the crowd heard her say a few words, followed by the sound of Fawn Eyes bursting into tears. Two Arrows stuck his head inside the tepee. Breanna whispered something to him, and he began to weep, rushing inside to his squaw and daughter.

Breanna stepped outside the tepee and lifted her voice as she ran her tear-filled gaze over the crowd. "You will all be glad to know that Star Light's fever has finally broken. She is past her crisis. She is going to live!"

The people cheered and whooped at the news.

Iron Hawk saw Silver Moon and went to her side. His voice held excitement as he said, "Sunshine Hair has prayed again, and another life has been saved!"

Silver Moon smiled slightly and nodded her head. "Yes, it is wonderful that Star Light is better."

By now the sun's warmth had melted the remaining hail on the prairie. There was a slight breeze, and the air smelled sweet and clean. Every shaman left his or her patient to assemble and learn of Star Light. There was no danger in leaving the patients now, for every one of them was doing better. All fevers had come down. This report was given to He-Who-Walks-in-Rain, who in turn told the chief.

Breanna started to go back inside the tepee when War Bonnet said, "Sunshine Hair, this chief has something to say to you."

She turned back. "Yes, Chief War Bonnet?"

Even the stalwart Cheyenne leader showed emotion. Tears filmed his eyes, and his voice cracked slightly as he said, "On behalf of my people, and as their chief, I want to say that we deeply appreciate what you have done for us. Many lives have been lost to the smallpox, as you whites call it. But since you came yesterday and began your treatments, our sick ones are on the way to recovery. I...can see that the God you serve must respect you very much. He listens when you pray, and He does as you ask. Our little Star Light and our Calf Woman are alive and will go on living because your Jesus Christ God has answered your prayers."

"Chief War Bonnet," Breanna said, "you honor me with your kind words. But the praise and honor go to my God for the fact that Calf Woman's fever went away when it appeared she would die. And the praise and honor go to my God for sending the hail that Star Light might live.

"When I say *my* God, I do not mean He is—as some believe—white man's God. When I say *my* God, I mean that He became my God and friend when I heard about His Son, the Lord Jesus Christ, and opened my heart to Him. The great God and Creator of this world made human beings with different colors of skin, yes. But He loves all of them, including the red men.

"All of us know there is evil in the world. This evil comes from a wicked being that God's Word calls Satan, the devil. According to God's Word, Satan tempted the very first man and woman God put on the earth. They followed the devil and sinned. This sin was passed on to the entire human race from that man and woman, who are our ancestors.

"God's Word tells us that because of this, all of us are sinners by nature and sinners by choice. God is holy, and He is righteous. He hates sin and will not allow it to come to His home in the sky. Sinful human beings like me, like you, must have our sins forgiven and washed away before we die, so we can go to God's home in the sky, which He calls heaven.

"God has provided the way for our cleansing and forgiveness. Many years ago, He sent His one and only Son, the Lord Jesus Christ, into this world to pay the price for the sins of all mankind...including the Cheyenne people. A price of blood and death must be paid because God's holiness and righteousness cannot ignore sin. That price must be paid by a perfect, sinless human being. There were none like this on earth, so God sent His perfect, sinless Son to take on human flesh, die the death, shed His blood, and pay the price. He did this because He loves us so very much. He wants to forgive us and cleanse us."

There was no sound except for a few low voices translating her words, and Breanna realized she had their full attention.

"God's Son, Jesus Christ, sacrificed Himself and shed His blood on an instrument of death to pay for the sin of all humanity. But He did not stay dead, Chief War Bonnet. He raised Himself from the dead and is alive—not only to send hailstorms when they are needed and to bring down fevers so that lives can be saved, but to save us from sin's penalty. He does this when we believe His Word, turn from our sin, put our complete faith in Him, and ask Him to save us. When we do this, He not only saves us, He washes away our sins in His blood, and He will take us to heaven when we die."

To nearly all the people, Breanna's words about the Lord were strange, but they smiled and nodded, showing respect to the loving woman who had saved them from the smallpox. War Bonnet thanked Breanna again for all she had done, and the crowd dispersed.

Silver Moon and Iron Hawk went to check on the patients, and Breanna went back inside the tepee to see how little Star Light was doing. The child was talking, though her voice was weak. With a little prompting from her parents she thanked Sunshine Hair for what she had done. She spoke in Cheyenne, and Fawn Eyes translated. Breanna took Star Light in her arms, kissed her cheek, and held her close.

At the sound of a hand clap outside the tepee, Two Arrows raised the flap and found Bull Elk standing there.

"I would like to speak to Sunshine Hair," said the shaman. He smiled when he saw Breanna holding the child. "Sunshine Hair said she would come to our tepee when she was able. Calf Woman and I want her to know we are looking forward to her visit."

Breanna warmed him with a smile. "I could come right now, Bull Elk, if it is all right."

"Yes. Right now would be very good."

As Breanna and the medicine man walked toward his tepee, Bull Elk said, "I told Calf Woman what you said after the hail came."

"You mean about Jesus Christ and His death for sinners?"

"Yes. We both want to hear more about your Jesus Christ."

Breanna's heart pounded with joy as she said, "Let's stop at Silver Moon's tepee. I'll pick up my Bible."

✦

There was a chill in the night air as darkness blanketed the prairie and the moon lifted its orange rim over the eastern edge of the earth. The coyotes began their haunting, mournful howls; the stars blossomed and grew brighter; and a light wind rustled the grass and toyed with the treetops.

Silver Moon had eaten the evening meal with Iron Hawk and several families and was being escorted to her tepee by the young warrior. The topic during the meal had been the miraculous arrival of the hailstorm, and Iron Hawk continued to talk of it as they walked along the path.

When they reached the tepee, Silver Moon noted there was no fire burning within. "Apparently Breanna is still with Bull Elk and Calf Woman in their tepee."

"They no doubt fed her," Iron Hawk said.

"Yes, but I hope she will come soon and take her rest tonight. She must be very tired."

"I am glad she will be sleeping in your tepee. You do have an extra pallet?"

"I will see that she is comfortable."

A mournful howl rode the night wind, coming from somewhere out on the prairie.

Iron Hawk ran his gaze over the moonlit land. "Coyote calling for his mate."

"Yes," said Silver Moon.

"Maybe he has no mate, but his eye is on a female coyote who greatly attracts him. Maybe—"

"I must go in now, Iron Hawk."

"I will live for the next moment I see you," he said softly.

"Good night," was all she said, then slipped inside the tepee, dropping the flap.

Iron Hawk waited until Silver Moon had a fire going, then moved like a shadow down the path to his own tepee.

Moments later, Silver Moon heard Breanna call to her from outside. "Come in," Silver Moon said, opening the flap. "The wind is cold."

Breanna's face shone in spite of her weariness as she entered the tepee and placed her Bible by her overnight bag. Silver Moon eyed the Bible and said, "That is your sacred Book?"

"Yes. The Book that gives us God's words to man."

"Two Arrows told Iron Hawk and me that you were spending some time with Bull Elk and Calf Woman."

"Yes."

"Did they feed you?"

"Yes. Bull Elk did the cooking. Calf Woman isn't quite up to it yet."

"I am glad you had supper. I know you are very tired. This pallet is yours. It is time you took your rest." Silver Moon paused and looked intently at Breanna. "Your face. It looks like the sun is shining on it."

"Is it that noticeable?"

"How can you look so happy and be as tired as I know you are?"

"Oh, I just had such a wonderful time with Bull Elk and Calf Woman," she said, smiling.

"It is good. I am sure that seeing Calf Woman alive when she would have been dead is a great help to you. And of course, the same with Star Light."

"Yes. A great help."

Silver Moon glanced at the overnight bag where Breanna had placed the Bible. "You were reading to Bull Elk and Calf Woman from your sacred Book?"

"They had some questions about Jesus Christ. I showed them what they wanted to know from its pages."

Breanna sat down on the pallet and began untying her shoelaces. Silver Moon eased down on her own pallet, keeping her eyes on the lady with the sunshine hair.

"How much longer will you be staying with us?"

Breanna slipped her right shoe off and laid it aside. "Well, honey, I guess I'll stay another day and night, just to make sure the sick ones are fully on the road to recovery. Then I'll ask Chief War Bonnet if there's a horse I can borrow to ride to Cheyenne City, and someone to ride along with me and bring the horse back. From there I'll take a train home to Denver."

"I am sure Iron Hawk would be more than glad to escort you there. Possibly some of the other braves will go along."

"That would be nice. I'll ask Chief War Bonnet about it tomorrow."

Silver Moon studied Breanna for a moment. "I am sure you will be very happy to be with your husband again."

Breanna's eyes lit up. "You're right about that! He's such a wonderful man, Silver Moon. I wish there was some way you could meet him."

"Is he handsome?"

"Very. And he's quite tall. I can always find him when we're in a crowd. He stands above almost everyone else. And like Iron Hawk, he is very muscular."

"Does…does he tell you he loves you quite often?"

"When we're together, many times a day."

"Does he find different ways to say it…like if he hears a coyote howl, that it is probably a lonely male coyote who is lonesome for the female he loves?"

Breanna scrutinized her friend and said, "I think maybe you've heard something like that before. Was it Bear Paw?"

Silver Moon looked down and said softly, "No. It was Iron Hawk."

"I see. Silver Moon…"

The young woman raised her black eyes to meet Breanna's gaze.

"When are you going to give in and admit that you're in love with that young man?"

"I…I am not in love with him. I am fond of him, but I am not in love with him."

A silence fell between them as Breanna finished untying her left shoe and pulled it off.

Silver Moon leaned toward Breanna and took hold of her hand. "I will miss you when you are gone. I will miss you very, very much."

Breanna squeezed Silver Moon's hand. "I will miss you too, young lady."

Tears were visible in Silver Moon's eyes. She fought down the lump in her throat and said, "You must get to sleep."

After they had changed into their nightclothes, Silver Moon lay down on her pallet, then noticed that Breanna had picked up her Bible.

"What are you doing?"

"I always read my Bible before I go to sleep."

"Oh. That Book that tells all about your Jesus Christ?"

"Yes."

"You said today that your Jesus Christ sacrificed Himself on an instrument of death for you."

"Yes. Not just for me. For Silver Moon too."

"What kind of an instrument of death was it?"

"It was a cross of wood. His arms were stretched out on the crosspiece and nails were driven through His hands to hold him there. His feet were nailed to the vertical piece."

"*Nailed?* Do you mean with iron nails like white men use to build wagons?"

"Yes. Exactly."

Silver Moon frowned. "Would you tell me about this cross of wood?"

Breanna smiled. "I would be most happy to do that." Breanna opened her Bible with a prayer in her heart that the Lord would give her wisdom.

18

SILVER MOON WAS STRUGGLING in her heart. To turn to this Jesus Christ Breanna had just told her about would mean she would have to turn her back on Heammawihio and Aktunowihio. How could she ever do that? She must never forsake her Cheyenne gods. To Breanna she said, "I do not wish to offend you, but it is very difficult for me to believe that your Jesus Christ raised Himself from the dead."

"It was no problem to Him, Silver Moon. Jesus is the giver of life. He said He is the resurrection and the life. Jesus is life itself. You exist because of Him, and you are alive because of Him. Jesus gives you every breath you take, and He gives you every heartbeat."

Silver Moon blinked in surprise at her words.

"He is alive, Silver Moon," Breanna said with conviction. "I know He's alive because His Book *says* He is. And I know He's alive because He lives in my heart, He moves and works in my life, and He answers prayer. Did a dead Jesus send the hail today?"

"Maybe it was Heammawihio who sent the hailstorm."

"I wasn't praying to Heammawihio. I was praying to Jesus."

Silver Moon lowered her head and rubbed her temples.

"Breanna, this is all so new to me. It is so different from what I have been taught all my life. I have been taught to believe that Heammawihio is the Wise One Above, that he is represented by the sun but is more powerful than the sun. Heammawihio is supreme because he knows more about how nature works than anyone else."

"But you see, Silver Moon, my God is the *Creator* of nature. His Book says all things were created by Him."

Suddenly there was a whisper outside the tepee: "Silver Moon! It is Iron Hawk."

Silver Moon excused herself to Breanna; she went to the flap and opened it just enough to expose her eyes. "Yes, Iron Hawk?"

"I heard your voices, so I knew you and Sunshine Hair were still awake. I just wanted to remind Silver Moon that I hold her in my heart."

Silver Moon held Iron Hawk's gaze in the dim light and said, "You are so kind, Iron Hawk. I am very fond of you."

Iron Hawk's voice was soft and tender. "I am living for the day when you will say that you love me. I will go now. Good night."

"Good night."

"And good night to you, Sunshine Hair."

"Good night, Iron Hawk," Breanna called.

Silver Moon returned to her pallet and sat down.

"What a fine young man he is," Breanna said.

"Yes, Iron Hawk is the best. He deserves the kind of love I can never give him."

"Cannot, or *will* not?"

The girl met Breanna's piercing gaze. "I cannot. Unless Heammawihio allows me to see justice done to John Chivington, I can never give my heart to any man. I close my eyes and I see Mother and Sky Eagle and Bear Paw very unhappy and unrestful in the land of Heammawihio because their murderer has never paid for his crimes."

"Silver Moon, do Cheyenne people sin?"

"Yes."

"Does Silver Moon sin?"

Silver Moon swerved her gaze to the fire, then back to Breanna. "Yes."

"And what has Heammawihio or Aktunowihio done for you that would cleanse these sins and provide forgiveness for them so there is no punishment when this life is over?"

"Well, I—"

"Crimes committed within the tribe are punished, aren't they?"

"Yes."

"And do you believe they should be?"

"Of course."

"And the crimes white men commit, whether against each other or against Indians—should they be punished?"

A spark of hatred flashed in Silver Moon's dark eyes. "When white men commit crimes against each other, they should be punished. But when they do as John Chivington did to the Cheyenne at Sand Creek, there should be very harsh punishment; there should be death!"

"But should crimes committed against the Creator of the world just be ignored? Do you think the Creator is less wise than the creature?"

While Silver Moon pondered this question, Breanna said, "Jesus Christ became the sacrifice for *your* sins as well as mine. He knew you would one day be born into this world as a sinner in need of salvation and forgiveness, so when He died on the cross, He was dying for Silver Moon. He died for you, honey, as if you were the only sinner in the world. He did the same for me."

Silver Moon batted her eyes. "Jesus Christ died for me? For *me?*"

"Yes. Scripture says, 'While we were yet sinners, Christ died for us.' That's because He loves us. Jesus loves *you*, Silver Moon. That's why He died for you."

Silver Moon pondered this, then shook her head. "Breanna, our shamans have taught us that only in exceptional cases is there any burden of guilt for wrongdoing to be borne beyond this life."

"Exceptional cases? What kind of cases?"

"There are only two. One is if a Cheyenne murders another Cheyenne. The other is if a Cheyenne takes his own life."

"And what happens to them in the afterlife?"

"They go to eternal punishment."

"Eternal punishment like the hell I have told you about?"

"Yes."

"So the shamans believe there's a hell, but it's only for those who have committed the sins you just noted."

"Yes."

"So any other kind of wrongdoing goes unpunished in the afterlife?"

"We believe that when a Cheyenne dies who has not committed either of the sins I mentioned, he or she travels up the Hanging Road—which white men call the Milky Way—to the land of Heammawihio in the sky. There they follow the Cheyenne way and live forever among their loved ones, friends, and ancestors. Life in the afterworld is much like that on earth. There the Cheyenne live in villages and camps, like we do here. They live close to the land, hunt game, and carry on familiar occupations. The homeland of Heammawihio holds no such terrors as judgment or hell."

"Except for Cheyenne who have murdered Cheyenne or taken their own lives."

"Yes."

"Remember what we read in God's sacred Book...that all of my sins and all of your sins were laid on Jesus when He hung on the cross. Christ died for *our* sins. That means you and I, and all the Cheyenne, and all the rest of humanity are responsible, as guilty sinners, for putting Jesus to death on the cross.

"I realize you're not convinced that what I've shown you from God's Book is true, Silver Moon. And I can understand that. You've been taught differently all of your life. But just suppose that what I've shown you *is* true. Then Silver Moon's sins nailed Jesus to the cross and caused His suffering and death. Unless this sin is cleansed and forgiven, you must go to an eternal hell when you die."

Silver Moon took a deep breath and said, "Breanna, it is time we get some sleep. I am very tired, and I know you are more tired than I, for you had no sleep last night."

Breanna yawned, covering her mouth, and said, "You're so right, honey. Let's get to sleep."

The Indian girl moved to Breanna on her knees and wrapped her arms around her neck. "Thank you for telling me about Jesus Christ and about the cross," she said, hugging her tight. "I love you."

"I love you too, Silver Moon."

Moments later, Breanna lay on her cot, thanking the Lord for the privilege of leading Bull Elk and Calf Woman to Jesus, and for allowing her to witness to Silver Moon. She prayed for God's protective hand on John and fell asleep praying for Silver Moon's salvation.

While the night wind slapped at the side of the tepee and

the fire dwindled to red embers, Silver Moon lay awake. She was deeply disquieted over what Breanna had shown her in the sacred Book and the things she had told her were in there. Breanna's words echoed through her mind.

"Just suppose what I've shown you is true. Then Silver Moon's sins nailed Jesus Christ to the cross and caused His suffering and death. Unless this sin is cleansed and forgiven, you must go to an eternal hell when you die."

The thought of going into eternal punishment burned in Silver Moon's mind. Fear filled her heart, but she fought it. This could not be. Heammawihio would not punish her. Why would Breanna's God punish her? But what if Breanna's sacred Book was right, and Heammawihio did not really exist? What if—?

Silver Moon rolled over on the pallet and realized that her hands were tightly clenched. She finally settled on her back, staring up at the stars through the opening at the top of the tepee.

Did Jesus Christ really rise from the dead? If He did, then everything Breanna had told her and shown her was true. If He really did go to that horrible cross for Silver Moon, then she needed to open her heart to him and ask Him to forgive her sins.

No! she told herself. Nobody rises from the dead. Breanna's Jesus Christ is the one who does not exist! I must remain true to Heammawihio and Aktunowihio. They have been my gods since I first learned of them from the shamans in my father's village.

Her father. Dead at the vile hands of the man named Custer. Little Sparrow, her stepmother, dead too. And then there was her real mother, Gentle Dove. And her little brother, Sky Eagle. And the brave Bear Paw...

Silver Moon's hatred toward John Chivington surged once more. She clamped her jaw until her teeth hurt.

Chivington. If ever anybody deserved to be punished, it was him! If only she could be the one to do it!

She listened to Breanna's soft, even breathing and turned to look at her by the dim red glow of the dying embers. Moving her lips in a low whisper she said, "Breanna, what an unselfish, loving person you are. You came to this village so you could save lives with your medicine and your knowledge of inoculation, and you have asked for nothing in return. And you have so kindly told me of your Jesus Christ because you believe what your sacred Book says about Him. You believe what it says about sin and forgiveness and salvation...and eternal punishment. You have to be wrong, though you believe it so sincerely. You have to be wrong because Heammawihio and Aktunowihio do exist. They are the gods of the Cheyenne. They are the gods of Silver Moon."

The night wind buffeted the sides of the tepee in a rhythmic pattern, and soon the young woman fell asleep.

19

⬥

DENVER COUNTY SHERIFF Curt Langan looked up from his desk as Deputy Steve Ridgway came through the door from the cell block. Ridgway was hooking handcuffs to his belt as he said, "I wish we could close down every saloon in this town."

"Me too," said the sheriff, running fingers through his sand-colored hair. "Our jobs would be a whole lot easier, that's for sure. That guy give you trouble back there?"

"You mean getting him into the cell?"

"Mm-hmm."

"Nah, he's too drunk."

"I thought I heard sounds of struggle."

"Oh...that. When I took the cuffs off him, he took a swing at me. He's...ah...sleeping peacefully in cell number 6."

"*Induced* sleep?"

"Well, I did sort of put my shoulder behind the punch."

Langan nodded. "So that makes five cowboys in each of the first six cells."

"I believe that's right. Five in each occupied cell, now that I put this last one in number 6. What are we gonna do if we fill up the other two before they face Judge Brillhart and pay their fines?"

"Well, I guess we'll pack them tighter, and more than one

255

will have to sleep on the floor."

The rawboned, black-haired Ridgway shook his head. "Why is it that when these cowhands finish a cattle drive they have to beeline for the saloons and tank up on whiskey?"

Langan chuckled. "Well, they say they have to unwind after the long trail drive."

Ridgway looked back toward the cell block. "Wonder how they like unwinding in a crowded jail cell?"

Suddenly there were gunshots from outside and rapid footsteps on the boardwalk. Then the door burst open and a small, wiry man gasped, "Sheriff! There's a coupla drunk cowboys shootin' up the sign on the Bullhorn Saloon! They started trouble inside, and Mack threw 'em out. Now they're shootin' up his sign."

"Come on, Steve," Langan said and bolted out the door. Ridgway was right behind him.

The sheriff's office was located in the heart of Denver's business district, on Tremont Street. There were seven saloons in a four-block section of Tremont. The Bullhorn was the closest to Langan's office.

Two staggering cowpokes were standing in the middle of the street, swearing as they blasted away at the sign above the saloon door.

Langan ran at them, shouting, "Hey! That's enough!"

Both watery-eyed cowboys wheeled and looked at the sheriff with scorn as the deputy drew up beside him.

Langan extended his hand. "Give me your guns."

Mack Duggins, the owner of the Bullhorn, came through the batwings, anger darkening his face and bald head. "Sheriff, they gotta pay for that sign!"

"They will, Mack," said Langan. Then he turned to the reluctant cowhands. "I said, give me those guns."

The two drunks looked at each other. Langan grabbed the gun hand of the closest man and twisted the weapon free, keeping the muzzle pointed toward the ground. The other cowboy saw Ridgway coming toward him and said, "Okay, okay!" and handed the deputy his gun.

While the men were being cuffed Duggins said, "When am I gonna get the money to pay for the sign, Sheriff?"

"Right now would be a good time. How much you think it'll cost to get a new sign made?"

"Well…at least thirty dollars."

"These boys just got paid," said Langan. "I'm sure they've got that kind of money on them."

"Hey, Sher-rf!" complained the one Langan had disarmed. "That ain'—" he burped—"that ain' right! We worked hard for our…we worked hard for our money."

"No doubt you did, but it wasn't right for you to shoot the man's sign, either." Sheriff and deputy extracted a wad of bills from the pocket of each drunk. "Let's give Mack forty dollars, Steve. Twenty from each."

By this time, a crowd had gathered.

Ridgway took twenty dollars from the wad he held and handed it to Langan.

"Take them and lock them up," said the sheriff.

Ridgway led the staggering, sour-faced drunks up the street as Langan handed the bartender forty dollars.

"Thanks, Sheriff," said Duggins. "Maybe someday guys like them'll learn they can't get liquored up and just start shootin' at private property."

"Who sold them the liquor, Mack?"

"Well, I did. Why?"

"Then you're as much to blame as they are. You whiskey sellers don't mind at all taking their money, but you cry your eyes out when the stuff you sell gets them in a troublesome mood and you have to throw them out of your place."

Duggins's bald head turned red again. "A man has a right to make a living selling liquor if he wants to."

"I'm aware of that. And since your property is under my jurisdiction, I'll protect it because I'm sheriff here. You hold proof of it in your hand right now."

Duggins looked at the forty dollars and nodded. "I appreciate you makin' 'em pay, Sheriff, even if you don't approve of the saloon business."

"The whole world would be better off if there was no liquor. And you know it." Langan turned and headed back down the street.

Duggins stuffed the money into his pocket and stepped up on the boardwalk, only to find two elderly women barring his way.

"What the sheriff said about the whole world being better off if there wasn't any liquor is right, Mr. Duggins," said one frail-looking woman.

Then the other woman chimed in. "My husband was killed when a drunken cowboy was shooting up a saloon just like those two were doing. Happened in Wichita, Kansas. A stray bullet hit him in the heart. The drunk who killed him was sold the whiskey by a bartender just like you."

"Excuse me, ladies."

The women parted, and Duggins plowed through the batwings, leaving the doors to swing and clatter.

"Looks like we've got a good start on filling up cell number 7," Steve Ridgway said when Sheriff Langan returned to the office. "If this keeps up, the county'll have to build us a new jail."

Langan took off his hat, tossed it on a peg behind his desk, and sat down. "The way people are moving into this county—especially to Denver—we're going to need a bigger jail, anyhow. With greater population come more lawbreakers. Seems to go hand in hand."

"It's a good thing the county officials approved the enlargement of your staff, Sheriff. Another deputy in this office will really help out."

"You're right about that."

"Speaking of more staff," said Ridgway, "how're the applications coming along since it hit the newspapers you're looking for a new deputy?"

Langan sighed. "Well, so far every man who's come to the office or written to me about the job has been too young, too inexperienced, or both. The man I hire must have been a deputy sheriff or deputy marshal somewhere, or at least have experience as an army officer. You know…someone who's seen combat, can handle a revolver, and can deal with people."

"Makes sense. Denver's not the place for a greenhorn."

Langan picked up an official-looking envelope. "Here's that court summons Judge Throckmorton wanted delivered to the rancher on Turkey Creek. Might as well get it out there."

"Okay, boss. When the new man comes on, how 'bout we let him do these menial tasks?"

"Sure. You can chase the bad guys and do the gunfighting…that kind of stuff. That is, after you handle all this paperwork I'll be assigning you."

"Get outta here!" said Steve with a laugh. He took the envelope. "I'm no good at paperwork. That'll still be your department."

Just before Ridgway reached the door, it opened. A tall, slender man entered, stepped to one side, and said, "Excuse me."

"Can I help you, sir?" Steve said.

The man glanced at Curt Langan. "I wanted to see the sheriff."

"Yes, sir," said Langan, rising to his feet. "I'm Sheriff Langan."

Ridgway went out the door, closing it behind him.

"I understand you're taking applications for a deputy position, Sheriff," the man said.

"Yes, I am."

"I'd like to apply."

"I'll tell you right up front, sir, that I'm looking for a younger man. I assume you have experience, and that's very important, but when a man is pushing sixty-five or better, the job's just too much."

"I'm only fifty-one, Sheriff. I was an officer in the United States Army for nearly twenty-two years. I've seen plenty of combat, fighting Confederates in the Civil War, and fighting Indians here in the West. I can handle a gun well enough to be a lawman. I'd really appreciate the opportunity to show you I can handle the job."

"What about your health? You look like you're not feeling well."

"I...I've been through a lot the past few years, Sheriff. But I assure you, I can handle the job. All I ask is that you give me the opportunity to prove it."

Langan shrugged. "Well, sit down, sir." The sheriff eased into his chair and said, "You married?"

"No, I'm not."

"I haven't seen you around town. You live nearby?"

"Ah...in the mountains."

"You'd be required to live within Denver County if you were hired for the job."

"That wouldn't be a problem, Sheriff."

"All right." Langan reached into a drawer and took out a printed form. He shoved it and a pencil across the desk and said, "Fill this out for me."

The man smiled. "Thank you, Sheriff. I really appreciate your letting me apply."

Langan placed his elbows on the desk and watched as the man picked up the pencil and began printing his name. When he saw *John M. Chivington* he said, "Are you the John Chivington who was *Colonel* John Chivington at Camp Weld?"

"Yes. That's me."

Langan spoke in a kindly tone as he said, "Mr. Chivington, I'm sorry, sir, but if I hired you as my deputy, it would cause all kinds of problems. There would be real trouble, not only from the county officials who've authorized me to hire a new deputy, but from the people of this county and this territory. Your name is too well known here in connection with the incident at Sand Creek."

Chivington dropped the pencil on top of the printed form and shoved both toward Langan. "I guess I'll never live it down, Sheriff. Thanks for your time." As he spoke, he rose to his feet and headed for the door.

"Mr. Chivington…"

The tall man stopped and turned around slowly. "Yes, Sheriff?"

"Perhaps you should get into a line of work where you don't meet or deal with the public."

"I'm already doing that."

Langan stood up and rounded the desk. "Oh? What are you doing for a living?"

"Panning gold. I've got a small cabin up near Granby. I

work the creeks that feed the Fraser River. Just eking out a living. I've really had my heart set on wearing a badge. I'd hoped the Sand Creek affair was far enough in the past that it wouldn't be a millstone around my neck anymore."

"There's still a lot of talk about it around Denver," said Langan. "That's why even though I wasn't here in '64, I know a lot about it. It's probably best that you keep panning gold."

Chivington sighed. "Looks like that's what I'll have to do."

"There is one other option, if you really want to get into law enforcement."

"And that is?"

"Go where your name isn't known."

"Wouldn't work, Sheriff. Congress made the Sand Creek story national news. There's nowhere to go."

"Tell you what, Mr. Chivington...I just thought of something."

"Yes?"

"Maybe you could make it as a deputy U.S. marshal. They travel most of the time. It wouldn't be the same as walking the streets of Denver as a deputy sheriff where you're so well known. I do know that Chief Brockman is always looking for good men. You ought to talk to him."

"Brockman? There's a new chief U.S. marshal over the Western District?"

"Yes. John Brockman."

"What happened to Solomon Duvall?"

"He retired. Felt like he was getting too old for the job. He goes into the office now and then to help in one way or another, but mostly he's just taking it easy."

Chivington rubbed his bearded jaw. "Well, I guess it'd be worth a try. Thanks for the suggestion."

Langan nodded. "Hope it works out for you."

Deputy U.S. Marshal Barry Shores was on duty at the front desk in the Federal Building when a stout man in his midthirties entered the office. He approached the desk and said, "I'm Dexter Wilson. I have a nine o'clock appointment with Chief Brockman for a job interview."

"Yes, Mr. Wilson," said Shores, rising from the desk. "The chief said to bring you in when you arrived. Come with me."

Shores stepped to the door of the inner office and tapped lightly.

"Yes, Barry?" came a voice from inside.

He opened the door a few inches. "Mr. Wilson is here, sir."

"Bring him in."

The deputy ushered Dexter Wilson into Brockman's office, and after the chief and Wilson had shaken hands, Shores said, "Remember, Chief, you have to be at the depot by ten-fifteen."

"I'll make it all right, Barry," said the tall, rugged man. "Mr. Wilson and I will be done in less than half an hour."

Shores returned to the outer office to find a tall, stoop-shouldered man with silver-white hair standing before his desk. "Good morning, sir. May I help you?"

"I'd like to see Chief Brockman, if I can."

"I'm sorry, sir, but Chief Brockman has someone in his office right now, and when he's finished he has to catch a train. Is there anything I can do for you?"

"Well, maybe I could speak with someone else. I have many years of experience as an army officer and would like to be in law enforcement. Sheriff Langan told me Mr. Brockman was looking for new men to hire as deputies."

"He is, sir, but Mr. Brockman is the only one who does the interviews. He'll only be gone a few days. If you'd like to check back—" Shores stopped speaking. He squinted at the tall man, then blinked in surprise and said, "Don't I know you?"

"It's possible. I've been around."

Suddenly Shores snapped his fingers. "Of course! You're John Chivington! You've really changed, sir. You used to be much heavier, and your hair was black."

"Where do you know me from?"

"I was a teenager when you were pastor of Broadway Methodist Church, right here in Denver. Maybe you remember Darrell and Jessica Shores...my parents. I have two older brothers. We were all members of the church."

"Shores...Seems like I should remember. Oh, yes. Your father was a carpenter—a furniture builder."

"That's right. My brothers are married now. One lives in Maryland and the other is in business with Dad in Missouri. Mom's doing fine."

"Well, that's good to hear, Barry. Give them my regards next time you see them."

"I sure will, sir." Barry paused. "Tell you what...I can give you an application to fill out. Like I said, Mr. Brockman will only be gone a few days. I'll see that it's on his desk when he returns."

"Instead of that," said Chivington, "I'll just come back in a week or so."

"All right, sir. It's nice to see you again."

Just then, a middle-aged man walked in, dressed in suit and tie, carrying important-looking papers. The man glanced at Chivington, looked at him a second time, then handed the papers to Shores. "Barry, Chief Brockman is expecting these. Would you see that he gets them?"

"Sure will, Mr. McCallister."

Chivington was headed out the door, but he froze in place when he heard the name. Slowly he turned to look at the man.

In the same instant, Duane McCallister said, "I know you! You're *Chivington!*"

Chivington's scalp prickled as he recognized Duane McCallister, who had been a captain under him during the battle of Glorieta Pass, and also in the First Colorado Cavalry at Camp Weld.

"Hello, Duane," said Chivington, licking his lips nervously.

"I see you two know each other," Barry Shores said.

Chivington nodded. "We haven't seen each other in almost ten years."

"Well, then, you don't know that Mr. McCallister is head of the Federal Department of Legal Affairs, which is located here in the Federal Building."

"No. I didn't know that."

McCallister's face twisted into harsh lines as he said, "I don't know what you're doing here, but whatever it is you'd better make it fast." McCallister turned to Barry Shores and said, "This is the man I served under in the First Colorado Cavalry. His favorite saying was, 'The only good Indian is a dead Indian, men! Let's go out there and make us some good Indians today!' He beat me to a pulp one day after I refused to help him carry out his bloody deeds." McCallister turned back to Chivington with a look of loathing. "I hardly know you, Chivington. You're looking old and haggard. Maybe you haven't had all the peace and quiet you were after."

Chivington looked at a stunned Barry Shores and said, "What we were discussing won't work, Deputy. I can see that now." With that, he pivoted and left the federal offices.

The Colorado sun was setting over the mountains when a somber-faced John Chivington eased himself from the saddle at his corral gate. It seemed a great effort to remove the saddle and bridle, then pour grain into the feed trough inside the barn and pitch a generous amount of hay in the trough. He left the corral gate open so the horse could forage and go to the river for water anytime he pleased.

He shuffled into the cabin and hung his hat on a peg by the door and draped his coat over the back of one of the chairs at the table. He unbuckled his gun belt and wound the belt around the holster, then laid it on the table and sat down. He put his elbows on the table, buried his face in his hands, and wept.

After several minutes, he pulled the revolver from its holster and laid it before him. He then went to a crude cabinet across the room, took out an old yellowed envelope and pencil, and went back to the table to write.

To whomever finds my body—

I can't stand it any longer. Judge Joseph Holt was right. I have lived these years with indelible infamy, and it is more than I can bear.

I am sorry for what I have done to the Plains Indians, especially for the massacre at Sand Creek. I wish I could turn back the hands of time and start over. I would do it all differently. I would not disgrace the church that ordained me, nor the army that commissioned me.

I wish I could talk to the survivors of Sand Creek—however many are still living—and ask their forgiveness.

Chivington ran out of space and flipped the envelope over.

I have lived alone in these mountains for years in cold fear, expecting any time that one or more of the Cheyenne men who survived Sand Creek would track me down and kill me.

Now I will do for them what they would like to do. I will end my life as a gesture of contrition for my awful deeds at Sand Creek.

To the person or persons who find my body, I ask one favor. Will you please see to it that the survivors of Sand Creek who are still alive are shown this note? I beg their forgiveness.

John Chivington

With trembling hand he picked up the Colt .45, eased back the hammer, and placed the muzzle to his temple.

20

✟

"IT'S WONDERFUL TO SEE YOU doing this well, Essie Bird Woman," Breanna said. The Cheyenne woman was feeling well enough to sit up. "Like most everyone who has smallpox, you'll have some tiny scars, but at least you're alive and doing well."

"Yes, thanks to you, Sunshine Hair."

Breanna and Silver Moon then left Essie Bird Woman to continue their rounds through the village, going from tepee to tepee to examine the smallpox victims.

In War Bonnet's tepee, Painted Flower and the chief were just finishing their midday meal when a hand clap sounded outside the flap. The chief rose from his sitting position, opened the flap, and saw one of his shamans standing there.

"What can I do for you, Bull Elk?"

"I need to talk to you, Chief War Bonnet. It is very important."

War Bonnet flicked a glance at Painted Flower.

"In private," said Bull Elk.

"I will go see how little Star Light is doing," said Painted Flower, and whisked through the opening past Bull Elk.

War Bonnet gestured for Bull Elk to enter. As both men sat

down cross-legged, War Bonnet said, "This is something very important, I assume."

"Yes. Very important."

"Speak. Your chief is listening."

"I am sure you have heard that Calf Woman and I have become Christians because of what Sunshine Hair has told us and shown us from her sacred Book."

"Yes. This is known by all in the village, I believe."

"In order to become a follower of Jesus Christ, I had to renounce Heammawihio and Aktunowihio. I felt I should be honest with you. This means I am no longer a shaman."

There was no change of expression on War Bonnet's face, and Bull Elk could see no reaction in his chief's eyes. Bull Elk waited. What seemed like hours passed, then War Bonnet said, "It is very difficult for me to grasp how you could forsake Heammawihio and Aktunowihio, Bull Elk. Is there not room in your heart for more than one deity?"

"No. When a person becomes a Christian, his full allegiance is to Jesus Christ. Calf Woman and I have a deep peace in our souls that we never had before."

War Bonnet was silent again.

When a long moment passed, Bull Elk said, "Does the chief want us to leave the village?"

War Bonnet blinked, then rubbed a hand over his mouth and said, "Does your allegiance to Jesus Christ force you to renounce me as your chief?"

"No. We love and admire our chief, but we do not worship him. We worshiped Heammawihio and Aktunowihio. It is them we have renounced."

The shadow of a smile appeared on War Bonnet's lips. "Then I do not want you and Calf Woman to leave the village. I want you to stay."

"Are you angry that we have turned to Jesus Christ and that I am no longer a medicine man?"

There was a pause as the chief pondered the question. "I am not angry, Bull Elk. Bewildered, yes, but not angry."

"Are you angry at Sunshine Hair for showing us Jesus Christ?"

"I am not angry at Sunshine Hair. This dear white woman has come to us and saved so many lives. I cannot be angry with her. And even if she makes Christians of more of our people while she is here, I cannot be angry with her."

"Chief, it really was Jesus Christ who brought Calf Woman's fever down. And it was He who sent the hail so little Star Light's life could be saved. This only happened because Sunshine Hair prayed to Him."

War Bonnet, perplexed as he was, nodded. "I cannot dispute this, Bull Elk. I will not try."

When Breanna and Silver Moon had seen the last patient, they walked together toward Silver Moon's tepee, happy that everyone was recuperating and doing well.

"Do you think anyone else will come down with the smallpox?" asked Silver Moon.

"It's possible," Breanna said. "Until everyone has passed the incubation period, they are not safe from it."

"Incubation period? What is that?"

"The length of time someone who is exposed to the disease has until it is no longer a threat. This is ordinarily about twenty-one days."

"But you are going to leave us tomorrow. What if others get the sickness?"

"Then *you* can be their nurse."

"Me?"

"Yes. You know how to mix the salicylic acid, which I'll leave with you. And you know how to bathe their wrists and necks with cool water. I would stay if I could, but I have a husband, a home, and a job to go to."

Silver Moon's face twisted. "But what if I should have a case like Star Light? What if I need hail?" Even as the words left her mouth, Silver Moon realized she had said the wrong thing. "Oh! Yes, of course. I can pray to Heammawihio for hail."

At sunset the aroma of cooking food wafted through the air. Breanna was inside Silver Moon's tepee alone, brushing her hair, which she had just washed. Silver Moon was visiting another tepee on the other side of the village. The flap was back, and Breanna looked up to see Iron Hawk appear in the opening.

"Hello, Iron Hawk," she said. "Silver Moon isn't here at the moment."

"I know. I saw her at Two Arrows's tepee, talking to Fawn Eyes. I want to talk to you."

"Oh. All right." She laid the hairbrush down and stepped outside. "What can I do for you?"

"Last night, when you were talking to Silver Moon here in the tepee about Jesus Christ and His death on the cross of wood, I...I was standing out here, listening. I hope you will not be angry."

Breanna smiled, shaking her head. "Of course I'm not angry. I'm glad you were listening."

Iron Hawk's tension eased. "Thank you, Sunshine Hair. You told Silver Moon that God's Son paid the price His Father demanded for sin."

"That's right."

"And you said He died for all of us...all sinners. Even Indians."

"Yes, He did."

"Could...could I talk to you about it some time tonight?"

"Why, of course. I'll ask Silver Moon—"

"Here she comes now," said Iron Hawk, looking beyond Breanna.

"Hello, you two," said Silver Moon.

They greeted her, then Breanna said, "Iron Hawk just told me that while I was talking to you last night, he was listening outside."

"Oh?" There was a slight hint of displeasure in the young woman's dark eyes.

"He wants to talk to me further about it. Since it wouldn't be proper for the two of us to talk alone, I want to ask if it's all right if Iron Hawk comes to the tepee after supper so we can talk with you present?"

Breanna saw a flash of emotion in Silver Moon's expressive eyes.

"Yes, of course. Right after supper."

That evening, Silver Moon, Breanna, and Iron Hawk sat cross-legged around the fire, and Breanna opened her Bible. Silver Moon struggled to keep her composure when Iron Hawk began asking questions about salvation, which Breanna answered from the Scriptures.

As the evening wore on, Breanna could see that the Holy Spirit had used her testimony and the Scriptures she gave Silver Moon the night before to convict Iron Hawk that Jesus Christ was the Saviour of the world, and that to be saved, Iron Hawk must open his heart to Him.

While Silver Moon looked on apprehensively, Iron Hawk told Breanna he wanted to be saved. Breanna took him to Romans 10:13, read the verse to him, and said, "Now tell me, Iron Hawk, what does it say right here that you must do to be saved?"

"It says I must call upon the name of the Lord."

"Are you willing to call on Him and ask Him to save you?"

"Yes, I am."

Silver Moon clenched her fists as she watched Iron Hawk bow his head and ask Jesus to save him. She told herself there could be nothing between them now. Iron Hawk had betrayed his Cheyenne gods. What would happen to him for turning his back on Heammawihio and Aktunowihio?

When, through tears, Iron Hawk finished calling on the Lord, someone clapped outside the tepee. Silver Moon opened the flap and saw Two Arrows.

"Is Sunshine Hair with you?" he asked.

Silver Moon nodded.

Breanna moved to the side of the young maiden and smiled at Two Arrows. "Is something wrong with Star Light?"

"No. She is fine. Fawn Eyes and I would like to talk to you, if you could come to our tepee."

"Certainly," said Breanna, then turned and looked at the new convert. "Iron Hawk, I'm so glad for you."

"Not as glad as I am! Thank you for talking to me."

"I love to talk to people about the Lord Jesus."

As Breanna walked with Two Arrows toward his tepee, Silver Moon left her tepee and Iron Hawk followed her.

"I have long heard of Jesus Christ," he said, "but I have never been able to learn of Him from the sacred Book. I am so glad Sunshine Hair came to the village and— Is the beautiful Silver Moon angry at me?"

"I am not angry at you."

"I have become a Christian, Silver Moon, but I still love you very much."

"I am very fond of you," she said, "but I am afraid. Very much afraid."

"About what?"

"About your becoming a Christian."

"What is it that makes you afraid?"

"What Heammawihio and Aktunowihio are going to do to you for turning your back on them. Maybe they will punish you severely...even kill you."

"There is nothing to fear, Silver Moon. Heammawihio and Aktunowihio are false gods. They only exist in the minds of the Cheyenne people who have been taught wrong by their shamans and their ancestors. I know now who the true God is. He is the great God of the universe, and His Son is the Lord Jesus Christ."

Silver Moon's features crumpled and tears filled her eyes. Her lips quivered as she said, "How do you know this? You are only taking Breanna's word for it, and what her Book says. She is a wonderful person, and I love her very much, but she could be wrong, Iron Hawk. Tell me how you *know* what is the truth."

"I...I do not know how to explain it. But I will try. As I listened to Sunshine Hair talk to you last night, and as she read to me from the sacred Book tonight, something—how do I say it?—something or *Someone* spoke to me down deep inside. It was not a voice I could hear with the ears of my head but with the ears of my soul. I just knew what I was hearing was the truth, and I saw that what I had been taught by the shamans was *not* the truth. It is very hard to explain. It is something you need to experience for yourself."

Silver Moon drew in a deep breath and let it out slowly as she looked up at the stars.

"Now that I know Jesus Christ, Silver Moon, I want my Cheyenne people to know Him too. I love my people with all of my heart, and I want them to have the peace I have. I want *you* to be saved. I want *you* to have this peace."

Silver Moon wiped tears from her cheeks and sniffed.

Iron Hawk wished he could take her in his arms. Instead he moved closer and said, "I have not meant to bring unhappiness to you."

Silver Moon looked at him through her tears and said, "Even though you now believe that our gods do not exist, I know they do. They are going to punish you. I do not want to see you punished."

There were footsteps on the path, and they looked up to see Bull Elk. "Is Sunshine Hair in the tepee?" he asked.

"No," Silver Moon said. "She is with Two Arrows and Fawn Eyes in their tepee."

"Good. Then I can talk to Iron Hawk without her hearing."

"What do you want?" asked Iron Hawk.

"Sunshine Hair needs someone to escort her to Cheyenne City tomorrow. I thought it would be good if you and I did that. She could ride one of the ponies, and we could bring it back with us."

"I would be very happy to do that. And may I tell you something?"

"Of course."

"Sunshine Hair helped me this evening, and I became a Christian, just like you and Calf Woman!"

A smile broke over Bull Elk's craggy face. "This is good, Iron Hawk! This is good! Sunshine Hair taught Calf Woman and me that when we receive Jesus, we are born into the family of God. So you and I are not only Cheyenne brothers, we are Christian brothers!"

"Yes, that is true," said Iron Hawk.

"And, of course, I am no longer a medicine man. I can deal no more with the mystic spirits, nor will I ever pray to Heammawihio or Aktunowihio again."

Silver Moon's eyes widened. "Bull Elk, the gods will punish you!"

"I do not fear gods who do not exist, Silver Moon."

She glanced at Iron Hawk, who had said the same thing. "But do you not fear Chief War Bonnet? What will he do when he learns you are no longer a shaman?"

"I have already talked to Chief War Bonnet. He is disturbed that I have become a Christian, and saddened that I am no longer a medicine man. But when I asked him if he wanted Calf Woman and me to leave the village, he said he did not. He said he is not angry at us for becoming Christians, and he is not angry at Sunshine Hair for causing us to follow Jesus Christ. He said he could not be angry at her because of what she has done for our people."

"This is very good," said Iron Hawk. "I am glad to hear that Chief War Bonnet is being reasonable about it. I am hoping that one day all of our people become Christians...even our chief."

"Silver Moon too," said Bull Elk, swerving his gaze to the young maiden.

"I cannot turn my back on my gods," Silver Moon said. "I fear for you and Calf Woman, Bull Elk. Even as I fear for Iron Hawk. Heammawihio and Aktunowihio will punish you severely."

"Do not be afraid for us, sweet Silver Moon," Iron Hawk said. "We are in no danger from the gods."

"Then it is agreed," Bull Elk said to Iron Hawk. "We will escort Sunshine Hair to Cheyenne City tomorrow."

"Yes."

"I will go to Two Arrows's tepee and tell her," said Bull Elk.

When Bull Elk was gone, Iron Hawk said, "I must go to my tepee now, Silver Moon. I wish to say again that my heart still holds you, and it always will. Please do not forget that."

Silver Moon managed a weak smile. "I will not forget it. And I will beg Heammawihio and Aktunowihio not to punish you."

"Good night. I will see you tomorrow."

It was late when Breanna returned to the tepee. The fire was burning low, and Silver Moon lay on her side, eyes closed. Breanna changed into her nightclothes as quietly as she could, but Silver Moon rolled onto her back and looked at her.

"I'm sorry," said Breanna. "I tried not to wake you."

"I was not asleep. I was lying here wishing you could stay longer. I dread seeing you leave tomorrow."

"Maybe you could ride along to Cheyenne City. Bull Elk said he and Iron Hawk would escort me there. They have a horse for me to ride and one to carry my luggage. It would be a pleasant thing if you went along with us."

Silver Moon sat up. "That would help me very much. I could be with you a little longer if I went along."

"Then I can count on it?"

"Yes, unless Iron Hawk and Bull Elk would not want me."

"I'm sure they would not object. Especially Iron Hawk, who loves you so very much."

"I will ask them in the morning. Breanna, is everything all right at Two Arrows's tepee?"

"Oh, yes. They wanted to talk to me about knowing the great God who sent the hailstorm so their little daughter's life could be saved."

"Are you going to tell me that Two Arrows and Fawn Eyes have become Christians too?"

"Yes, they have!" Breanna said, smiling broadly. She sat down on her pallet and reached over to touch the girl's arm. "My concern now is for you, Silver Moon. I would like to see my young friend become a Christian before I leave."

Silver Moon's muscles tensed, and Breanna saw the fear in her eyes. "I cannot betray Heammawihio and Aktunowihio. I do not want to hurt you, Breanna, but there is no room in my heart for Jesus Christ."

Breanna put her arms around Silver Moon, who responded quickly by embracing her.

"Silver Moon, I love you, and I want you to be saved. But I cannot force this on you, and I won't try. All I can ask is that you consider all the things I have told you about Jesus and your need to know Him."

When Silver Moon remained silent, Breanna said, "Will you do that?"

"Yes," came a weak reply.

"All right. Let's get some sleep now."

The night wind whined around the tepee as Breanna lay on her pallet, praying that the Lord would draw Silver Moon to Himself, and thanking Him for those she had been able to lead to Him while in the village.

She was about to drift off to sleep when she heard Silver Moon say, "Breanna…"

"Yes, honey?"

"I love you."

Breanna smiled in the semidarkness. "I love you too."

While Breanna slept, Silver Moon remained awake, praying to her gods, begging them not to punish Iron Hawk and the others who had betrayed them by turning to Jesus Christ.

After breakfast the next morning, Iron Hawk and Bull Elk were at the rope corral, tying Breanna's luggage on a pony in preparation for the ride to Cheyenne City. A pinto had been bridled for Breanna, as well as one for Silver Moon.

Breanna had made the rounds, telling all her patients goodbye. The rest of the people were gathered near the rope corral to bid Sunshine Hair farewell.

When the luggage was secured on the pinto's back, Chief War Bonnet stepped to the front of the crowd and said, "Sunshine Hair, it is with deepest gratitude that I say for these people, and for this chief, thank you. Thank you for coming to us and saving so many lives. You have labored hard, even giving up your sleep in order to help us."

War Bonnet paused, searching for the right words. The morning breeze tugged at the feathers in his long, full headdress. Then he cleared his throat and said, "It is my wish that your Jesus Christ God will put His blessings upon you for what you have done here. Though you will leave us and be gone from our sight, you will never be gone from our hearts."

Breanna was about to respond when she saw War Bonnet nod at Painted Flower, who stood with a group of women. Painted Flower stepped forward, carrying a beautiful bright-colored blanket. She extended it to Breanna, with tears filming her eyes, and said, "Sunshine Hair, I wish to present you with this blanket, woven by my own hands—a token of love and appreciation for what you have done. Please accept it as from all the people of the village."

Breanna blinked as sudden tears filled her eyes. "Thank you, Painted Flower. I will cherish it always, and it will serve to bring back sweet memories of my brief stay in your village."

"Chief War Bonnet!" came the cry of a young warrior. "A rider comes!"

Every eye turned to see two huge black horses trotting toward the village from the west. A tall man in black rode one, and he led the other on a lead rope.

Breanna's jaw dropped. "It's John! It's my husband!"

When Breanna's great black stallion saw her, he whinnied a shrill greeting and bobbed his head. She stepped forward to meet John as he reined in. The badge on his coat flashed in the sun.

While John dismounted, Breanna wrapped her arms around the stallion's neck and said, "Chance! Mommy's big boy! I'm so glad to see you!"

Ebony whinnied and flicked his ears.

"I'm glad to see you too, Ebony," Breanna said, reaching to pat his muzzle.

While the Cheyenne looked on, Breanna hugged her husband and said, "Darling, what a surprise!"

Chance nickered again, swishing his tail and shaking his head.

"I can sure tell who comes first between us boys!" John said, chuckling.

"He's got us figured out, sweetheart," Breanna said to Chance. She took John by the hand and smiled at the crowd. "I want all of you to meet my husband, John Brockman." She then led him to the man in full headdress and said, "John, this is Chief War Bonnet."

The two men shook hands Indian style, and War Bonnet welcomed John warmly, saying, "This people and their chief are deeply indebted to Sunshine Hair. She has saved many lives and relieved much suffering."

"I'm glad, Chief," said John. Then to Breanna he said, "Looks like you were about ready to leave. Is the smallpox in check?"

"Yes, thank the Lord."

"I couldn't wait any longer. I had to come and see how it was going for you, and to take you back home whenever you could go. I noticed several fresh graves in the burial ground as I rode up. Been pretty bad, has it?"

"Many died with the smallpox, John, but the Lord has also done some wonderful things the past couple of days. I'll tell you all about it on the trip home."

"I'll look forward to hearing it, and I think I know what you're going to say. Now what did the chief call you...Sunshine Hair?"

"Yes."

"Fits, doesn't it?"

"Well, they sure couldn't call *you* Sunshine Hair!"

John laughed. "What I was going to say was that I know my wife well, and though she's been busy saving lives, there's no doubt some *souls* have been saved around here too."

Iron Hawk, who was standing beside Silver Moon, stepped forward and said, "Mr. John Brockman, I am one of those souls who has been saved because Sunshine Hair told me about Jesus Christ."

John grinned, shook his hand, and said, "Just what I thought!"

21

BREANNA BROCKMAN HAD THE JOY of introducing her husband to those Cheyenne she had led to Christ. Two Arrows and Fawn Eyes took a moment to describe for John how Sunshine Hair had prayed down the hailstorm and used the hail to save their daughter's life. Bull Elk and Calf Woman told him how Sunshine Hair had prayed and God had saved Calf Woman's life when she was nearly at the point of death. John was elated to see how the Lord had used Breanna as she labored among the people of War Bonnet's village.

"John," Breanna said, "Bull Elk and Iron Hawk were about to escort me to Cheyenne City so I could catch a train to Denver. Oh! And here's someone else I want you to meet."

She motioned for Silver Moon to come forward and took her by the hand. "This is Silver Moon. She and I have become close friends."

John smiled down at the dark-haired beauty. "Hello, Silver Moon. I am very glad to meet you."

"It is my pleasure to meet *you*, John Brockman." She gave him a warm smile. "You have a very wonderful squ—ah... wife."

"She helped me care for the sick, John," said Breanna. "Did a great job too. And something else you'll be interested to know: Silver Moon's father was Chief Black Kettle."

"Black Kettle!"

"Yes," said Silver Moon proudly.

"Your father was a great man, Silver Moon. A real champion for peace."

"Thank you."

"John Brockman," Bull Elk said, "Iron Hawk and I will still escort you and Sunshine Hair to Cheyenne City, if you wish. We can leave the luggage on the pinto, then we will bring the pinto back with us."

"We'll take you up on it, Bull Elk. I appreciate it very much."

"May I still go along, Breanna?" asked Silver Moon.

"Yes, of course."

"Before you go, John Brockman," said War Bonnet, "I have something else for Sunshine Hair."

The chief held up a colorful Cheyenne headband that looked like the ones all the women in the village wore.

The people moved a little closer as their chief stepped up to Breanna and said, "Sunshine Hair, this headband, as you already know, is designed to show that the wearer is Cheyenne."

Breanna nodded, her throat tight with emotion.

"As a chief in the Cheyenne tribe, I hereby declare you, Sunshine Hair, an honorary member." As War Bonnet spoke, he placed the headband on Breanna's head. He took a step back and said, "In the eyes of the entire Cheyenne tribe, you are now one of us, Sunshine Hair. You are Cheyenne."

Tears streamed down Breanna's cheeks, and she seemed at a loss for words. There were tears in the eyes of many of the people, too, including the men.

"Chief War Bonnet," John said, "as you can see, my wife is deeply touched by this marvelous gesture on your part. The honor you have bestowed on her is something she will proudly carry the rest of her life. She—"

Breanna touched his arm. "Thank you, darling. What my husband has said, Chief, is so true. I am humbled and deeply honored by this. I will cherish my relationship to the Cheyenne tribe always. Thank you all…and good-bye."

It was late in the afternoon when John and Breanna stood beside the Denver-bound train in Cheyenne City. Ebony and Chance were in the stock car, and the conductor was calling for the passengers to board.

While John was saying good-bye to the two men, Silver Moon embraced Breanna and said in her ear, "I love you, Breanna. I will miss you very, very much."

Breanna pulled back so she could look into Silver Moon's teary eyes and said, "You will keep your promise, won't you? To think on everything I showed you in the Bible?"

Silver Moon nodded. "I will."

"Remember that Jesus loves you and He died for you so you could be forgiven for your sins and saved from that awful place called hell."

Silver Moon nodded.

"If you ever come to Denver, I would love to have you stay with us. John and I have a big house."

"It is possible that I could do that…someday."

"Well, if you come, anyone at Mile High Hospital could tell you how to find me, and anyone in town could tell you where the hospital is."

"Maybe, someday."

They embraced again, and Breanna said, "I love you, sweet girl."

"And I love you, my dearest friend."

"Good-bye, Silver Moon," John said. "I heard what Breanna said to you about staying at our house. Please know that you are most welcome."

"Thank you."

John turned to Breanna. "Well, *Sunshine Hair*, we'd better get aboard."

The Brockmans took a seat on the platform side of the depot and waved at the Indians as the train chugged out of the station.

Breanna kept Silver Moon in sight until the platform passed from view, then turned around on the seat, blew into a hankie, and said, "Such a sweet girl, John."

John took his wife's hand. "I think you've found a real friend there, honey. But it appears she didn't respond to the gospel as the others did."

"No. She has a strong sense of loyalty to her pagan gods. I just wasn't able to reach her."

"But you sowed plenty of seed, if I know you."

"That I did."

"Then we'll just water that seed with prayer and ask the Lord to open her blinded eyes and let her see the light."

"Yes," said Breanna, dabbing at her eyes. "And while we're praying, let's ask the Lord to somehow let us know when she gets saved."

"He's big enough to handle that." John eyed the headband. "Well, my life will never be the same again."

"What do you mean?"

"I wasn't married to an Indian before, and now all of a sudden, here I am married to a Cheyenne! With sunshine hair to boot!"

Breanna giggled, punched his upper arm, and said, "And

don't you forget it, mister! Get out of line and I'll clonk you between the eyes with a tomahawk!"

During the next several days, Silver Moon kept herself busy, tending to the smallpox victims, doing what she could to help them recover.

Essie Bird Woman was finally back on her feet, though she was still too weak to perform any spiritual ceremonies. Late one afternoon, the aging shaman was sitting in her tepee when she heard hands clap outside and Silver Moon call, "Essie Bird Woman, may I come in and talk to you?"

"Of course. The flap is not hooked inside. Enter."

Though Essie Bird Woman's eyesight was not as good as it had been before she was stricken with smallpox, she could tell by the look on the young maiden's face that she was troubled.

"Silver Moon's heart is heavy," said the shaman. "What is the matter?"

Silver Moon sat down on the earthen floor of the tepee, facing her mentor. "I need your help."

"Yes?"

"When Sunshine Hair was here, did she talk to you about her Jesus Christ God?"

"Yes. When we were alone. Three or four times."

"Did it bother you?"

"In what way, child?"

"Did you wonder if what her sacred Book says about Jesus Christ is true?"

"It cannot be true, child, or our gods are false."

"I have tried to tell myself this same thing, but something in my heart keeps cutting me, like I am being stabbed with a sharp knife."

"I see. And this has been ever since Sunshine Hair was here?"

"Yes. It seems to get worse as each day passes."

"We must seek the aid of a dream helper who can give me the power to drive this stabbing pain from your heart. You will concentrate on Aktunowihio as I pray to the dream helper, Silver Moon. When enough spirit force is upon me, I will drive the stabbing pain from within you."

The night sky was a black velvet dome blazing with white stars as Silver Moon left Essie Bird Woman's tepee and walked the path toward her own. It was all over now. No more stabbings in her heart. No more thinking about Jesus Christ on the cross, bleeding and dying for her. No more worrying about punishment for her sins in the afterworld. No more trembling at the thought of an eternal hell.

Aktunowihio, the true god on earth, had answered Essie Bird Woman's prayer.

When her tepee came into view, Silver Moon saw Iron Hawk waiting for her, leaning against a cottonwood tree. Moving toward her he said, "I could not go to my tepee for the night without telling Silver Moon that my heart still reaches for her and always will."

"It is kind of Iron Hawk to wait for me, and it is nice to see him, but I am so very tired, I must go to my pallet quickly."

"I will not detain you. But when you close your eyes, please remember that I love you."

Silver Moon heard the wordless cry from her own mouth as she awoke with a start and sat up on her pallet. The fire had died out, and the darkness that surrounded her seemed thick and suffocating. She could barely get her breath, and her heart pounded wildly as if trying to tear itself from her body.

She had dreamed of Sand Creek again. John Chivington with those evil eyes was pointing his gun at her. Just as he pulled the trigger, she felt the bullet rip into her chest.

Silver Moon shook her head to throw the terrifying picture from her mind, and her shoulders twitched with a shudder. Gasping for breath, she wiped perspiration from her brow, and the name came out in a low growl through her clenched teeth. *"John Chivington."*

She lay back down and stared into the pitch black darkness, then hissed aloud, "I hate you, John Chivington! I hate you!"

Sleep eluded Silver Moon as she lay there. She placed shaky fingers to her temples as horrible thoughts assaulted her mind. On that cold day in November 1864...what if the bullet that buzzed by her ear had been on target? What if Chivington had killed her then and there? Would she have walked the Hanging Road to the home of Heammawihio in the sky? Or would she have dropped into a burning hell?

Suddenly another scene appeared before her imagination. She could see Jesus Christ on the cross, bleeding and dying for her. She could hear Him crying that He was forsaken of God.

And then it seemed as if He looked down from the cross directly at her and said, "Silver Moon, why have you not opened your heart to Me? I did this for you because I love you. I paid the price for your sins so you could be saved and escape eternal punishment, but still you reject Me. Come, Silver Moon! Come to Me. I love you. I want to save you!"

The moan of the night wind blended with the sorrowful lament in the depths of Silver Moon's soul. Essie Bird Woman's plea for power from the dream helper to drive the stabbing pain from her heart had not lasted.

As dawn's gray light spread across the east side of her tepee,

Silver Moon knew she could stand the discomfort of mind and heart no longer. There was only one thing to do.

Breanna Baylor Brockman stood over the operating table at Mile High Hospital, administering ether to the seven-year-old girl while her brother-in-law, Dr. Matthew Carroll, performed the delicate surgery. While playing with neighbor children, little Marylou Morgan had fallen from a tree onto a picket fence, driving one of the pickets dangerously close to her heart. In addition to administering the ether, Breanna provided instruments from a nearby tray as Dr. Carroll called for them.

Breanna had been back in Denver for nearly two weeks after her stay at War Bonnet's village, and her mind frequently drifted to the young Cheyenne maiden. Breanna's burden for Silver Moon had not eased. She had prayed earnestly several times a day that the Lord would draw her to Himself.

Marylou Morgan had been in surgery for just over four hours when Dr. Carroll said, "All right, Breanna. Let's close her up."

"What do you think, Doctor?"

"She's going to be fine." Matt Carroll ran a sleeve across his sweaty brow. "If that picket had pierced her chest a half inch farther to the right, I couldn't have saved her."

Breanna looked at her brother-in-law with admiration. "And even then, if Marylou hadn't been so fortunate as to have the West's most skilled surgeon, she might have died on the operating table."

"Maybe you're just a little prejudiced."

"Not at all. I've worked with a lot of doctors, sir. I know the best when I see him."

Matt grinned, shaking his head.

When they were finished, Marylou was placed on a cart and

taken to the recovery room. The doctor went to the waiting room to give the parents the good news, and Breanna headed down the hall toward the front door, slipping into her coat. It was after 5:00 P.M., her shift was over, and she was tired.

Dr. Eldon Moon stopped her and said, "How'd the surgery go on the little girl, Breanna?"

"Perfectly, Doctor. She's going to be fine."

"Wonderful! She had the best surgeon this side of the wide Missouri."

"That's what I told Dr. Carroll," Breanna said.

"You look weary."

"I am. I'm going to talk John into taking me out for supper tonight. I'm too tired to cook."

Breanna moved on, and as she neared the end of the hall, Nurse Veronica Clyburn waved her down.

"Oh, Breanna! I was just coming to see if you were out of surgery yet. There are some friends of yours in the waiting room out front. They've been here for over two hours and are eager to see you."

"Oh? Who might that be?"

"Some Cheyenne from that village you were at a couple of weeks ago. Seems they've ridden all the way from the village to see you."

"Thanks, Veronica," Breanna said, hurrying away. As she reached the end of the hall she said, "Dear Lord, could it be? Have You answered my prayers about Silver Moon?"

She rounded the corner and headed toward the lobby, where she could see Silver Moon and Iron Hawk sitting, dressed in their best buckskins. They smiled and stood up when they saw her. Just as Breanna passed the receptionist desk, Silver Moon ran to meet her, opening her arms.

"Oh, Breanna," she said, "I have had a miserable two weeks!

Everything you have shown me from the sacred Book, and all the things you told me—somehow I know they are true! Heammawihio and Aktunowihio do not exist. They are false gods. The true God is the God of the sacred Book, and the true Saviour is His Son, Jesus Christ. I asked Iron Hawk to ride with me to Denver, and he was glad to do it."

Breanna looked at Iron Hawk as she embraced Silver Moon. He was smiling from ear to ear.

"I have renounced the false gods, Breanna," Silver Moon said. "I realize how wicked I have been not to believe in Jesus Christ. I am ready to repent of it and to open my heart to God's Son. I want you to help me."

Breanna was struggling to stay composed. Pulling back so she could look at Silver Moon, she said, "You two come with me to my house. We'll take a look at some verses again in my Bible, and you can get this thing settled."

"Breanna..." came the voice of the receptionist.

Breanna turned. "Yes, Vickie?"

"I have a note here that was brought in about an hour ago by Sheriff Langan."

Breanna took the note and found it was actually from Stefanie Langan, inviting Breanna to supper. Curt had already told John, and John would meet Breanna at the Langan house at six-thirty.

Breanna stuffed the note in her coat pocket. "I'll have to stop one place on the way." She took two steps, stopped, and said, "Wait a minute...how did you two get out of the village for this trip by yourselves? The tribal rule—"

"We are not by ourselves, Sunshine Hair," said Iron Hawk. "We have a chap— chap— What is it?"

"Chaperone. Who is your chaperone?"

"Come, and we will show you," said Silver Moon.

When they stepped out the front door, Breanna saw Bull Elk at the hitch rail with the three pintos. She gasped his name and hurried to welcome him.

Breanna put the Indians in her buggy with their horses tied behind, and while driving to the Langan house, she explained the situation. When they learned that she planned to cook for them, they said they had brought along buffalo jerky and bread. Breanna told them they could eat those provisions on their way back to the village, but they were going to eat *her* food while they were there.

Bull Elk chuckled. "Sunshine Hair is very stubborn, like Indian."

Breanna laughed. "Bull Elk, have you forgotten? I *am* Indian! Chief War Bonnet *made* me an Indian!"

"Mmm! I did not think of that!"

The four had a good laugh, and soon the buggy pulled up in front of the Langan house.

"I'll be right back," said Breanna, climbing down.

Jared, the Langans' oldest boy, answered the doorbell. He hugged Breanna, then called toward the back of the house, "Mom! Miss Breanna's here!" Then to Breanna, "Come on in."

"I can't right now, Jared. But I need to see your mother."

Stefanie appeared at the end of the long hallway and walked toward the door, motioning her inside.

Suddenly, Jared's attention was drawn to the buggy. "Hey! Indians!"

"Stefanie, I need to explain something," Breanna said.

Stefanie was elated to know that Silver Moon wanted to be saved. When Breanna said she and John would come to supper another time, Stefanie wouldn't hear of it. Breanna was to bring the Indians to supper with her. She would be happy to have them. She'd just throw some more stew in the pot.

293

Breanna gratefully accepted and said they would come back by six-thirty.

As the buggy pulled into the driveway of the Brockman place, Iron Hawk said, "This is very nice, Sunshine Hair. You have a beautiful home."

"Thank you. We enjoy it, and there's plenty of room for all three of you."

Breanna led her guests into the house, and they were all eyes. They had never seen anything like it.

"Come into the kitchen," said Breanna. "We'll sit at the table."

When her guests were seated, Breanna removed her coat and hurried to the parlor to get the Bible she and John kept on an end table. She returned and sat beside Silver Moon and said, "All right, sweetie, let's just go over some basic things. From what you've already said, I think you're just about ready."

Within half an hour, many tears were shed as Silver Moon opened her heart to Jesus and called on Him to save her. Breanna followed with a prayer for Silver Moon as she began her new life in Christ. When the amen was said, Iron Hawk was so excited he left his chair to throw his arms around Silver Moon. When he realized what he was doing, he sucked in a sharp breath, let go of her, and backed away. "Oh, Silver Moon," he said. "I am sorry. Please forgive me."

"Please do not feel bad," Silver Moon said. "You have not offended me."

"But I have broken tribal rule. We are not married. I am not allowed to embrace you."

"Tribal rule allows brother and sister to embrace, does it not?" she said, smiling.

"Ah…yes."

"I just became your sister in Christ, did I not?"

"Yes."

"So it was not wrong for you to embrace me."

Iron Hawk took a deep breath. "Then, my sister in Christ, it would not be wrong if I embraced you again to celebrate the occasion, would it? I mean, especially with our chaperone looking on?"

Silver Moon blushed. "I…I do not see any reason that would not be allowed."

When they embraced again, Bull Elk smiled broadly and Breanna brushed tears from her cheeks.

22

IT WAS 6:30 ON THE DOT when Breanna Brockman and her Indian friends arrived at the Langan home. The chief U.S. marshal had not yet put in an appearance but was expected at any moment.

Neighbors looked on wide-eyed as Sheriff Langan and his family stood on the front porch and welcomed the Indians as Breanna introduced them. Nathan and Susan Langan, who were seven and eleven, were a bit nervous about having Indians in their house, but thirteen-year-old Jared was elated.

As Curt and Stefanie led their guests inside, Stefanie smiled at Breanna with a question in her eyes.

"Yes!" said Breanna. "She got saved!"

The entire Langan family had known about the spiritual results in the Cheyenne village and that Breanna was very burdened for Silver Moon. They had prayed for her and now rejoiced over her salvation.

John Brockman arrived moments later, shook hands with Bull Elk and Iron Hawk, then turned to Silver Moon.

"John Brockman," she said excitedly, "I am a Christian now. Breanna brought me to Jesus at your house a little while ago!"

"Hey, that's great! Did you have Bull Elk and Iron Hawk

bring you all the way from the village so you could talk to Breanna?"

"Yes, I did. Both of them told me I could call on Jesus Christ right there at the village, but I wanted Breanna to help me, so I would do it right."

"Nothing wrong with that," said John. "It's the most important decision you will ever make."

Everyone sat down around the large table in the Langan dining room, and Curt asked John to thank the Lord for the food.

As the meal progressed, Iron Hawk said, "I am very heavy in my heart for my Cheyenne people. Now that I am a Christian and realize what spiritual darkness I was in, I so much want my people to come out of the darkness too."

"Yes," said Bull Elk. "I feel the same way."

"I was so blinded by Satan," Silver Moon said. "I want my people to realize how blinded they are too."

"I feel especially that it is my responsibility to take the gospel to my people," said Iron Hawk, "but I need training to deal with them properly. And I need a Bible."

"Iron Hawk," said John, "Breanna and I will provide all three of you with Bibles. And if you would like more to take with you when you go back, we'll provide those too."

"That is most kind of you," said Iron Hawk.

"John," Breanna said, "I showed Silver Moon, Iron Hawk, and Bull Elk the Bible's teaching that they need to be baptized. And they want to do it. I told them I'd take them to meet Pastor Bayless tomorrow, so they can give him their testimonies and he can plan to baptize them on Sunday."

"Good," said John. "Sunday is five days away...I'm glad they can stay that long. If you could stay in Denver even a little longer, Iron Hawk, I'm sure Pastor Bayless would work with you and train you. He can help you go back to your people with the gospel and present it tactfully and prayerfully."

"That is exactly what I want, John Brockman," said Iron Hawk, "but I am not sure how to make it happen. I know Bull Elk must get back to Calf Woman soon, and it is against tribal law for him to travel alone with a woman unless she is a blood relative, so I will have to go back with him and Silver Moon, then return alone."

"There is another way to handle it, Iron Hawk," said Silver Moon.

"Yes?"

"I would like to stay while you are here and learn more about Jesus Christ and the Bible. If we had separate places to stay, we could set a time for Bull Elk to come back and chaperone us as we travel back to the village."

"That's a marvelous idea!" said Breanna excitedly. "You could stay in our house, Silver Moon. I'll make time to teach you every day."

Curt looked at his wife. "Steffie, we could keep Iron Hawk in our house."

"We have two spare bedrooms. He could have his choice. We'd love to have you stay with us, Iron Hawk."

"Wow!" said Jared, no longer able to contain his excitement. "We sure would! Just think of it! I could tell all the kids at school we've got a real live Cheyenne warrior stayin' at our house!"

"Is this all right with you, Bull Elk?" asked Iron Hawk.

"I will be glad to return and be the chaperone again."

"Okay," said Curt. "It's settled. Why don't we go ahead and have Bull Elk and Iron Hawk stay here with us starting tonight?"

"That is fine," said Bull Elk. "You have a barn in the back of the house that I saw."

"Yes."

"Iron Hawk and I will ride in the buggy when Sunshine Hair and John Brockman go home this evening and ride our horses back, if we can keep them in your barn."

"Of course," said Curt.

John added, "I'm sure that after we talk to Pastor Bayless about some training for you, Iron Hawk, he'll tell you how long he thinks it'll take. Then Bull Elk will know when to come back for you and Silver Moon."

As they continued eating, Iron Hawk said, "Sheriff Curt Langan, I have never seen the inside of a white man's jail. Would I be allowed to see yours?"

"Of course. I'll take you to work with me in the morning...give you a special tour and answer any questions you might have."

"I would like to see it too," said Bull Elk.

"Then I'll take both of you to work with me."

"Tell you what," said Breanna, "I'll take the day off tomorrow. Silver Moon and I will go see Pastor Bayless and set an appointment so all three of you can talk to him about baptism. That way you men can do the 'man thing' and look the jail over."

"Sounds good to me," said Curt.

"Dessert time," Stefanie said. "I've got chocolate cake, and I've got pumpkin pie."

The Cheyenne men looked at each other blankly, then Bull Elk said, "What is chocolate cake and pumpkin pie?"

Stefanie laughed. "It would be too hard to tell you. You can have both, then you'll know."

When everyone had been given their dessert and the Indians were enjoying food they had never tasted before, Stefanie said, "Children, I think there's something you should know about Miss Silver Moon. She had a very famous father, and all three of you know his name."

"Really?" said Susan. "Who was your father, Miss Silver Moon?"

Stefanie watched the young woman's reaction and was relieved to see the young woman smile.

"My father was the Cheyenne chief whose name was Black Kettle."

"Black Kettle!" exclaimed Nathan. "Wow! We just read about him in my class a few days ago!"

"This is great, Miss Silver Moon!" Jared said. "I did a paper on the Battle of the Washita last May. Wait'll everybody finds out I have personally met a survivor of that battle and that she's the daughter of Black Kettle! How old were you then, Miss Silver Moon?"

"Jared," said Curt. "Haven't your mother and I taught you that you don't ask a lady her age?"

"But I didn't ask her age *now*, Dad. I asked how old she was then."

"And when did the attack take place?"

"November 27, 1868."

"And that was how long ago?"

"Almost four years."

"So if Miss Silver Moon told you how old she was in November 1868, you'd know her age now, wouldn't you?"

The boy's face turned crimson, and his chin dipped. "Oh. I'm sorry, Miss Silver Moon."

Silver Moon touched his hand with her fingertips. "It is all right, Jared. I do not mind your asking. I was nineteen grasses when the attack was made on my father's village on the Washita River."

"Grasses?" repeated the boy. "What are grasses?"

"Those are *years,* big brother," Susan said.

"Years? How do you know that?"

"Because I listen when Mrs. Martin teaches us about the North American Indians. You know she's part Cherokee."

"Yeah, but I don't remember her saying anything about grass years."

"It's not grass years, Jared," said Susan, giving him a sister-is-smarter-than-brother look. "One grass means one year. Isn't that right, Miss Silver Moon?"

"Yes. That is how we count our years, Jared. By the grasses."

"I don't get it."

"You know how when winter comes, the grass turns brown. And when spring comes, the grass turns green."

"Yes."

"When the grass turns brown again, another year has passed, so we call a year a *grass.*"

"Oh," said Jared. "Now I get it."

Little sister covered her mouth and snickered.

"Susie, that's enough," said Curt.

"Yes, sir."

"Girls always think they're smarter than boys," said Nathan. "Molly Sue Compton always thinks she's smarter than me."

"Enough of that," said Curt.

Nathan shrugged his narrow shoulders and stuffed a forkful of chocolate cake into his mouth.

Silver Moon looked at the oldest Langan boy and said, "Jared, I must disappoint you concerning your having met a survivor of the Washita Battle. I was not there when the attack came. I was many miles from Oklahoma."

"Were you at Sand Creek when Colonel Chivington attacked your father's village?" he asked.

"Yes, Jared. I was there."

Breanna was trying to think of a way to change the subject when Jared said, "That Colonel Chivington really treated your people bad, didn't he, Miss Silver Moon? I read what Congress said about it."

"Colonel Chivington did, indeed, treat my people bad. Congress told the truth, Jared, but they did not know the half of it."

"My dad had Colonel Chivington at his office a couple weeks ago, Miss Silver Moon. He wanted a job as a deputy sheriff. But Dad didn't hire him because of what he did to your village."

Silver Moon felt Breanna's eyes on her, and Iron Hawk stole a quick glance at the woman he loved.

That beast of a man was in Denver so recently? How close might he be now?

"Chivington came to my office after he was at yours, Curt," John said. "From what Barry Shores told me, you turned him down but sent him to me."

"Yes, he really wanted to wear the badge. I knew it'd only cause problems if he were wearing a badge around Denver. But I figured maybe he'd make it as a deputy U.S. marshal, since they travel most of the time."

"I see your reasoning," said John.

"So how'd it go when he talked to you?" asked Curt.

"Never did get to. I was in my office interviewing a prospective deputy when Chivington came in. Barry said Duane McCallister came into the outer office while Chivington was there. Turned out they knew each other but weren't on good terms. Anyway, when Chivington learned that McCallister was head of the Department of Legal Affairs, he told Barry there was no point in interviewing for a deputy position, so he left. I don't have any idea where he went or what he's doing now."

"Probably still panning for gold," said Curt.

"Oh? So that's how he's making his living."

"Yep. Told me he's got a cabin up near Granby. Said he works the creeks that feed the Fraser River. Since he didn't get on with you, I imagine he's back up there panning gold."

"Been a while since I've been up around Granby," said John. "Beautiful country."

Curt nodded. "Snowcapped peaks up there on every side, all year round."

Breanna and Iron Hawk watched Silver Moon, but she seemed to listen only casually to what John and Curt were saying.

Afterward, John drove the Brockman buggy out of town with Ebony tied behind. Iron Hawk and Bull Elk rode in the back seat, and Silver Moon sat next to Breanna in the front seat as Breanna snuggled close to her husband.

Breanna leaned toward Silver Moon and said quietly, "You all right, honey? All that talk about Chivington and all?"

Silver Moon smiled. "I am fine, Breanna."

Later, at the Brockman home, Silver Moon was in one of the guest rooms on the second floor preparing for bed when she heard Iron Hawk and Bull Elk ride away. Moments later there was a tap at her door and she went to open it.

Breanna entered. "It's all set. John will leave for town a little early in the morning so he can go by the hospital and tell them I won't be in for the day."

"Will this cause any problems?"

"No. I'm not on a permanent schedule with the hospital since I travel some, and I also work for a doctor in town. I know you're tired, so I want you to sleep as long as you need to in the morning. When you get up, I'll feed you breakfast, then we'll take a buggy ride into town and see Pastor Bayless." Breanna picked a Bible up from the small table beside the bed. "Now, let's have a short Bible reading together, then we'll pray and you can get to bed."

Moonlight came through the south window of Silver Moon's room, illuminating everything it touched with a soft glow. When all was still in the house, she left the bed and put on her clothes.

Moving silently as a shadow, Silver Moon walked down the hall past John and Breanna's room and descended the stairs. Inside John's den at the rear of the house, there was enough moonlight to guide her to the gun rack. She stopped a moment to listen for sounds from upstairs, then lifted a Remington .44-caliber repeater rifle from the rack and moved down the hall toward the back door. Moments later she was astride her pinto.

She guided the horse quietly around the grove of cottonwood and willow trees that surrounded the house, then angled across the fields and finally passed through the gate onto the road.

Breanna kissed her husband good-bye as the Colorado sun lifted off the eastern horizon. She stood on the wide front porch and threw him a kiss when he reached the gate and turned in the saddle to wave. As soon as John was out of sight, she went back inside and washed the dishes she'd used for his breakfast. She would wait and eat breakfast with Silver Moon.

When nine o'clock came, Breanna had read her Bible, had her prayer time, and was beginning to wonder if Silver Moon was all right.

She mounted the stairs and stopped in front of Silver Moon's room, pressing her ear to the door. Tapping lightly, she called, "Silver Moon, are you up?"

Silence. She tapped louder.

"Silver Moon?"

When there was no reply, Breanna turned the knob and eased the door open. Silver Moon's bed was unmade. Breanna moved inside and looked around. She found the nightgown she had loaned Silver Moon draped across the foot of the bed.

She ran down the hall toward the stairs and hurried to John's den. She dashed to the gun rack and saw that one of the rifles was missing. She ran to the barn. The buggy horse and Chance both greeted her with friendly nickers, but there was no sign of the pinto.

The sun was on its downward slant toward the mountain peaks west of Granby as Silver Moon topped the rise overlooking John Chivington's cabin. She had found people in the eastern foothills of the Rockies who were kind enough to tell her how to find Granby, and the people in Granby were kind enough to tell her how to locate Chivington's cabin, though no one could recall having seen the man for a while.

Learning this, Silver Moon was afraid Chivington had deserted the cabin and gone elsewhere, looking for a job as a lawman. Had she wasted her time and energy to ride here from Denver, only to find that she had come close—as in Ohio—but missed him again? Would the justice that was due him after all these years still not be served?

Silver Moon gripped the rifle in her hand and nudged the pinto forward. She rode down the slope toward the cabin, with the sound in her ears of the Fraser River racing down the mountainside. She could see no sign of life.

When she was about thirty yards from the cabin, which stood amid tall pines and evergreens, she slid from the horse's back and tied it to a bush. Easing down the steep slope, she looked for movement at one of the windows, but there was none.

When she got near the side of the cabin, her line of sight went to the small corral and barn out back. The corral gate was open, swaying in the breeze. There were no horses or pack mules to be seen.

He's out panning for gold, she told herself. But the sun would soon be down. Certainly he couldn't work in the dark. He would be back soon. She decided to check the cabin just to be sure.

The boards of the front porch squeaked under her feet as Silver Moon eased up to the door. She pounded it with the palm of her free hand, then took two steps back, gripping the rifle with both hands, and pointed it straight at the door.

There was no answer.

She pounded on the door again, but still there was no response.

Silver Moon tried the latch. To her surprise it was unlocked. She freed the door from the latch, then gripped the rifle with both hands and gave the door a shove with her foot. It swung open freely.

The mountain air seemed to take on a sudden chill and swept up behind her, rushing through the door. It rustled the silver hair of the gaunt, almost skeletal figure before her.

23

↑

SEATED IN HIS BATTERED, overstuffed chair was the rail-thin Chivington. A jagged pink-white scar ran down the middle of his forehead, put there by the rock Silver Moon had thrown at him eight years ago.

She held the gun aimed at his frail chest and stepped through the door, her fierce eyes fixed on him. Could this wasted, hollow-eyed man be John Chivington? He resembled the man she remembered, but— Yes. *The eyes.* Sunken deep in his head, they were the same eyes, though they had lost their demonic look.

Chivington's thin arms lay on the ragged chair arms, his blue-veined hands gripping the edges. His eyes were dull as he looked at her headband and said, "I always thought it would be a Cheyenne warrior who would come after me. Why have they sent a woman?"

"No one sent me. I came on my own."

"But...who are you? I—" Chivington gasped. "The girl! Oh, I've seen those eyes in my nightmares for all these years. You're the girl!"

"Yes, the girl whose brother and mother you murdered. I am Black Kettle's daughter, Silver Moon. You tried to kill me too, remember? You shot and missed. Then you fired again, but Bear Paw, whom I was to marry, jumped between us and took the bullet."

Chivington nodded slowly. "Yes. I remember, Silver Moon. I have lived that moment over and over in my mind. It has come to me in nightmares a hundred times. You threw a rock and hit me on my forehead, didn't you? I carry the scar."

"I see it." She kept the black bore of the Remington .44 pointed at his heart. "I have lived for one thing all these years, Chivington…to find you and kill you. I traveled to Columbus, Ohio, to kill you, but you had come back to the West by the time I got there. But now I have found you. Finally…finally… justice can be served!"

"My life has been nothing but misery since I led the massacre at Sand Creek. I am an outcast of society. I have never been able to live down what I did. I was wrong. Very wrong. Go ahead, child. Shoot me. You'll be doing me a favor. I wanted to kill myself, but I just didn't have the guts. But first, may I show you something?"

"What?"

"It's on the table."

She saw the yellowed envelope underneath the holstered revolver and said, "I see a revolver and an old envelope. You do not expect me to bring you the revolver, do you?"

"No. I want to show you the envelope."

"Stay where you are."

Silver Moon inched her way to the table, keeping the rifle trained on him. She picked up the envelope and returned to where she had been standing with her back to the open door.

"That's the suicide note I wrote several days ago. I was going to end it all by putting a bullet through my head, but I just couldn't do it."

Silver Moon kept Chivington in view above the top of the

envelope while she read of his contrition for the Sand Creek Massacre. Her features grew slack when she read the words: *I wish I could talk to the survivors of Sand Creek—however many are still living—and ask their forgiveness.* When she reached the part that requested the note be shown to the survivors of Sand Creek and that he begged their forgiveness, she lowered the envelope and stared at him.

"Go ahead," he said. "Pull the trigger. Have your final justice."

Tears filmed Silver Moon's eyes. She lowered the rifle and said in a low voice, "I am not going to shoot you, Mr. Chivington. In fact, I did not come here to shoot you."

"What then?"

Silver Moon let the envelope flutter to the floor and reached into her coat pocket, taking out ten live cartridges. "This rifle holds nine bullets in the magazine, and one in the chamber. Is that correct, Mr. Soldier Man?"

"Yes. It holds ten cartridges."

Silver Moon dropped them on the floor one at a time, watching Chivington's lips move as he counted them. She then worked the lever of the rifle and displayed an empty chamber.

"If you didn't come here to kill me, why did you come?"

"To make you *think* I had come to kill you. To see the fear of dying leap into your eyes."

"That's all?" he asked in disbelief.

"Yes. You see, Mr. Chivington, yesterday I became a Christian. The dearest friend I have in this world led me to Jesus Christ. God's Son came into my heart and changed me. Until that moment, I held a hatred toward you that ate like a cancer at my soul."

Chivington licked dry lips and blinked.

"Mr. Chivington, I no longer hate you. With Jesus Christ

living in my heart, I cannot hate you. He has forgiven me of all my sins because in repentance I asked Him to. I believe you are honestly sorry for your wicked deeds at Sand Creek and have repented of them. You asked in the note that the survivors of the Sand Creek Massacre forgive you. As one of those survivors, sir...I forgive you."

Tears filled John Chivington's eyes and spilled down his cheeks. He raised a shaky hand to wipe them away.

"I can see that you have paid dearly for what you did," Silver Moon said. "Final justice has been served."

"Silver Moon, there are other Sand Creek survivors, aren't there?"

"Yes. About fifty. They live in the same village I do. War Bonnet is our chief. The village is a few miles east of Cheyenne City."

"Would you take me to them?"

"I will see that you get that opportunity, Colonel Chivington," came Iron Hawk's voice from behind Silver Moon.

Silver Moon whirled about, speechless. She finally found her voice and said, "Iron Hawk! Breanna! John Brockman! How long have you been standing out there?"

Breanna moved to Silver Moon's side and wrapped her arms around her. "Long enough to hear that you couldn't kill this man because you have Jesus in your heart."

Silver Moon handed the rifle to John, then looked at Iron Hawk and said, "The hatred I carried for John Chivington is gone. Bear Paw is a sweet memory, but I can honestly say that I love you, Iron Hawk, and I always will."

Breanna took a step back to allow the happy young warrior to move in. Tears marred her vision and she almost stumbled, but John caught her and held her close.

Iron Hawk took Silver Moon's hands in his own. "Pastor

Robert Bayless could do a simple ceremony while we remain in Denver for my training. If you are willing, we could tell Bull Elk not to come back for us. When we go home we will be husband and wife and not need a chaperone."

Silver Moon smiled. "Then let us tell Bull Elk not to come back for us."

EPILOGUE

COLONEL JOHN M. CHIVINGTON'S Sand Creek Massacre cost the Indians heavily in blood and sorrow, but it cost the white man more. After the massacre, a party of Southern Cheyenne chiefs went north to powwow with the chiefs of the Northern Cheyenne. This powwow brought about another one with Arapaho and Sioux chiefs. One of the Sioux chiefs attending was Sitting Bull of the fierce Hunkpapas, who was just coming into prominence.

Upon hearing the details of the Sand Creek Massacre, Sitting Bull became an implacable foe of the white man, more than any Sioux chief before or after him. He stirred the Cheyenne and Arapaho tribes to put on their war paint, and in the years that followed, hundreds of white people were slaughtered by vengeful Sioux, Cheyenne, and Arapaho warriors.

The Little Big Horn massacre of Colonel George Armstrong Custer and his entire Seventh Cavalry unit on June 25, 1876, was masterminded by Sitting Bull and had its deadly roots in Sand Creek.

John M. Chivington was never able to live down Joseph Holt's prophesied label of "indelible infamy." The populace of the United States in the last half of the nineteenth century never forgave him for the horrid massacre at Sand Creek. He died a lonely, forsaken man in 1894, at the age of seventy-three.

OTHER COMPELLING STORIES BY
AL LACY

Books in the Battles of Destiny series:

☞ *A Promise Unbroken*

Two couples battle jealousy and racial hatred amidst a war that would cripple America. From a prosperous Virginia plantation to a grim jail cell outside Lynchburg, follow the dramatic story of a love that could not be destroyed.

☞ *A Heart Divided*

Ryan McGraw—leader of the Confederate Sharpshooters—is nursed back to health by beautiful army nurse Dixie Quade. Their romance would survive the perils of war, but can it withstand the reappearance of a past love?

☞ *Beloved Enemy*

Young Jenny Jordan covers for her father's Confederate spy missions. But as she grows closer to Union soldier Buck Brownell, Jenny finds herself torn between devotion to the South and her feelings for the man she is forbidden to love.

☞ *Shadowed Memories*

Critically wounded on the field of battle and haunted by amnesia, one man struggles to regain his strength and the memories that have slipped away from him.

☞ *Joy from Ashes*

Major Layne Dalton made it through the horrors of the battle of Fredericksburg, but can he rise above his hatred toward the Heglund brothers who brutalized his wife and killed his unborn son?

☞ *Season of Valor*

Captain Shane Donovan was heroic in battle. Can he summon the courage to face the dark tragedy unfolding back home in Maine?

Books in the Battles of Destiny series (cont.):

☞ *Wings of the Wind*

God brings a young doctor and a nursing student together in this story of the Battle of Antietam.

☞ *Turn of Glory*

Four confederate soldiers lauded for bravery mistakenly shoot General Stonewall Jackson. Driven from the army in shame, they become outlaws...and their friend must bring them to justice.

Books in the Journeys of the Stranger series:

☞ *Legacy*

Can John Stranger bring Clay Austin back to the right side of the law...and restore the code of honor shared by the woman he loves?

☞ *Silent Abduction*

The mysterious man in black fights to defend a small town targeted by cattle rustlers and to rescue a young woman and child held captive by a local Indian tribe.

☞ *Blizzard*

When three murderers slated for hanging escape from the Colorado Territorial Prison, young U.S. Marshal Ridge Holloway and the mysterious John Stranger join together to track down the infamous convicts.

☞ *Tears of the Sun*

When John Stranger arrives in Apache Junction, Arizona, he finds himself caught up in a bitter war between sworn enemies: the Tonto Apaches and the Arizona Zunis.

☞ *Circle of Fire*

John Stranger must clear his name of the crimes committed by another mysterious—and murderous—"stranger" who has adopted his identity.

Books in the Journeys of the Stranger series (cont.):

☞ *Quiet Thunder*

A Sioux warrior and a white army captain have been blood brothers since childhood. But when the two meet on the battlefield, which will win out—love or duty?

☞ *Snow Ghost*

John Stranger must unravel the mystery of a murderer who appears to have come back from the grave to avenge his execution.

Books in the Angel of Mercy series:

☞ *A Promise for Breanna*

The man who broke Breanna's heart is back. But this time, he's after her life.

☞ *Faithful Heart*

Breanna and her sister Dottie find themselves in a desperate struggle to save a man they love, but can no longer trust.

☞ *Captive Set Free*

No one leaves Morgan's labor camp alive. Not even Breanna Baylor.

☞ *A Dream Fulfilled*

A tender story about one woman's healing from heartbreak and the fulfillment of her dreams.

☞ *Suffer the Little Children*

Breanna Baylor develops a special bond with the children headed west on an orphan train.

☞ *Whither Thou Goest*

As they begin their lives together, John Stranger and Breanna Baylor place themselves in danger to help a friend.

Books in the Hannah of Fort Bridger series (coauthored with JoAnna Lacy):

☞ *Under the Distant Sky*

Follow the Cooper family as they travel West from Missouri in pursuit of their dream of a new life on the Wyoming frontier.

☞ *Consider the Lilies*

Will Hannah Cooper and her children learn to trust God to provide when tragedy threatens to destroy their dream?

☞ *No Place for Fear*

A widow rejects the gospel until the disappearance of her sons and their rescue by Indians opens her heart to God's love.

Available at your local Christian bookstore